William Wilder Wheildon

Memoir of Solomon Willard

Architect and superintendent of the Bunker Hill monument

William Wilder Wheildon

Memoir of Solomon Willard
Architect and superintendent of the Bunker Hill monument

ISBN/EAN: 9783337318741

Printed in Europe, USA, Canada, Australia, Japan

Cover: Foto ©Raphael Reischuk / pixelio.de

More available books at **www.hansebooks.com**

MEMOIR

OF

SOLOMON WILLARD,

ARCHITECT AND SUPERINTENDENT

OF THE

BUNKER HILL MONUMENT.

BY WILLIAM W. WHEILDON.

. . . "But the work is done ; and posterity ought to know that they are more indebted to Solomon Willard than to any other person for the monument."—[Amos Lawrence.

. . . . . "The merits of this noble-spirited man deserve permanent record.—[Professor Packard.

PREPARED AND PRINTED
BY DIRECTION OF THE MONUMENT ASSOCIATION
1865.

TO THE

LADIES OF BOSTON AND VICINITY,

BY WHOSE PATRIOTIC EFFORTS AND PERSONAL SACRIFICES,

THE

Bunker Hill Monument Association

WAS ENABLED TO COMPLETE

THAT MAJESTIC MEMORIAL

To the Principles and Bravery of the Fathers,

IN THE ERECTION OF WHICH

SOLOMON WILLARD,

AS ARCHITECT AND SUPERINTENDENT,

BY HIS GENIUS, SKILL AND LABOR, GRATUITOUSLY RENDERED,

SO LARGELY CONTRIBUTED,

THIS MEMOIR

IS

RESPECTFULLY INSCRIBED.

AUTHOR'S NOTE.

It will be seen by reference to the published proceedings of the Bunker Hill Monument Association, for June, 1861, that a committee was then appointed to prepare a Memoir of Solomon Willard, the Architect and Superintendent of the Monument and one of the earliest and largest contributors to the work.[*]

It was thought by the Association that Mr. Willard's eminent and unrequited services in its behalf, and his extraordinary devotion to the work which they had inaugurated, entitled him to the distinctive honor proposed. A brief notice of his life, perhaps a short analysis of his character, and a mere statement of the services specially rendered by him, was at first all that was contemplated; but it soon appeared to the Committee that a narrative of his life; of the self-education and self-elevation which he accomplished; of the industry, economy and exemplary habits which he cultivated; of his liberal, public-spirited and magnanimous conduct, as well as a detailed account of his labors in relation to the Bunker Hill Monument, in every stage and step of its progress, and which did so much to secure its completion, was due to him, would meet the approval of the association and at the same time furnish, in the life of an excellent and worthy man, an example of industry, perseverance and fidelity, which would be profita-

---

[*] William W. Wheildon, Amos A. Lawrence, Uriel Crocker, Nath'l. Cotton, and F. H. Stimpson, Committee.

ble to the youth of the country and a bond of faith to the faithful. They have not hesitated to act upon this conviction, and with such means as were open to them, attempt the performance of the work proposed.

The reader will not fail to observe that the narrative of Mr. Willard's life, for many years, is so intimately connected with the progress and history of the monument, that a detailed account of the one is necessarily the history of the other. Even during the periods of suspension, and when Mr. Willard was officially discharged from the service of the association, he was repeatedly consulted and called upon for information and advice in relation to the work, its resumption or its completion. For this and other reasons, it has been thought best to pass over the periods of suspension, in order to give, in a connected form, the narrative of the building of the monument, resuming the personal history after the completion of that great work.

There are two matters connected with the erection of the monument, in regard to which it was desirable that justice should be done to Mr. Willard without doing injustice to any other party. — These relate to the authorship of the design and the name of the architect — two matters that have been controverted. The authorship of the design has been denied to him and earnestly claimed for another; and the plate under the corner-stone bears the name of a gentleman as architect who never had anything to do with the planning or execution of the work, and does not bear the name of Mr. Willard. Although these were matters of more or less notoriety during the progress of the work, Mr. Willard spoke of them only on one occasion, never preferring any claim in his own behalf; and, as the real and only architect, with his own hands, placed the untruthful deposit under the present corner-stone, without a murmur of displeasure. Few men, we think, with less faith in the justice of a final public judgment, would have passed these matters over in silence.

In the course of the narrative, wherever it has been practicable to do so, the author has preferred to allow all parties to speak for themselves, quoting letters not intended for the public eye, rather than using language of his own; and very rarely has he taken the liberty of changing a word or making any correction in style. This rule has been applied particularly to Mr. Willard and his letters; and most of the statements made are in the words of their authors or the record. In one or two instances, the chronological progression of the narrative suffers some violation, but it was thought better to submit to this irregularity than to anticipate reliable authorities and disturb other connections.

In regard to the preparation of the memoir, the author deems it only justice to himself to say that it has been prepared at moments of time taken from other duties, or while making daily passages in the railroad cars to and from a residence out of the city. It may also be interesting to some readers to know that the setting of the type for the entire volume, reading proof-sheets, &c., have been performed by him in the same way — portions of the work having been composed in type without any previously written copy.

The press work and printing of the plates, have been done at the office of Messrs. George C. Rand & Avery, to whom personal acknowledgments are due for many kindnesses during its progress.

The materials used in the preparation of this volume have been obtained from papers and books of Mr. Willard, furnished by his brother and administrator, Mr. Cephas Willard of Petersham; from a portion of the letters and papers of the late Mr. Amos Lawrence; and from the records of the Monument Association. The author is also indebted to Mr. G. Washington Warren, President of the Association, for the use of valuable papers, and to various individuals who were personally acquainted with Mr. Willard, for facts and information which have been of service.

W. W. W.

May 1st, 1865.

STATEMENT OF CONTENTS.

10

STATEMENT OF CONTENTS.

CHAPTER IV.

VISITS TO THE SOUTH — STATUE OF WASHINGTON.

Mr. Willard visits the South ; Spends three months in Richmond, engaged in
Carving, &c. ; Also at Baltimore and New York ; Proposed Statue of Washington; Model in Wax after Houdon's Statue at Richmond ; Destroyed in
its transportation from Richmond to Boston, and the undertaking relinquished ; Chantrey's Statue at the State House ; Visit to Mr. Rush at Philadelphia ; Drawing of the "Water Nymph" ; Mr. Rush's compliment ; Alpheus Carey's opinion of Mr. Willard.   34 — 37

CHAPTER V.

MODELLING — THE CAPITOL AT WASHINGTON.

Letter from Mr. Charles Bulfinch ; Visit to Washington ; Model of the Capitol ; Exhibited to Mr. Willard's friends at Washington, (not Boston, as in the
text) ; Invitation to carve the ceilings of the Congressional Rooms declined ;
Rooms in New York ; Models of the Pantheon and Parthenon.   38 — 41

CHAPTER VI.

CARVING IN STONE — ST. PAUL'S CHURCH — TEACHING.

New studies ; Carving marble panels for Mr. David Sears ; Stone work on St.
Paul's church ; Its portico and pediment ; Proposed Scripture piece ; the
U. S. Branch Bank at Boston ; Teaching ; Designing and building Suffolk
County Court House.   42 — 44

CHAPTER VII.

NEW HEATING APPARATUS — THE HOT-AIR FURNACE.

Pursuits in Boston ; Building and warming houses ; Franklin's fire-place
and Count Rumford's cooking range ; Use of Sea coal ; Development of
coal in this country ; Invention of a hot-air furnace, and its introduction ;
English inventions ; Furnaces for the capitol at Washington.   45 — 51

CHAPTER VIII.

BOSTON MECHANICS' INSTITUTION.

Harmony between the Mercantile and Mechanical professions ; The spirit of
the Revolution exemplified in the formation of the Mechanics' Institution ;
Officers and members ; Mr. Willard one of the Vice Presidents ; Mr. Everett's lecture, 1827 ; Mr. Webster's lecture, 1828 ; After ten years of exist
ence its effects given to the Mass. Charitable Mechanic Association. 52—57

14   STATEMENT OF CONTENTS.

CHAPTER XXVII.

CELEBRATION OF THE COMPLETION OF THE MONUMENT — 1843.

CHAPTER XXVIII.

COST OF THE BUNKER HILL MONUMENT.

CHAPTER XXIX.

LOCATION AND DESCRIPTION OF BUNKER HILL MONUMENT.

CHAPTER XXX.

MR. WILLARD AS ARCHITECT AND BUILDER — 1824 — 1835.

CHAPTER XXXI.

NEW YORK MERCHANTS' EXCHANGE — 1836 — 1841.

CHAPTER XXXIII.

THE STONE BUSINESS — MR. WILLARD AS A FARMER.

CHAPTER XXXIV.

INTRODUCTION OF GRANITE AND MACHINERY.

CHAPTER XXXV.

CLOSING LABORS OF MR. WILLARD'S LIFE — HIS DEATH.

CHAPTER XXXVI.

PERSONAL APPEARANCE AND CHARACTER OF MR. WILLARD.

APPENDIX. ·

1. BEACON HILL MONUMENT.
2. WILLARD MEMOIR — LETTER TO THE PRESIDENT OF THE MONUMENT ASSOCIATION.
3. FIRST REPORT OF THE COMMITTEE.
4. PUBLIC MONUMENTS IN MASSACHUSETTS.
5. STATUARY IN MASSACHUSETTS.

ILLUSTRATIONS.

VIEW OF BUNKER HILL MONUMENT — From a Photograph.
VIEW OF BEACON HILL MONUMENT — From a painting by Sully.

———

1. Diagram of the First Course and Corner-Stone (○) of Bunker Hill Monument.
2. Sectional View of Bunker Hill Monument.
3. Diagram of the Lifting Jack, — with side, interior and front views of the same.
4. Diagram of the Pulling Jack, for removing large and heavy blocks of stone.
5. Diagram of the Hoisting Jack, for loading columns, pilasters and other heavy blocks.

MEMOIR

OF

SOLOMON WILLARD.

———•◦•———

CHAPTER I.

INTRODUCTORY—BOSTON.

SOLOMON WILLARD was not a native but a voluntary citizen of Boston; and although at one time disposed to take up his residence in another city, and actually locating himself there, he soon returned to Boston as his most congenial home.

Bostonians are proud of their city, its history and its honor-·able names in the various walks of business, in public and private life. Her citizens have been distinguished as patriots and heroes, and professionally as lawyers, statesmen, clergymen, and in the departments of art, science and literature. They are known in history and biography, and bear a fame down to posterity as enduring as language, which, whatever may be said of the self-complacency of the people, will forever justify the right of the city to appreciate its own. It is a testimonial to her liberality and the generous nature of her people that no distinctions are made, in the award of merit or in the contest of excellence, between native and voluntary citizens; those of the household and those who seek its shelter and its consideration. The road

3

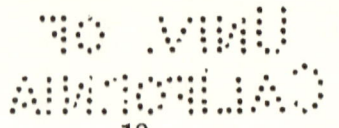

to distinction has been ever open to all competitors, titled or not titled, and merit, made more apparent by the obstacles it has to encounter, is assured of its position and its honor. Pretension everywhere has its achievements and for a time revels in success, but true worth always finds its appreciation and reward among an intelligent people. It may not be entirely peculiar, but it is deemed characteristic of the people of Boston, that those who have come into her fold have found as ready employment, consideration and honor, as those born into it. This is her early and later history, and numerous illustrations, more or less conspicuous, are to be found in her annals. Commendable as this may be in her life and honorable to her judgment, her generosity and her patriotism, it is almost too much to believe that mistakes or omissions have not happened in which injustice has been done to worthy motives and a reasonable ambition. But as the rule, encouragement and appreciation have been bestowed upon all who have taken up their abode with her people, whether coming to them over the hills of New England or the waves of the Atlantic. The guerdon of learning, the stamp of genius, the odor of sanctity, the oriflamme of patriotism, have been recognized by the citizens of Boston, more readily and more surely than any hereditary claims to position or consequence, or the flaunting of any token of imperial favor. And not this alone, not merely achieved prominence or distinction, but humble effort, immature merit, aspiring hopefulness, in science or art, in learning or labor, have rarely failed to meet that encouragement which rightly and earnestly directed effort is entitled to receive.

Boston has honored herself in this : The list of worthy names which adorns her history, of men who have ornamented her society, directed her councils, represented her in the state and federal governments, graced and honored her professions, promoted her wealth and prosperity as merchants and mechanics, and who have in a more than poetic sense, lived in her life, includes those of many who were not born on her soil and inherited none of her greatness though they now bear a proud share in it. Revere and

Franklin were her's; Hancock and Otis were her's; Samuel Adams and the Phillipses, the Jacksons, the Sullivans and the Lowells, were her's; but the names of Warren, Adams, Quincy, Dexter, Gerry, Mason, Story, Webster, Bowditch, Choate, the Lawrences and others, and many more among the living, are her's only by voluntary residence and adoption : in the whispered words of another to our private ear, "they had their nests in the woods." She has welcomed and nurtured and honored these, as her own children, and they have faithfully given back to her their labors, their success, their thoughts, their unforgotten names, and side by side with her own, and as her own, they stand upon the pages of her history. They are no less than others, her jewels, and form with them her chaplet of fame, her constellation of patriotic and high-souled men.

The subject of this memoir, in other countries, where other laws prevail, where different institutions exist, where merit attaches to position, or is compelled to seek it for countenance and support, would hardly be considered as entitled to this distinction, by the higher classes, nor would it be demanded by those less favored who could not bestow it. The class, — it seems as though we might almost say race, — to which Mr. Willard most unequivocally belongs, though not wholly unknown in some other of the civilized and progressive nations, is believed to be peculiar to our own country, born with its birth—existing even before its birth as a nation—and growing with its growth, with a vigor which proves its congeniality, if not its indigenousness to the soil. The laws, it is true, or the absence of them, have undoubtedly something to do with this : neither making or allowing any distinctions between elder and younger sons, or men as men ; but leaving every one at liberty to seek his own improvement, promote his own welfare, work out as it were, under God alone, his own destiny, making his mark if he can, or writing his full name as he may, upon the page of history or the scroll of fame. Born, it may be, in obscurity or retirement, with no inherited claim to prominence, often with no education but that furnished

by a half yearly public school; with no endowment of wealth
or prestige of position; in fact often amidst deprivation, labor
and hardship — those parents of perseverance and skill — men
among us have worked their way to high positions of usefulness
and honor, — as if the very point from which they started, and
the way they were compelled to travel, were alike necessary to
that developement of energy and intellect which has made them
men among men equal with the highest peer of them all.   The
lives of such men are of great advantage to community, in all
the departments of science, learning, literature and the arts of
life, for they are inventive and progressive men ; and the lessons
they afford are by no means the least of the benefits they confer
upon the whole human family.   They adorn the times in which
they live, and leave, besides the wealth of their intellect, an example to be followed by succeeding generations, which the histo-
rian of men should not fail to record.

Mr. Willard was one of this class of men and minds — so received, so welcomed, so encouraged, so appreciated by the people
of Boston.   He was endowed by nature with a mind of original mechanical and artistic thought, combining tact and talent,
which were developed by self-effort and judicious self-cultiva-
tion, — some of processes and means and results of which we
shall see and endeavor to illustrate in the course of this narrative of his life and labor.

CHAPTER II.

MR. WILLARD'S ANCESTORS—HIS EARLY LIFE.

MR. WILLARD came to Boston in early life, a "rough ash-lar," to seek employment, to learn a trade, labor and obtain an honest living,—and see, as many others have done and thought, what shall come of it. Not as "waiting for something to turn up," but rather to turn something up and see what activity, energy and industry, directed by the best lights open to him, might be able to accomplish.

He was born at Petersham, Worcester County, Massachusetts, on the 26th of June, 1783. His father, known as Deacon William Willard, was a native of Biddeford, Maine, and his mother, Katherine Wilder, of Lancaster, Massachusetts. They were married November 22, 1763. William Willard was the son of Rev. Samuel Willard of Biddeford, who was the son of Maj. John Willard of Port Royal, Jamaica, and grandson of Rev. Samuel Willard, D. D. pastor of the Old South Church and Vice President of Harvard College. As the last named Samuel was a son of Major Simon Willard, the first emigrant and military leader of his time, Solomon Willard, the subject of this memoir, was a direct descendant from that noted man, of the sixth generation, as follows : 1. Simon, the first emigrant ; 2. Samuel, the Vice President of Harvard College ; 3. John, of Jamaica, trader ; 4. Samuel, of Biddeford ; 5. William, of Petersham ; 6. Solomon, the architect.

William Willard had two brothers, Rev. John Willard, D. D.

of Stafford, Connecticut, and Rev. Joseph Willard,* the fourteenth President of Harvard College, father of Joseph Willard,
Clerk of the Superior Court, Suffolk Co., at the present time,
(1863,) and author of the "Willard Memoir." William was
the father of eleven children, and Solomon was the youngest but
one : two of them died in early life. The Rev. Samuel Willard,
of Deerfield, known as the Blind Preacher, and yet remembered by many persons in this vicinity, who have listened to his
discourses with peculiar interest, was a brother of Solomon. His
blindness was caused by grief and over-use and a similar cause
brought the same deprivation upon his son. His familiarity with
the Bible and Psalm Books was remarkable, and his memory
was so retentive and firm that he was able, with slight preparation, to perform all the services of the pulpit without authorizing
a suspicion of his blindness.

Major Simon Willard, above mentioned, was a native of Hors-
monden, County of Kent, England, and was baptized on the 7th
of April, 1605. He came to this country with his sister Mar-
gery and his half brother George, in the year 1634, and was
three times married — his second and third wives being near relatives of President Dunster, of Harvard University. It seems
that he held a military commission in England. Soon after his
arrival here he was engaged in the public service, and besides
filling numerous civil offices, as a military teacher and leader
served the colony for nearly forty years. He first settled at
Cambridge; was the principal purchaser of Concord from the
Indians; removed from Concord to Lancaster; thence to Groton — and finally to Charlestown, where he died. He was a
leading man in all these towns, and a large landholder, having
received several grants of land for his various public services.

---

* This uncle of Solomon Willard was inaugurated as President of the College
on the 19th of December, 1781, under Governor Hancock, and held the office
until his death, September 15th, 1804, within a few days of the coming of his
nephew to seek his fortune in Boston.

It would require a large space simply to enumerate the various public offices held, and public duties performed, by Major Simon Willard, during the forty years of his public life. He was 'Clerk of the Writs' at Concord, for nineteen years, by election; deputy and representative for fifteen years; assistant for twenty years. He was the surveyor of arms; superintendent of the fur trade; commissioner and negotiator for numerous important purposes relative to towns, boundaries, the Indians, &c. He was for more than twenty years in command of the Middlesex Regiment; for much of the time on the frontier towns, defending them against the incursions of the Indians; was the leader of the expedition against Ninigret, the Narraganset sachem, and near the time of his death, unable to discharge his civil duties by reason of his military services, he was actively engaged in King Philip's War. Twice he had the subject of " the Concord and Sudbury meadows" in his hands — an important interest, not yet after the lapse of more than two centuries, finally disposed of. There is scarcely any kind of service needed of a public man in those early times, that Major Willard did not render to the colony : in making and administering the laws, preparing for war and conquering peace, regulating trade, settling controversies and town difficulties, buying and dividing lands, &c. His house at Groton having been burnt by the Indians, in March, 1675, his family fled to Charlestown, where he died on the 24th day of April, 1676, (4th of May, N. S.) Major Willard was the father of seventeen children, and his descendants of the 6th generation are estimated at 10,976; of the 8th generation, 239,057.

In speaking of one of his descendants, Major Willard Moore, it is said, "At the battle of Bunker Hill, he was a Major in a new regiment raised at Cambridge, of which Colonel Doolittle was commander. In the absence of the Colonel, the command of the regiment devolved upon Major Willard Moore. 'He was early in the field, and took a prominent post of danger. . . . He was wounded, and fell in the second charge of the enemy upon

the lines.   He received another wound through the body, as his
men were carrying him from the field, which proved fatal.'   At
the foot of that hill reposed in peace the remains of his great-
grandfather, Major Simon Willard."*

The Rev. Samuel Willard, D. D., was the seventh President
of Harvard College, the General Court, by its votes having excluded President Increase Mather and appointed Dr. Willard,
on the same day, 6th of September, 1701.   He held the office
under the title of Vice President, for more than six years, and
discharged the duties of the office to great acceptance.   "Willard
was quiet, retiring, phlegmatic and unpretending.   .   .   .
His life had been devoted to professional research and pastoral
duties.   His study was the scene of his private labors ; his
church the theatre of his public action.   These had constituted
a sphere of usefulness, to which his ambition had been limited ;
which he did not quit until after repeated legislative applications,
for one higher and wider, and then with reluctance."†

It is remarkable how nearly some of these personal characteristics were reproduced in the subject of this memoir, a hundred
years later.   The Doctor's independence of character, as illustrated in the following extract, was not less conspicuous in Mr.
Solomon Willard : "Amid the agitations consequent on that in-
sanity of the age, denominated 'The Salem Witchcraft,' the conduct of Willard was marked by prudence, firmness and courage.
He neither yielded to the current, nor feared to cast the weight
of his opinion publicly in opposition to the prevailing delusion ;
an independence the more remarkable and honorable, as Stough-
ton and Sewall, two of the Judges of the Court of trial, men of
great influence in the Province, both his personal friends, and
the latter a principal member of his church, were deeply infect-
ed by the distemper of the times."‡   He died on the 12th of

---

* Willard Memoir, or Life and Times of Major Simon Willard, by Joseph
Willard, p. 391.   1858.

  † Quincy's History of Harvard University.   ‡ Ibid.

September, 1707. His son Josiah held the office of Tutor in the University, and was afterwards Secretary of the Province of Massachusetts Bay, earning in this office the sobriquet of "the good Secretary."

Of Solomon Willard's early life we have only some general information ; and this, of small importance in most cases, is perhaps less essential in Mr. Willard's, whose early career was of a most common character — and yet, bred a man of industry, perseverance, self-reliance and energy, he was sure to leave an impress of himself upon whatever he touched. His brother, Cephas Willard, of Petersham, writes of him, "My brother had no advantages but a common school of that day. He acquired easily and made good proficiency. His employment was mainly agricultural. His father was a carpenter and joiner, and in dull weather and in winter, Solomon was employed in the shop,— not with the expectation of learning a trade, but to fill up his time in some useful employment. He was very ingenious and would perform skilfully many things in the mechanic arts. He labored upon the farm until about the first of August after his majority, and in October, 1804, he left home for Boston."

These few lines indicate Mr. Willard's birth, parentage and education — such as belong to the history of thousands of young men born and nurtured, i. e. made useful, in New England.— There is nothing peculiar in it — nothing important, unless it be in the general absence of all advantage of position, means and influence, sometimes supposed to be necessary to success. It is no disparagement to the boy — no reflection upon the interest of the parent — to say that, besides being occupied "in some useful employment," he was left to develope himself, like a tree in the field, expected and permitted, in due time, to bear its own fruit, with such care alone as the husbandman can give it in common with the rest.

There is no doubt that he labored faithfully for his father during his minority, and it is equally certain that the latter was required to do nothing for him after that period. He attended the

4

town school in winter, and employed such portions of time as
were granted to him, with a borrowed book or two, for his own
improvement in gratifying his thirst for knowledge.   He is said
at this time to have been persevering and indefatigable in whatever he undertook to accomplish; achieving triumphs, under the
circumstances, in mechanical and intellectual pursuits,— opening
the doors of knowledge and invention to himself; often no doubt,
surprised by the discovery of things and their relations, principles and their application, known long before his renowned military ancestor was born.   It is no marvel that in after years, the
mind which had worked out old discoveries for itself, should
work out new ones for others.   The latter were no more discoveries to him, from the original workings of his mind, than the
former, as both were the result of the same thoughtfulness and
study, the same combinations and the same capacity for investigation and calculation.

In his youth Mr. Willard exhibited other qualities, which afterwards became characteristic of his life and conduct.   He was
of gentle manners, amiable, kind and obliging; careful, faithful and considerate.   Ready, we imagine, as in after life, to en-
ter upon any new undertaking which promised to call forth the
energies and inventive powers of his mind, and more especially
if something no one else would undertake, or in which others
had failed.   In such a case he would accomplish the desired object or end, or show how it could be done, as a matter of course
and not as a success, much less as a triumph for himself.   His
brother relates of him that in his study of Euclid, a copy of
of which some way came into his possession, the problem which
puzzled him at night, as he pored over it after the rest of the
family had retired, was sure to be found mastered on his slate
in the morning.

CHAPTER III.

HIS EMPLOYMENT IN BOSTON.

MR. WILLARD's first work in Boston has been variously stated. Mr. Alpheus Carey, who knew him well for many years, says he "commenced to learn the trade of a carpenter and the first work he did was to fit with the broad axe a set of piles for the building of a wharf, and notwithstanding the coarseness of the work, he said his master taught him one good habit, and that was to keep his tools always in good order." He never forgot this lesson, or failed to give the principle it inculcated a broad application. Mr. Willard's own record, probably of this transaction, shows that he worked for Pond & Gale, ten days at fifty cents per day (and board,) and the amount is entered under the date of 10th November, 1804. The next thirteen days he was employed by Salmon Morton, at the same rate of compensation. But this kind of labor and its proportionate pay could not long engage the attention of a mechanic of Mr. Willard's capacity. He was one who always worked with his head as well as hands, and in doing a piece of work himself, or seeing another do it, his immediate thought would be whether it could not be done in some easier, quicker, or cheaper way, or in a more perfect manner.

Before the end of his first year in Boston, Mr. Willard had worked for several parties, had paid his personal expenses, made purchase of tools, books, &c. and on the 12th of October, 1805, "received of Salmon Morton two hundred dollars, due for eight

months' work, with money lent." It would appear that he had
supported himself and furnished his employer with a part of his
working capital in the first year of his freedom. Three months
later, besides visiting the paternal roof and making — what
was then a journey — a visit to Providence, he had money to let,
and took a note of William Willard for two hundred and five
dollars, which was subsequently paid by installments. It must
not be inferred from these statements of his prudence and thrift
that Mr. Willard was a penurious or an avaricious man, — he
was neither the one or the other, — but free and liberal always,
spending his money for useful, practical and profitable purposes,
and not otherwise ; often for means of instruction and improvement, but seldom for mere recreation.

In 1808, Mr. Willard, still working at the trade of a carpenter, was employed upon the famous Exchange Coffee House, an
immense and costly structure, in the rear of State-street, and
extending from Congress to Devonshire-street. This building,
combining the hotel and merchants' exchange, was at the time
of its erection, one of the largest and most pretentious buildings
in the country, and was almost as remarkable for its architectural designs and arrangements as for its great height, numerous
apartments and spacious accommodations. There were in this
edifice three principal stair-cases, of which the grand spiral pile,
on the southerly side of the building, which extended from
the basement story to the roof and intended especially for the
hotel, was built by Mr. Willard, and was a work of considerable
calculation, judgment and skill in the joiner's art. Probably
there was no piece of joiner's work in the country at that time
which would compare with it, in spaciousness, achitecture or
finish. It was some slight preparation for the construction,
many years afterwards, of the winding steps leading to the top of
Bunker Hill Monument. Mr. Willard was engaged upon this
edifice for several months, until the 8th of December, 1808.
He had previously had some experience in stair-work, which
has since then become a distinct branch of carpentry. As this

building was seven stories high, and contained a central rotunda with galleries and an immense dome, it included much elaborate work in various styles of architecture by the best artists of the time, and was a very useful study for Mr. Willard. No doubt he profitted by the opportunity it afforded. This costly building was destroyed by fire on the 3d of November, 1818, and the light of the conflagration was seen at the distance of a hundred miles from Boston.

Although Mr. Willard had worked these three or four years to considerable pecuniary profit, and had also learned his trade, without any regular apprenticeship, he had by no means neglected the improvement of his mind and the acquisition of knowledge intended to be made available in the future. He early provided himself with the most approved works on architecture and perspective drawing; purchased an Encyclopædia and other standard books, and paid for his tuition at a drawing academy for at least two terms — some years later becoming a teacher himself.

Mr. Willard had also during the same years, in the improvement of that time which so many others waste, qualified himself not only as a draughtsman but as a carver in wood. His first charge for this kind of work was made in February, 1809, to A. Dexter, for six capitals, probably for a door-way. The same year he carved a set of Ionic capitals for the Brighton meeting house; and other sets for E. Preble and Richard Hills. In the latter part of this year, so much had this business grown in his hands, Mr. Willard seems to have been constantly employed, carving besides other work all the capitals, Ionic and Corinthian, for the steeple of Park-street Church, of which Peter Banner, a well-known architect of that time, was the designer.* He re-

---

* Peter Banner was a native of England, and followed his profession as an architect previously to coming to this country. One of the best preserved evidences of his skill and taste in this vicinity, is a private mansion house admi-

ceived from Mr. Banner, in November, 1809, nearly four hundred dollars for his work on this church ; and in December hired
a room in Somerset Place and employed two workmen to assist
him.

For the following years, 1810, '11 and '12, Mr. Willard was
still engaged in carving, commencing the first of these years on
work for the Federal-street Church, (Dr. Channing's,) lately
taken down, of which Charles Bulfinch, afterwards employed to
finish the capitol at Washington, was the architect.   He also
purchased some "anatomical apparatus"; attended a course of
lectures on that subject; commenced the study of the French
language, and secured admission to the Library of the Boston
Athenæum.

In 1810, in the spring, Mr. Willard carved at the establishment of Mr. Goodrich, organ builder, a colossal spread Eagle,
which was placed upon the apex of the pediment of the old Custom House in Boston, and still ornaments the warehouse which
now occupies the same site on Custom-house street.   As this
figure was designed to be elevated to the height of some sixty
feet, it was of colossal size, measuring five feet from wing to
wing, and about five feet in height.   It was in these measurements admirably adapted to the proportions of the building which
it was designed to embellish and indicate as national in its purposes.   Of this kind of work at that time, it unquestionably possessed considerable merit, and probably to-day in its

---

rably located on the northerly slope of Parker's Hill, Washington Street, in
Roxbury, built for Mr. Eben. Crafts, in 1805.   At that time it was quite noted
for its proportions and classic style, was visited by the Cambridge students and
is still much admired for its rich and massive front elevation ; its fine fluted
Corinthian columns, in pairs, on pedestals, and reaching to the height of two
stories, and for its general purity of style.   The interior finish is also elaborate
and the ornamentation profuse but still tasteful and classic.   It has been for
the last twenty years, the residence of George Howe, Esq., and has recently
been purchased by other parties, who we trust, will long preserve it and its
delightful grounds and venerable elms from the vandal hands of "progress"
and "improvement."

porportions and execution, for the purpose intended, will stand the test of a reasonable criticism. This Eagle is said to have been one of several, more or less prominent, that were cotemporary in the early history of Boston. The first of these was that which was placed upon the top of Beacon Hill Monument, erected by the Citizens of Boston, in 1790, upon the hill then existing and lying between Dearne street and the State House, the present site of the Reservoir. The gilded Eagle, still preserved, is suspended in the Representatives' Hall, while the large tablets of slate-stone, covered with historical data, are in the Doric Hall below, still calling the attention of the people to the independence and prosperity of their country and admonishing them to "forget not those who, by their exertions, have secured to them these blessings." The Eagle carved by Mr. Willard was damaged by fire in May, 1862, but has since been repaired, and while its cotemporary, taken in from the storms of the elements, overlooks the legislation of the State, this proud bird still calmly gazes upon the evidences of an extended commerce and peers into the dim distance of the ocean beyond.

The Beacon Hill Monument, built two years after the Beacon itself,* its frame and "skillet" had been blown down, was probably the first public or historical monument erected in the coun-

---

* The Beacon was erected in 1635, the next year after the completion of the fortifications on Fort-hill by the people of Boston, Charlestown, &c., and was intended to alarm the neighboring towns in case of an attack by Indians. As it was standing during the revolutionary war, it may have been used to alarm the country had occasion required. The Beacon was therefore ante-revolutionary by a hundred and forty years, while the Monument was subsequent to the adoption of the Constitution.

In 1768, when it was expected that British troops were coming to Boston, a meeting was held to consider the subject and adopt measures for "the peace and safety of his [Majesty's] subjects in this Province, &c. At this time, September 10, an officer arrived from Halifax "whose mission was rightly judged to be to make arrangements for quartering troops in the town. Immediately after his arrival a tar-barrel was discovered in the skillet of the Beacon on Beacon Hill. This, it was understood, was to be fired when the King's ships containing the troops from Halifax, should make their appearance in the bay.— Construing the elevation of a tar-barrel, under such circumstances, to be a gross

try, and as it no longer exists, a brief notice of it here may not be out of place. The hill, according to drawings reproduced in 1859, was nearly as high as the dome of the State House, and was dug away between 1806 and 1810, and the monument taken down. It was pyramidal in form, ascended in part by a flight of steps from Dearne street, and said to be 138 feet above tide-water. The monument was a plain Doric column, 4 feet diameter, on a pedestal of 8 feet, 60 feet high, and surmounted by an Eagle, bearing the arms of America. It was of brick masonry, plastered. In the panels of the pedestal were four inscriptions : that on the south side stated the purpose of the monument thus : "To commemorate that train of events which led to the American Revolution, and finally secured Liberty and Independence to the United States, this column is erected by the voluntary contributions of the citizens of Boston, MDCCXC." On the west side, these events were named, commencing with the Stamp Act and ending with the Declaration of Independence ; and on the north side, they were continued, including the Confederation, the Constitution, Treaty of Peace, Inauguration of Washington as President, &c. On the east side, an appeal which ought to mark the spot to day : "Americans ! while from this eminence scenes of luxuriant fertility, of flourishing commerce, and the abodes of social happiness, meet

---

insult, in his military capacity, the Governor [Bernard,] summoned the Council, which was held at a gentleman's house half-way between the Governor's at Jamaica Plains and Boston." Here the tar-barrel question was debated, and it was " resolved that the Selectmen should be desired to take it down ; but they would not do it." " However, Sheriff Greenleaf had private orders from the Governor and Council to remove it, using his own discretion as to the proper time to do it. He, therefore, taking about a half-dozen men with him, proceeded stealthily to the hill, just at dinner time, and effected the important object in about ten minutes. This was a victory over the Sons of Liberty, gained while they were not expecting the enemy." Drake's History of Boston.

     It seems from this account that the engraving in Dearborn's peculiar book, " Boston Notions," representing the Beacon with a full-sized tar-barrel on the top of the pole besides that in miniature in the " skillet" suspended from the crane, is an unauthorized addition of the artist.

your view, forget not those who, by their exertions, have secured to you these blessings."

This just monition of the early fathers might with great propriety and good sense be inscribed upon Bunker Hill Monument.
It was the original intention to put inscriptions similar to those
above mentioned on this structure, as the first circular of July
9, 1823, declares : " It is intended to erect a monument which
shall be consecrated to the great leading characters and events,
civil and military, of the American Revolution, up the 17th of
June, 1778, to bear appropriate inscriptions of names and dates."
It is not unlikely that the inscriptions already quoted suggested
this idea, but the purpose, if really entertained, to make Bunker Hill Monument personal or individual, in any degree,
never met with public favor, and upon a full consideration and
discussion of the subject, it was thought best to leave it without
inscription of any kind. If, however, the original intention
should ever be carried into effect by the association, we know of
no more fitting words for a portion of the inscription than those
just quoted. Better, perhaps, even than this would be the re-
erection of Beacon Hill Monument on the Common, a very
suitable place for it, or on the grounds in front of the State
House.

Mr. Willard continued the business of a carver, as a profession, for several years, having in 1813, as we find by his first
charge for such work, added to his architectural work that of
ship-carving. His anatomical studies, his observation and his
practice had prepared him for this new branch of art, and among
the figure-heads carved by him are mentioned those of a native
" Tartar," for the ship of that name — a vessel of celebrity in
her time — and an Arab, for a schooner called the " Caravan."
In January, 1816, Mr. Willard completed a colossal bust of
Washington, for the United States 74-gun ship Washington,
built at Portsmouth, N. H. and launched that year, and for this
work he received one hundred dollars.

5

CHAPTER IV.

VISITS TO THE SOUTH — STATUE OF WASHINGTON.

On the 18th of December, 1810, Mr. Willard paid for his passage by vessel to Norfolk, in Virginia, and arrived at Richmond on the 21st. He was at the " Cape" on the 9th of December, and probably sailed from there, paying his passage on board the vessel. He passed about three months in Richmond, engaged in carving, and also spent some time in Charlotteville, Washington, Baltimore, Philadelphia and New-York,— returning to Boston on the 16th of May, 1811. In 1814, Mr. Willard did considerable carving for parties in Providence, and in the latter part of this year was again at the south. In November, 1817, Mr. Willard left Boston, and returned again on 31st of October, 1818. He spent about six months in Baltimore, and vicinity, and three or four months in New York, (thinking to locate there permanently,) and seems to have prosecuted his business very successfully.

About this time it was proposed to erect a Statue of Washington in Boston, by the Washington Monument Association, which was organized some time previously. An Equestrian Statue was at first proposed, to be placed on Flagstaff Hill, on the Common, but the idea was subsequently abandoned and a simple statue determined upon, to be placed in the Doric Hall of the State House. Mr. Willard, who had already made a colossal bust of Washington, in wood, had a strong desire to engage in this work, although we have found no mention of any work in stone by him previously to this time. He was consulted by some of the gentlemen entrusted with the duty of procuring the statue, and was induced to make a journey to Richmond, Virginia, where the State Government had erected a Statue of Washington, by Houdon, under the superintendence of Mr. Jefferson. This was made at Mount Vernon, in 1785, by actual "measurements of the hero's person" taken by the artist himself, who had come to this country on the invitation of Franklin and Jefferson, expressly to execute this work and a bust which he took home with him.

Reaching Richmond, by a sailing packet, in about ten days from Boston, Mr. Willard, who was accompanied and assisted by his friend, Mr. Alpheus Carey, (to whom we are indebted for these particulars,) proceeded at once in taking measurements and in the construction of a model on a miniature scale in wax. In this he succeeded much to his satisfaction, and also obtained a life-size bust in plaster, a copy of that by Houdon. With these means, under the inspiration of the subject and his own genius, it is believed that Mr. Willard would have been able to produce a Statue of the Father of his Country creditable to him and worthy of the subject. Unfortunately, perhaps, for Mr. Willard's fame, the model although packed with great carefulness, was broken and rendered worthless in its transportation to Boston. Mr. Willard thereupon, — probably finding the work a greater task than he had calculated, and with his little experience, more than he would be justified in assuming, — relinquished the undertaking. A conscientious fear of failure, which would be injurious to himself and a much more serious wrong to his employers, we have no doubt prevented Mr. Willard from recommencing the work. The statue, as is generally known, was executed by Chantrey, a distinguished English sculptor, in London, and occupies the room constructed for it by the Association in the Doric Hall of the State House, where it was placed in 1828. It is of pure white marble, grace-

fully clothed in a military cloak.   Chantrey, like Willard and
Rush, commenced his career in art as a carver.

After leaving Richmond, Mr. Carey relates that they visited
Baltimore and Philadelphia.   In the latter city they presented
letters of introduction to Mr. William Rush, these having been
furnished to them by Mr. Robert Mills of Baltimore, the distinguished architect of the Washington Monument, erected in
that city in 1815-16.   Mr. Rush had at this time acquired considerable reputation as a carver in wood, and especially of figure-
heads for ships.   These were favorably spoken of in the periodicals, and had also been noticed in England — where, it is
said, they had been in some instances purchased and transferred
to the bows of English vessels in Liverpool.   Mr. Rush succeeded "admirably with Indian figures," and these would be likely
to attract attention abroad.   He subsequently wrought a Statue
of Washington for the State of Pennsylvania, which is now in
the State House at Philadelphia.*   Mr. Mills was a prominent
competitor for the premium offered by the Bunker Hill Monument Association for a design for the monument, and appears to
have thought he had a strong claim to it.

During this visit to Philadelphia, Mr. Willard made a drawing of the "Water Nymph," a piece of statuary by Mr. Rush,
which surmounted the building of the Fairmount Water Works,
(a labor of singular insignificance in these days of artistic skill
and photography,) with which Mr. Rush was much pleased, and
which gained his consideration.   In speaking of this matter the
next day, Mr. Rush said to Mr. Carey, "that gentleman is a
man of high talent; I wish I could draw as well as he does, but
I cannot."   Mr. Willard had an accurate eye and a facility in
drawing quite remarkable for that time and the slender opportunities he had enjoyed.   Mr. Rush was a Director in the Pennsylvania Academy of Fine Arts, and a member of the City

---

* Vide Dunlap's History of the " Arts of Design."

Council of Philadelphia. The remark made by him was considered by Mr. Carey as a very high compliment to his friend. We have no doubt that it was well merited.

Architectural drawing, carving in wood, various studies in chemistry and geology, teaching in drawing and perspective, occupied Mr. Willard's time, until he added to these pursuits those of modelling and sculpture. His taste, industry and general accomplishments in all these arts, induced Mr. Carey to say in a letter of June, 1861, "I have been acquainted with nearly all of the principal artists and mechanics who have resided in Boston for the last fifty years, and I think I have never known a man of greater original powers of mind, combined with uncommon practical skill in execution, than Solomon Willard. He was indefatigable in whatever he undertook, and seldom if ever failed to accomplish his object. Whether the material on which he wrought was clay, wood, marble or granite, he was equally successful in all." Similar testimony is offered by others who knew Mr. Willard personally and professionally. "Combined with uncommon practical skill in execution," we doubt if his place has even yet been filled.

CHAPTER V.

Mr. WILLARD seems to have adopted modelling as an auxiliary to designing and drawing, in architecture, and appears to have applied it to private as well as public enterprises. The first mention of modelling found in Mr. Willard's books is under the date of June, 1817, where he mentions having worked five days upon a model, at three dollars per day. He probably did other work of this kind before he left for the south.

The next mention of the subject is in the following letter from Mr. Charles Bulfinch, at the time engaged as architect upon the capitol at Washington :

"Washington, January 30, 1818. ·

"Mr. Willard, — Sir, I understood from Mr. Towne, when he passed through this place, that you were in Baltimore and intended soon to come on here and with a wish to obtain employment. There are a number of sculptors employed on the public buildings — very superior workmen, brought from Italy by the agents of the government, and whom they are under contract to keep employed. But I have a wish to have a Model made of the capitol building, both of the parts already erected and finishing and of the different designs for the centre. To be on a scale of one inch to eight feet would require a model of four feet long and about fourteen inches high, or to be more exact, forty-five inches long, fifteen deep and ten high in the walls. Should you like to undertake this? I wish you to consider and let me know as soon as convenient, whether you incline to come for the purpose, and on what terms you would undertake it, and how long time it would require. Perhaps the doing that would introduce to other work. The model I propose to be of wood, similar to one of a hospital, done by you in Boston for Dr. Parkman.

"Your answer would oblige your friend and humble servant,
"CHARLES BULFINCH.

"On consulting the Commissioner he is willing to engage you for one month, if you think you can complete the model in that time, at three dollars per day."

Mr. Willard at this time was engaged on the ornamental work of the Independent Church, in Baltimore, and to Mr. Bulfinch's friendly invitation sent the following reply :

"Baltimore, February 16, 1818.
"Sir, — Previous to receiving your letter I had engaged to execute some ornamental finishings for the Independent Church, in this place, designed by Mr. Godfrey, and which will probably require a month to complete.

"I have a desire to be engaged at the public buildings and on a part which will not interfere with others. The time necessary to make the model which you mention would depend on the mountings of the representation ; but I should think that it might be done sufficiently so in about eighteen days. The compensation per day should be from two hundred and fifty to three hundred cents.

"It would oblige me if you would let me know soon, by the way of the post office, if the terms are acceptable, or if the delay will occasion any inconvenience.
"Yours, &c.,   SOLOMON WILLARD."

The correspondence, so characteristic of Mr. Willard in the

foregoing letter, was further continued by Mr. Bulfinch, on the
twenty-fifth of February, who then informed Mr. Willard as
follows : " Since I have mentioned to the Committee of Congress
and to the Commissioner of Public Buildings the advantages of
having a model, they have become impatient to have it made,
and wish it to be undertaken immediately." Urging Mr. Willard to make an arrangement to come on and begin the work,
he says, " there will be no difficulty about the terms, . . .
and I think there will be an opening for you here in the line
you are fondest of, that is worth your attention."

Mr. Willard replies that " the committee of the church have
consented to release me for the present, . . . and I shall
have the necessary implements for executing the work transported by land, and shall be happy to serve you to the extent of my
ability."

The work was accordingly undertaken and completed early
in April. In a letter to a friend under the date of Baltimore,
April 9th, 1818, Mr. Willard speaks of the work as follows :

" I have just returned from Washington, where I have been
engaged in executing a model of the public buildings, under the
direction of Mr. Bulfinch. The model though slight, seems to
give satisfaction, and Congress has shown uncommon liberality
in the appropriations for carrying the work into effect. This
model was executed in the architect's room, where we had the
honor of a visit from Mr. Latrobe."

Some years afterwards the model was in the possession of Mr.
Bulfinch, at Boston, and was shown by him to his friends and
commended as an evidence of the genius and ability of Mr.
Willard. It is presumed to be still in existence, but now representing only a small portion of the present building.

Some months previous to the execution of this work, Mr. Willard visited Washington for a few days, and it is understood then
rendered valuable assistance to Mr. Bulfinch in making drawings
and working plans of Mr. Latrobe's designs.

In June of the same year, while yet engáged in Baltimore, Mr. Bulfinch invited Mr. Willard to come to Washington "to undertake the carving on the ceiling of the Senate and Representatives' rooms," and adds, "I hope your engagements will not interfere with your coming here, as I should derive great confidence and pleasure from your engaging in the work, and would do all in my power to render it agreeable and profitable to you." But, notwithstanding his formerly expressed desire to be engaged on the public buildings and the kindness of his friend, Mr. Willard, evidently thinking he might "interfere with others," under date of June 19th, 1818, wrote as follows: "The ornaments of the church are not quite completed and when they are finished I do not think of returning to Washington, as there are a sufficient number of my profession already there; but I shall make New York my residence, as I think that my ultimate views will be best promoted in that place." What were the ultimate views entertained by him at this time, we have no means of ascertaining. This correspondence shows that he regarded carving and ornamental work as comprising his profession; but modelling, as connected with architecture and as he practiced it, was an art which seems to have been undertaken and pursued by him partly as a matter of taste.

In July, Mr. Willard hired a room in New York of Mr. Van Buren, — but returned to Boston in October of the same year. He was no doubt fully employed while in that city. Subsequently and for a number of years, in Boston, Mr. Willard occupied a portion of his time in modelling designs and plans of his own, and, in addition to these, made models in plaster of the Pantheon and Parthenon, of exact proportions, which were used by Mr. Edward Everett, in a course of lectures delivered by him, in the winter of 1821-2. These models are yet in existence, in the basement room of the Boston Athenæum.

6

334642

CHAPTER VI.

CARVING IN STONE — ST. PAUL'S CHURCH — TEACHING.

AFTER his return from the south, Mr. Willard who had previously paid some attention to the subject of geology, now connected this study with chemistry, and attended a course of lectures on the latter science. He made himself familiar with the
different kinds of stone and their component parts, and devoted
much time and labor to a practical investigation of the science —
which like his other studies and pursuits, proved available in
aftertime, both in quarrying and building. He continued also
to meet all the demands made upon him in carving, making designs and drawing plans, and added to his other pursuits that
of carving in stone, or sculpture in its limited and popular sense.
The first work of this kind mentioned by him in his memoranda
of accounts, excepting a single tablet for Mr. Carey, is the
" modelling and executing of five panels in marble for Mr. David
Sears, at one hundred dollars per panel," in October, 1816.—
These are to be seen in the front of his fine granite mansion
house on Beacon street, in Boston, and as specimens of scroll-
work and foliage are quite equal to the best outside-work of the
present time.

In January, 1820, Mr. Willard was engaged on the stone-
work of Saint Paul's Church, Tremont street, of which Captain
Alexander Parris was the architect. He had previously been
an inmate of Capt. Parris's family, and undoubtedly gave him

friendly assistance in the arrangement and preparation of the plans for this edifice, which was regarded as a very decided improvement, in material and style, on the churches of half a century ago, — resulting, as it certainly did, partly owing to its cramped situation, in disappointing the expectations of its proprietors. Its completion, we think, was not regarded with much satisfaction : in point of fact it never has been completed, and since its erection, has been overshadowed by the Masonic Temple, now the United States Court House, and other buildings near it. The masonry of this church was the work of Mr. Carey, who thinks Mr. Willard made some of the drawings, though Capt. Parris prepared the working plans. The front elevation, — its Ionic portico and pediment, — is of Potomac sand-stone, from the quarries near Aquia Creek, which were visited by Mr. Carey on occasion of his trip to Virginia with Mr. Willard, two or three years previously. The massive columns, in blocks, are the work of Mr. Carey, but the wrought capitals are by Mr. Willard, who worked them out on Mason street, on land afterwards occupied for many years until his death, by his warm friend Mr. Amos Lawrence. It was originally intended to have a Scripture-piece, executed in bass-relief, in the pediment above the portico, for which purpose the blocks of stones are left projecting at the present time. The subject proposed was, " Paul before King Agrippa," and it was to have been executed by Mr. Willard; but the edifice having cost more than the original estimate, the proprietors did not feel warranted in incurring any further expense, and the work was not undertaken. They also thought the kind and quality of the stone inferior and unsuitable for the work ; but, as it can be worked with facility and will of course be as durable as the columns and capitals of the portico, — notwithstanding the unfavorable location of the edifice, — the original design may yet be completed. It would greatly enrich and improve its appearance.

During the following years, Mr. Willard, — besides furnishing plans, designs and models ; including plans of improvements for

the Second Church and Brattle-square Church, (1823-4) ; a
plan and model for the United States Branch Bank ; plans and
outlines for many private houses and blocks, — received pupils
at his studio near St. Paul's Church, and gave lessons in architecture and drawing. Mr. Nathaniel Cotton, a member of the
committee to prepare this memoir, was an attendant in one of
his classes in drawing, and speaks of him in high and appreciative terms as an instructor and a gentleman. He says, "Mr.
Willard's ability as an architect having become more generally
known, he was induced to devote a portion of his time to impart-
ing instruction in architectural drawing ; and by his experience
and perfect familiarity with his subject, was a competent and
thorough teacher, especially for those who were disposed to begin at the beginning. He was always interested in the progress
of his pupils and encouraged them by the kindness of his manners. He endeavored to teach them the first principles of geom-
etry and of perspective, and as they progressed he gradually
brought them to comprehend and understand the orders of architecture and their true application and appropriate purposes. He
was familiar with the works of the old masters of the art and
had a high appreciation of proportion and harmony. He not
only had his juniors as his pupils ; but many, who for a score of
years had been practical architects and mechanics, were solicit-
tous of his instruction, and to some of these he gave private
lessons. They all profitted by his instructions, knew well how
to appreciate his ability and still retain a lively and interested
recollection of him." Mr. Charles Wells, who was afterwards
associated with him as a member of the Bunker Hill Monument Association, and still is one of its Vice Presidents, was
one of his private pupils. During the administration of Mr.
Wells, in 1832, as Mayor of Boston, Mr. Willard was employed
to design and build the County Court House, in Court street,
which was enlarged in 1862, in a manner according with the
original plan.

·.

· CHAPTER VII.

NEW HEATING APPARATUS — THE HOT-AIR FURNACE.

WE have seen that Mr. Willard came to Boston at the age of twenty-one years, and without having served any regular apprenticeship, soon became master of his art, — his third piece of work being one of the most difficult in carpentry.   Devoting himself assiduously to labor and study, we have found him rising in his pursuits and securing the means unaided to improve his mind, cultivate his taste and qualify his hand for still higher service.   Taking lessons in art-work, attending lectures in science, seeking the privileges of the best library in Boston, studying volumes of history and of the masters of design — supporting himself by his industry and absolutely lending his employer money — we soon see him laying aside the broad-axe and fore-plane and occupied as a draughtsman and carver.   Architecture and modelling, sculpture in wood and stone, are next adopted and successfully practiced, while geology, anatomy, chemistry and the French language are pursued as studies, and teaching a little later almost as a pastime.

As much of Mr. Willard's attention for a number of years had been given in some form, to the construction of buildings, both public and private, it was natural that he should bestow some thought upon the existing methods of warming these — imperfect, inadequate and unsatisfactory as such methods were admitted to be.   Nearly all the fuel used for producing artificial

heat was wood, furnished from the neighborhoods of our cities
and towns and from the almost boundless forests of Maine.   The
Franklin fire-place and Count Rumford's cooking-ranges, were
in use in the best dwelling-houses;   and large cast-iron stoves,
with extensive pipes ranging through rooms and halls, were . in
use in the public buildings and churches.   Some better means
of warming these last was even more necessary than in private
dwellings where open fire-places and iron stoves with moderate
lengths of pipe could still be used with comparatively satisfactory
results.   In public halls, school houses and churches, large iron
stoves in the coldest weather, were kept at a red-heat, — thus
burning up and destroying the air for all purposes of sustaining
life, and still failing to keep these large apartments comfortable
or maintaining any reasonable equanimity of temperature.   Some
few merchants and others of the wealthy classes, were able to
procure a supply of " Sea Coal" from England, for use in their
counting-rooms and perhaps for the parlor grate, but the total
amount of English coal imported into the city of Boston, at that
time, was a small item in the aggregate amount of fuel used.—
It was not until 1820, two hundred years after the first settlement of the country, that our own immense supplies of coal were
developed and during that year only three hundred and sixty-
five tons of anthracite were used in the whole country.   It was
some years after this before it could be used to any considerable extent, for want of experience and suitable apparatus : its
successful introduction required an apprenticeship in the consu-
mers ; its use was a new art; it was not easily ignited and the
traditionary methods of hastening combustion in wood fires were
sure to extinguish one made of stone-coal.   The lesson, however,
was learned ; new apparatus came with the experience, and
the increasing use of mineral coal has continued ever since, until it now reaches an amount exceeding in annual value the sum
of twenty millions of dollars.

It may well be believed that there was at this time need of
some improvement in the methods as well as means of warming

and ventilating dwelling-houses and public buildings — and the earnestness with which these were sought is manifested in every letter and record we have upon the subject. Numerous improvements were made in stove-patterns and stove-manufacture, as. is sufficiently attested in the patent office, but they were stoves still and required the usual quantity of pipe in exposed situations, and in various ways increased the danger of fire. To Mr. Willard belongs the credit of originating in this country the first step towards the complete, adequate and almost perfect contrivance of the present day for the production of artificial heat, — namely, the Hot-air Furnace, — placed in the basement of the building, having communication with the external air, and pipes leading to the various apartments to be warmed. — The system thus introduced for warming dwelling-houses, office-buildings, school houses or churches, easily, readily and equably, and of obtaining the required ventilation, was completely successful. Progress and improvement had been planned and made upon the results attained in the scientific experiments of Dr. Franklin and Count Rumford. Although we do not find that Mr. Willard ever obtained or applied for a patent for his invention, we are not aware of any claim of prior right existing in conflict with that now made for him. Many patents for new furnaces, and for improvements, in both cases involving the same general plan and principles, have been obtained since Mr. Willard's furnaces were introduced — of course all these are designed for the use of the modern mineral fuel.

Mr. Willard's furnaces were manufactured by Mr. Daniel Safford, a well-remembered mechanic of Boston, at his establishment on Devonshire street, between Water and Milk streets : they were made chiefly of wrought and sheet iron, and as we have intimated, were intended for the use of wood as a fuel. — Two of these were constructed in the Old South Church ; two in Saint Paul's Church ; one in Rev. Dr. Lowell's Church, and one in Mr. Davenport's factory, in the fall of 1823. There was one in the Rev. Mr. Coleman's Church, in Salem, and the Rev.

Benjamin Abbott, of Exeter, N. H., (whose society had just completed a small church on a plan furnished by Mr. Willard,) applied for one for that building.   The inventor has not left any description of this furnace or account of his interest in it : the following letter from Mr. Bulfinch, two years later, is the only writing containing any notice of it which we have seen :

" Providence, Rhode Island, October 8, 1825.

" Dear Sir, — I intended to have called upon you once more before my leaving Boston, but was prevented by a variety of engagements in which I found myself involved.   I called according to your advice at Mr. Safford's work-shop.   He was not within, but his foreman explained to me the construction of the various parts of the furnaces now in use.   I also saw at Salem, one set up in Rev. Dr. Coleman's church — so that I have a very complete general idea of them; but there are some further particulars that I wish to be informed upon, and will thank you to answer the following, as soon as you conveniently can :

" The dimensions of size, in breadth and height, of the square inside stove ; the same of the external cover containing the tubes, its base, its diameter in the middle and its height.

" The size of the cold-air tubes — admitted at the bottom — and the best size of the openings to convey warm-air to the rooms, both for churches and for private houses to warm separate rooms. The size of the openings in the floor to promote circulation, and whether they are necessary in every room.

" Is it best to admit the warm-air near the floor ?   In Mr. Coleman's church the openings were about five feet from the floor.

" Do you find any necessity for ventilators, and how do you construct them ?

" What is the difference in size, of furnaces for churches and for private houses, and the difference in expense?

" I wish for information on these points, because we are about taking measures for warming the centre of the capitol, and the

President is desirous of adopting the most approved mode for warming the entrance-hall of his house : it opens to the north and is not only cold in itself but keeps the whole house uncomfortable. There is a basement room under this hall, in which a furnace could be set very conveniently. I want to be able to do it in the best manner, and to convey pipes to any room where they may choose to admit them. In these rooms I suppose they will continue their open fires, but as the rooms are very large a supply of warm-air must be very desirable.

" The dining-room is 30 by 40, and the banqueting-room 40 by 90 feet, and 22 feet high. This large room has never yet been used.

" I will thank you to give the subject some consideration, and to favor me with all the information that your experience may suggest to be necessary ; and the sooner the better, as the season is fast advancing upon us. You will address your letter to me at Washington, where I expect to be in the course of this week.

" If upon conferring with the President, after his return, he should determine upon having a furnace for his house, I shall write to you again, and ask your attention to having it constructed in the best manner : and shall be happy to return the favor by any means in my power.

" Your friend and servant,   CHARLES BULFINCH."

We regret that we have not been able to find Mr. Willard's reply to this letter, as it would no doubt afford a more distinct idea of the construction and character of the furnace. It is evident, however, that it greatly resembled those in use at the present time, and may have been the model on which they are constructed. Some years previously to this time a stove had been invented in England, by Mr. William Strutt of Belper, in Derbyshire, which was called the " cockle" or " Belper" stove, which included the idea of the furnace. It was a cylinder stove, enclosed in a brick chamber, into which cold air was admitted at the bottom and heated air transmitted from the top to the

7

apartments to be warmed.   In 1792, Mr. Strutt applied it to
warm his large cotton factories.   An improvement of this stove
was made by Mr. Charles Sylvester for warming the Derby In-
firmary, and "was long regarded as a model of its kind for
a large building."*   This stove, notwithstanding the general remark that the use of heated air-chambers for warming adjoining
rooms is of very ancient date, is the first mention of any apparatus resembling the modern furnace for the same purpose, which
we have met with.   Mr. Willard's furnace differed materially
from the "cockle," being not a stove but an open fire-place,
with flaring jambs and back, covered with a hexagon chamber,
in which were the tubes, — the whole enclosed in brick work.
The smoke passed over the jambs and out of a smoke flue below.
Mr. Strutt's was a cylinder stove for burning "Sea coal."

Subsequently to Mr. Bulfinch's letter above given, probably
in 1827, two of these furnaces were manufactured by Safford
and Low, for the capitol at Washington, and their erection was
superintended by Mr. Low, in that year.   It is possible that these
were made for the burning of coal.   Some of these furnaces were
put up by Mr. Safford as late as 1843, in interior places where
wood was more easily obtained than anthracite.

This furnace, of course, in the onward march of improvement,
has been superceded; but for some twenty years, it answered
the public wants and was almost without a rival.   The demands

---

* Vide, "Treatise on Warming and Ventilation," by Charles Tomlinson.
London, 1858.   Franklin's and Count Rumford's experiments and improvements, are explained and commented on in this volume, but no mention whatever is made of any of the American anthracite burning stoves or furnaces for
warming and ventilating large buildings.   Nor are these mentioned with any
particularity or described in the "New American Cyclopædia," nor yet in the
"English Cyclopædia," 1861, while these works contain elaborate rehearsals
of early experiments, inventions and improvements pertaining to the subject.
Existing methods of warming buildings and ventilating rooms, in the United
States, by means of hot-air furnaces, hot water pipes, or steam, can hardly be
learned from any works which have fallen under our observation.

for it were pressing and constant, not alone for public buildings but for private dwellings; and in their manufacture the workmen of Mr. Safford's establishment were employed night and day exclusively on them.   Probably more than one thousand of them were made and put up — and we have been unable to discover that Mr. Willard ever received any income, royalty or reward for his invention.   Managed in the customary way, with the protection of a patent, it would have proved a fortune to him ; but, prudent and judicious as he was in his expenditures, he was not the man, by nature or habit, to accumulate property for its mere possession.   Such an instance of unselfishness and indifference to profit, on the part of an inventor, must be of rare occurrence, and in the present time, we judge, it would not be easy to find one person thus freely yielding up a fortune either from indifference or for the public benefit.   Mr. Willard has done more than this : he has given the labor of his whole life to the public, or individuals, in every way in which he has been engaged, having barely had his own personal expenses paid, " which were very small."

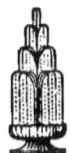

CHAPTER VIII.

BOSTON MECHANICS' INSTITUTION.

No association which was ever organized in Boston has more conspicuously illustrated the harmony of feeling and unity of purpose which prevailed at the time and has for many years subsisted between the mercantile and the mechanic interests, and we may add the professional also, than the Boston Mechanics' Institution. The evidence of this is seen in its list of members, in its organization and in its whole history. It has been thought that there was, at the commencement of the revolutionary war, if not during its continuance and at its termination, a feeling of opposition tinctured with some asperity, between the mechanic and the other interests in Boston, which was more or less manifested in the civil and political affairs of the time. It was natural, perhaps, that such a feeling should exist, when it is remembered that the mechanics were the first and most active in exciting and promoting the revolutionary spirit; which, of course, was looked upon by the merchants as destructive of the commerce and prosperity of the town, and which they were but little inclined thus early to encourage. — The " Liberty Boys" were mostly mechanics, or belonging to the working classes; the famous "Tea Party" company was similarly composed ; and General Gage seems to have believed that but for the greater numbers of the " lower classes," as he called them, the tea itself would have been accepted and the rebellious proceedings checked and possibly stayed altogether. But the purpose of the British government to make the colonies a source of revenue, became more apparent ; broader views began to prevail, and a truly patriotic feeling was soon engendered in the minds of the people. The different classes, if not acting together in the same private meetings, were cordially united in their purposes and measures. The mechanics had their clubs ; the merchants their clubs — and resistance to British injustice and coercion was the determination of each.

But whatever there was of this feeling, at any time, it was local and temporary, and had no deep-seated foundation in the sentiments or sober judgments of the people of either class or any section of the city. If it arose from a difference of opinion, as we have already suggested, it were impossible, in the incipient movements of the revolutionary war, that there should not be divisions of opinion and honest doubts on the momentous ques-tions of the day, — they were necessary to the issue, — but among those not absolutely tories, they were soon settled or exploded ; and the rebellious "lower classes" were fully and efficiently supported by the merchants and professional men. — The latter were privately invited to attend the secret meetings of the former, and the members of these were solemnly sworn not to communicate their proceedings to any persons excepting cer-tain prominent individuals, who were of the wealthy and culti-vated classes. So that when the revolution fairly broke out, the People of Boston, — excepting their natural enemies, the civil and military officers of the crown and their sympathisers, — were as a unit, and exerted their influence and directed their strength to the assertion and maintenance of their rights and ultimately to secure the national independence. The same spirit of har-mony and good feeling continued during the war — has been repeatedly and actively manifested since that period — is inter-woven with the domestic and political history of the city — and finds a striking exemplification in the formation and organization of the Boston Mechanics' Institution, in which, notwithstanding its distinctive corporate name, all classes and professions were united; and those other usually dividing lines in a community, religion and politics, were not considered.

The Boston Mechanics' Institution was originated by a few gentlemen in 1826, and was incorporated in 1827. The first meetings were held in a room in Boylston Hall. Mr. Willard was one of those engaged in its formation and was present at the primary meetings. When the subscription of membership was opened it was at once signed by Nathaniel Bowditch, Daniel Treadwell, David Moody, Solomon Willard, Alpheus Carey, Amos Lawrence, H. A. S. Dearborn, William Sullivan, Francis C. Whiston, Charles W. Moore, and others.

The act of incorporation was accepted on the 29th of June, 1827, and at the election of officers Nathaniel Bowditch was elected President; Daniel Treadwell, David Moody and Solomon Willard, Vice Presidents; Francis C. Whiston, Recording Secretary; George B. Emerson, Corresponding Secretary; Stephen Fairbanks, Treasurer, and the following equally well-known gentlemen a Board of Directors: Ebenezer Bailey, George Baldwin, Alpheus Carey, Timothy Claxton, John Cotton, George Darracott, H. A. S. Dearborn, Phineas Dow, James K. Frothingham [Charlestown,] William Lyman, Charles W. Moore, Alexander Parris, Charles C. Starbuck, Ezra Stone [East Cambridge,] William Sturgis and John W. Webster. Mr. Willard at this time was engaged in the erection of the Bunker Hill Monument.

In the formation of this Institution, which embraced among its members clergymen, professors in the college, lawyers, physicians, merchants and traders, and numbers from the manufacturing and mechanical pursuits, is seen with nearly all its characteristics, the Lyceum, which soon after occupied public attention; and in its annual courses of lectures by its own members, on scientific and literary subjects, the inauguration of the system of popular lectures which now forms an essential feature in the winter-recreations of our New-England communities. On the first season, commencing November, 1827, the introductory lecture was delivered by Mr. Edward Everett, " On the importance to practical men of scientific knowledge, and on the encouragement to its pursuit." In this interesting and valuable lecture Mr. Everett says, " The object of the Mechanics' Institute is, to diffuse useful knowledge among the mechanic class of the community. It aims in general, to improve and inform the minds of its members ; and particularly to illustrate and explain the principles of the various arts of life, and render them familiar to that portion of the community, who are to exercise these arts as their occupation in society. It is also a proper object of the Institute, to point out the connexion between the mechanic arts and the other pursuits and occupations, and show the foundations, which exist in our very nature, for a cordial union between them all."* The discourse was eminently calculated to encourage the institution and promote its purposes. Other lectures in the course were delivered by Professors Farrar and Treadwell, Dr. Jacob Bigelow, George B. Emerson, and Gamaliel Bradford.

In November, 1828, the second course of lectures was commenced with an introductory discourse by Mr. Daniel Webster, on the state of the mechanic arts, their usefulness and the purposes of the institution. Like that of the preceding year, it was an eloquent and scholarly production. In describing the purposes of the institution, Mr. Webster expands the view taken by Mr. Everett. The latter gentleman, rightly enough, spoke of it as intended to diffuse information among its members, and to promote a cordial union among all the pursuits and occupations

---

* " Orations and Speeches on Various Occasions, by Edward Everett."— Boston, 1856. Volume I.

of men.   Mr. Webster speaks of its purpose, in a far-seeing and
almost prophetic spirit :

" The distinct purpose is to connect science more and more with
art ; to teach the established, and invent new, modes of combining skill with strength ; to bring the power of the human understanding in aid of the physical powers of the human frame ; to
facilitate the co-operation of the mind with the hand ; to promote
convenience, lighten labor, and mitigate toil, by stretching the
dominion of mind farther and farther over the elements of nature, and by making those elements themselves submit to human
rule, follow human bidding, and work together for human happiness."*

How soon much of this was realized by inventions and improvements now so familiar !

After an eloquent explanation of the mechanical powers and
a brief sketch of the history of art, in speaking of the progress
of the mechanical arts — twenty-five years ago — Mr. Webster
says, " The slightest glance . . must convince us that mechanical power and mechanical skill, as they are now exhibited
in Europe and America, mark an epoch in human history worthy of all admiration.   Machinery is made to perform what has
formerly been the toil of human hands, to an extent that aston-
ishes the most sanguine, with a degree of power to which no
number of human arms is equal, and with such precision and
exactness as almost to suggest the notion of reason and intelligence in the machines themselves.   Every natural agent is put
unrelentingly to the task.   The winds work, the waters work,
the elasticity of metals works ; gravity is solicited into a thous-
and new forms of action ; levers are multiplied upon levers ;
wheels revolve on the peripheries of other wheels ; the saw and

* " The Works of Daniel Webster," Volume i.

the plane are tortured into an accommodation to new uses, and last of all, with inimitable power, and 'with whirlwind sound,' comes the potent agency of steam.   In comparison with the past, what centuries of improvement has this ·single agent comprised, in the short compass of fifty years !   Everywhere practicable, everywhere efficient, it has an arm a thousand times stronger than that of Hercules, and to which human ingenuity is capable of fitting a thousand times as many hands as belonged to Briareus."

These courses of lectures were continued with general 'success and satisfaction for some ten years.   They were popular and instructive ; the means of introducing a number of lecturers to the public, and afforded opportunities of association and intercourse which were highly valuable to the members and of much benefit to the community.   Mr. Willard, we have reason to believe, especially profitted by them, and we have no doubt, many others did also.   Some few books and scientific periodicals were collected by the institution, and considerable valuable philosophical apparatus was obtained from Europe and used to illustrate the lectures.   All these, together with the records and papers belonging to the institution, were transferred to the Massachusetts Charitable Mechanic Association in January, 1840, the members retaining certain conditional rights' in the property, and entitled to some privileges in the way of membership.

The institution flourished for ten or twelve years, successfully promoting its objects and preparing the way for other efforts in the same direction.

8

.

CHAPTER IX.

MR. WILLARD'S GREAT WORK — BUNKER HILL MONUMENT.

THE great work of Mr. Willard's life — for which he was prepared by circumstances; which comported with his taste and experience; into which he threw his energy and skill; and which, for the time, was as a part of himself, was the Bunker Hill Monument — the grand national memorial of the opening of the Revolutionary War and of the principles involved in that memorable contest for liberty and the rights of man. — As soon as the subject of erecting a monument was proposed to the public, Mr. Willard became interested in it. It seemed at once to seize upon his imagination and feelings — he labored for it in season and out of season — and notwithstanding all the difficulties, embarrassments and delays in the progress of the work, he never lost his interest in it or failed to do his utmost to secure its completion. He did not look upon it simply as a work of art, which might be supposed to be his stand-point, but regarded it as a high patriotic duty, sacred to the best and noblest sentiments of our nature, and one with which no selfish or sordid purposes of popularity or profit should be permitted to mingle. It was in his mind, — as surely in the minds of those eminent men who conceived, and by efforts and labors yet untold, promoted the enterprise, — to be a work of gratitude — the outpouring of appreciative and grateful hearts — as well as the memorial of an event, however important in its consequences. His ideas on this subject, in some respects, were peculiar : in order to make the work what it should be — the memorial of a grateful people — he thought all should contribute towards its necessary cost, according to. their means, but he did not believe in asking for or receiving money to pay a profit in such an undertaking.   In accordance with his feelings in this respect, he always refused for himself all compensation for services rendered, and, we think, to a large extent also for expenses incurred, and never sought for or accepted any pay or profit in any matter connected with the work, either during its erection or afterwards.   He seemed to feel that to undertake such a work for profit, to speculate in its contracts, or in any way diminish or misdirect its funds, would not only be a high misdemeanor to be punished by statute and a fraud upon the patriotic contributors, but would take from the structure itself a part of its sacred character as a work of gratitude and honor.   He took an early occasion to have his views on this subject known, as will be seen by his letter of June, 1825, before he was chosen architect and superintendent of the work.

With these feelings, Mr. Willard's interest in the monument became devotion to it, and there are, and have been, but few persons that know how arduous, continuous, self-sacrificing and public spirited have been his services in its behalf — from the beginning to the end.   There are but few persons if any, now living, who know how much we are indebted to him for the design and general plan of the monument ; for the massive and durable character of its material ; for the excellence and accuracy of the work ; for its low cost, and finally for its completion, with the means originally and ultimately at the command of the association.   Much of all this remains untold, and it is due to him, and to those with whom he was associated in the work ; to the truth of history, and as a faithful record of faithful services, that they should be stated and rendered as durable as the monument itself, and the deeds and principles it so sublimely commemorates.   He gave time, thought and labor to the work — its preparation, its management and its progress, — which as regards himself, money could neither command or compensate. — During his engagement upon it, he found his best reward in his own breast and in the approbation of those with whom he was associated in the patriotic service.

The first suggestion of the present monument is credited by Mr. Everett, without contradiction, to Mr. William Tudor, first editor of the North American Review ;* and it seems that Gen. H. A. S. Dearborn called attention to the subject of the battle-field in April, 1822, in one of the public papers, when a " lot of ground including the monument erected to the memory of Gen. Warren," was to be sold at auction.   He desired that " some patriotic gentleman of wealth in the town of Charlestown should purchase this American Marathon and have it enclosed with a stone or iron fence, to be held sacred, as the spot where the defenders of the Republic first met the shock of battle ' in times which tried men's souls.' "   Mr. Tudor thereupon consulted with Mr. Dearborn, and the result is stated as follows : "Dr. John C. Warren of Boston, purchased the land in November, 1822, and held it until the Monument Association, subsequently formed, took it from his hands."†   The Records of the Standing Committee, kept by Mr. Everett, make no reference to such a transaction, but state, under date of August 17, 1824, " that Mr. Knowles made a report on the subject of the Bunker Hill lands, exhibiting the proposals which he had received from the proprietors, and estimating the sum required to purchase them at $26,000.   This report was accepted, and it was voted, that the same committee be requested to proceed to make the purchase, and to procure a loan of the money required for the same on the credit of the corporation, secured by the joint obligation of such gentlemen as may be disposed to enter into it."   The lands were purchased and the next year rented as a pasture.

* Speech of May 28, 1833, in Faneuil Hall. Speeches, &c. vol. I.
† Prof. Packard's History of the Bunker Hill Monument.   Collections of the Maine Historical Society. 1852.

The act incorporating the Bunker Hill Monument Association was approved by the Governor, on the 7th of June, 1823, and was accepted by the corporation on the 13th of the same month. On the 17th, by-laws were adopted and the officers for the year elected. John Brooks, Governor of the Commonwealth, was chosen President of the association, and Daniel Webster first on the list of Directors. In his letter of acceptance, Governor Brooks said, " the object had always been a desirable one on his mind." Governor Brooks had himself served in the revolutionary war. He commanded a company of minute-men at Reading, and was on duty on the 19th of April, 1775 ; was a Major in Col. Bridge's regiment on the 17th of June, and as Lieutenant Colonel, stormed the entrenchments of the German troops at Saratoga.

In the first " address to the public," probably from the pen of Mr. Webster, published July 9th, 1823, the proposed erection of the monument is spoken of as follows :

" The erection of some public monument which should bear lasting testimony to national gratitude and cherish a national feeling, has often been the subject of discussion and conversation in this part of the country ; but none worthy of the name and purposes, has yet been executed. It is true that the public records, the productions of the press, history and poetry, are sure to preserve and perpetuate the remembrance of the great events of the American Revolution. Nevertheless, some grand and striking object, often recurring to the sight and impressing the mind with interesting associations, would be one, it is thought, neither useless nor unworthy for the present generation to rear to the memory of the past. . . . . Fortunately the scene of the battle of Bunker Hill possesses distinguished natural advantages for the site of a monument. It is high, conspicuous, and at present not covered with buildings.

" At present it is not practicable to define the character or magnitude of the monument which may be erected. This must

depend essentially on the extent to which the feelings of the
country shall be interested in the undertaking.   The general
view, however, is to erect a monument which shall be distinguished by simplicity and grandeur, rather than by elaborate
and elegant ornaments.   Like the events which it is to commemorate, we would wish it to exhibit the character of natural,
inherent, durable greatness."

At the expiration of a year, and after the recurrence of the
annual meeting, on the 27th of July, 1824, a Standing Committee was appointed, composed of H. A. S. Dearborn, John C.
Warren, Edward Everett, George Blake, and Samuel D. Harris, invested with authority " to exercise the powers of the Directors in managing the affairs of the association."

The first meeting of this committee was held at the Medical
College, on the 2d of August, 1824 : Gen. Dearborn, Chairman ; Mr. Everett, Secretary.   The first business before the
committee was a proposition from the Washington Benevolent
Society for transferring to the association its property and funds,
and these were subsequently received.   The next matter of record
is in the following words : " Plans of Monumental Columns,
drawn by Mr. Willard, architect, were submitted by Gen. Dearborn," with whom Mr. Willard had been in conference on the
subject.   The Standing Committee managed the affairs of the
association until April 29, 1825, — the date of its last meeting,
but the Building Committee did not have a meeting until the
last of October of that year.

Having shown his interest in the work, in various ways, Mr.
Willard was elected a member of the association in September,
1824, and received the following notice of the honor thereby
conferred upon him :

" Boston, September 8, 1824.
" Sir — You are hereby informed that you have been elected
a member of the Bunker Hill Monument Association, incorpo-

rated June 7th, 1823, for the purpose of commemorating the early events of the American Revolution, and especially for the erection of a Monument on the ground where the action of June 17, 1775, was fought.

"The intention of the association, in electing you a member, is to obtain your influence and aid in carrying into effect the design of the incorporation. These you are earnestly solicited to employ to the extent your situation and opportunity admit. Should you decline becoming a member, you will please to transmit a notice to this effect to the Secretary of the Standing Committee; otherwise you will forthwith receive a certificate of membership. By order,

EDWARD EVERETT,
Secretary of the Standing Committee of Directors."

The certificate subsequently received is as follows :—

"Be it made known by us, the President, Vice Presidents and Directors of the Bunker Hill Monument Association, instituted in 1823, for the purpose of commemorating the early events of the American Revolution, and especially for the erection of a Monument on the ground where the action of Bunker Hill was fought on the 17th of June, 1775, that Solomon Willard has been admitted to be a member of this association, and that this is to serve as a perpetual memorial of his having contributed to the execution of its patriotic design.

"John Brooks, President; T. H. Perkins, Joseph Story, Vice Presidents; Daniel Webster, George Blake, Benj. Gorham, H. A. S. Dearborn, Edward Everett, Samuel D. Harris, John C. Warren, Seth Knowles, Samuel Swett, George Ticknor, Theodore Lyman, Jr., Isaac P. Davis, Jesse Putnam, Directors; Nathaniel P. Russell, Treasurer; Franklin Dexter, Secretary."

On the 24th of September, the Standing Committee published a circular, "explaining the objects of the association," which was to be "circulated among the members of the community able to promote the design by their aid and interest." We should be

glad to copy this able and eloquent paper at length into these
pages, but for the reason that it will appear in a comprehensive
history of the monument, already in progress under a vote of the
association.   There are, however, two or three passages which
pertain so nearly to our subject, and which composed a part of
the material which artists would necessarily consider in making
a design for the work, that we feel justified in quoting them in
this place :

" The spot itself on which this memorable action took place,
is extremely favorable for becoming the site of a monumental
structure.   Competent judges have pronounced the heights of
Charlestown to excel any spot on our coast, in their adaptation
to the object in view.   Their position between the Mystic and
Charles, with the expanse of the harbor of Boston, and its beautiful islands in front, has long attracted the notice of the stranger.   An elevated monument on this spot would be the first
landmark of the mariner in his approach to our harbor ; while
the whole neighboring country, comprising the towns of Roxbury,
Brookline, Cambridge, Medford and Chelsea, with their rich
fields, villages and spires ; the buildings of the University, the
bridges, the numerous ornamental country seats and improved
plantations, the whole bounded by a distant line of hills and
farming landscape which cannot be surpassed in variety and
beauty, would be spread out as in a picture, to the eye of the
spectator on the summit of the proposed structure.

" Nor are these the only natural advantages of the spot. —
Though essentially rural in many of its features, it rises above
one of our most flourishing towns, the seat of several important
national establishments, where the noble ships of war of the
American Republic seem to guard the approach to the spot where
her first martyrs fought and bled.   Its immediate vicinity to
Boston, and its convenient distance from Salem, makes the access to it direct from the centres of our most numerous, wealthy
and active populations, and will be the means of keeping contin-

ually in sight, or bringing frequently to view, to the great masses of the community, the imposing memorial of an event which ought never to be absent from their memory, as its effects are daily and hourly brought home to the business and bosoms of every American citizen."

" In forming an estimate of the cost of the structure proposed, a single eye has been had to the principle which dictates its erection.   Everything separated from the idea of substantial strength and severe taste has been discarded, as foreign from the grave and serious character both of the men and events to be commemorated.   With this principle in view, it has been ascertained that a monumental column, of a classic model, with an elevation to make it the most lofty in the world, may be erected of our fine Chelmsford granite, for about thirty-seven thousand dollars."*

" The general propriety and expediency of erecting public monuments of the kind proposed are acknowledged by all. — They form not only the most conspicuous ornaments with which we can adorn our towns and high places, but they are the best proof we can exhibit to strangers, that our sensibility is strong and animated toward those great achievements and greater characters, to which we owe all our national blessings.   There surely is not one among us who would not experience a strong satisfaction in conducting a stranger to the foot of a monumental structure, rising in decent majesty on this memorable spot.

" Works of this kind also have the happiest influence in exciting and nourishing the national and patriotic sentiment.   Our

---

* This estimate refers to the earliest sketches made by Mr. Willard, of two columns " which had nearly the proportions of the Trajan and Antonine columns at Rome, excepting that the pedestals are higher in proportion than the Trajan and lower than the Antonine."   They were of less height and less diameter than the present monument, and the estimate was for small blocks and cheap construction.   The Trajan column is 106 feet in height with a pedestal of 19 feet ; that of Antoninus is 96 feet 6 inches with a pedestal of 26 feet 6 inches and a statue of St. Paul on the top of the column.

9

government has been called, and truly is a government of opinion; but it is one of sentiment still more. It is not the judgment only of this people, which dictates a preference for our
institutions; but it is a strong, deep-seated, inborn sentiment; a
feeling, a passion for liberty. It is a becoming expression of this
sentiment to honor, in every way, the memories and characters
of our fathers; to adorn a spot where their noble blood was spilt,
and not surrender it uncared-for to the plough. Years, it is to
be remembered, are rapidly passing away; and the glorious tra-
ditions of our national emancipation which we received from
them, will descend more faintly to our successors. The patriotic
sentiment, which binds us together more strongly than compacts
or constitutions, will if permitted, grow cold from mere lapse of
time. We owe these monuments, therefore, not less to the character of our posterity, than to the memory of our fathers. These
events must not lose their interest. Our children and our children's children have a right to these feelings, cherished and kept
by a worthy transmission. It is the order of nature that the
generation to achieve nobly should be succeeded by a generation
worthily to record and gratefully to commemorate. We are not
called to the fire and the sword; to meet the appaling array of
armies, to taste the bitter cup of imperial wrath and vengeance
proffered to an ill-provided land. We are chosen for the easier,
more grateful, but not less bounden duty of commemorating and
honoring the labors, sacrifices and sufferings of the great men of
those dark times.

"There is one point of view, in which we seem to be strongly
called upon to engage in the erection of works like that proposed.
The beautiful and noble arts of design and architecture have
hitherto been engaged in arbitrary and despotic service. The
Pyramids and Obelisks of Egypt; the monumental columns of
Trajan and Aurelius, have paid no tribute to the rights and feelings of man. Majestic and graceful as they are, they have no
record but that of sovereignty, sometimes cruel and tyrannical,
and sometimes mild; but never that of a great, enlightened and

generous people. Providence, which has given us the senses to observe, the taste to admire, and the skill to execute, these beautiful works of art, cannot have intended that, in a flourishing nation of freemen, there should be no scope for their erection. Our fellow-citizens of Baltimore have set us a noble example of redeeming the arts to the cause of free institutions, in the imposing monument they have erected to the memory of those who fell in defending their city. If we cannot be the first to set up a structure of this character, let us not be other than the first to improve upon the example ; to arrest and fix the feelings of our generation on the important events of an earlier and more momentous struggle, and to redeem the pledge of gratitude to the high-souled heroes of that trying day."

This noble appeal to the people, — in words which cannot be too often repeated, — could not have been unheeded by them, nor lost upon the artists of the country, and especially not upon Mr. Willard, whose feelings had already been awakened in behalf of the work. Those who read its eloquent sentences and happy illustrations, at this day, will be able to realize how forcibly and truthfully the subject was presented in it, and how clearly its reasonings have been fulfilled in the completion of the work.

Having thus presented the subject to the public, the next step was the initiation of active measures to obtain subscriptions for the work through the agency of the various town authorities, — accordingly a circular, dated October 1st, 1824, was addressed to the Selectmen of all the towns in the Commonwealth. This eloquent paper recounts the causes of the rebellion and the events which preceded the battle of Bunker Hill, and remarks of the battle and its consequences as follows :—

" Under cover of the night of the 16th of June, 1775, this detachment proceeded silently and cautiously, with such arms and implements as they had, and with a very small supply of powder, to take possession of the hills, and spend the night in

68 MEMOIR OF SOLOMON WILLARD.

the hurried labor of preparing for themselves some intrenchment, against the probable attack of the British. Poorly prepared, and wearied with labor, they met the shock on the following day, of the picked and chosen men of the British army !

" The consequences of the cool, undaunted, astonishing bravery, displayed on that day, we now feel and enjoy ; and they will continue to be felt and enjoyed, so long as we and our descendants shall be worthy of the name of Freemen.

" It is among these consequences, that we are now the citizens of a free and independent republic, not the degraded and despised subjects of despotic royal power ;

" That we live under laws made by rulers chosen from among ourselves, not under the orders of arbitrary authority, enforced by a ferocious soldiery ;

" That we dwell in security in our peaceful homes, in the full enjoyment of the fruits of our labor, instead of being liable to arbitrary taxation, and to personal service in wars of ambition, in which we could have no advantage, though subject to the most distressing evils ;

" That the community of which we are members, is thriving and expanding with the impulses of civil freedom, not creeping through an humble existence in the constraint of colonial dependence :

" In short, that we are citizens of a free, powerful and increasing nation, not a remote and insignificant appendage to a kingdom, and ruled by mandates issuing from a throne three thousand miles from our homes.

" What of gratitude, reverence and affection, do we not owe, fellow-citizens, to our countrymen who assembled and met the British on Bunker Hill on the Seventeenth of June ! It is to their manly resistance that we owe the precious blessings we call our own : ALL, ALL that we hold dear ! Had they turned and fled, as the British believed they would ; had a panic spread through the country from their flight, might not the germ of liberty have been crushed in the bud ; and the history of our country have been stained with disgraceful military executions, instead of being read as it now is, with emotions of inexpressible thanksgiving and praise !

" It is in honor of that glorious day that it is now proposed to raise a monument, worthy of those we commemorate, and to remind successive generations of the deeds of our fathers, and to evince the just and heartfelt gratitude of the present time."

. . . . " Such a monument will not only carry down to distant ages the memory of illustrious deeds ; it will also remind the generations, as they rise, of the origin of their social rights ; it will proclaim to them with awful grandeur, the sacred duty of preserving unimpaired the freedom which was purchased with precious blood."

CHAPTER X.

SELECTION OF A DESIGN FOR THE MONUMENT.

AFTER the purchase of the land, in behalf of the association, by the Directors, the next great questions to be considered were as to the plan of the monument and the means to meet its cost. The gentlemen who had conceived and undertaken the patriotic enterprise held frequent meetings, and immediately adopted measures to present the subject to the public and obtain subscriptions and donations for the work, as already described. The interesting question of a plan had of course been spoken of incidentally and was visibly presented at the first meeting of the Standing Committee, on 2d of August, 1824, by original designs from Mr. Willard, and it occupied the attention of the Directors and the public until July, 1825.

At the second meeting of the Standing Committee, on the 9th of August, "Dr. Warren having observed that Mr. Willard was prepared to make a drawing on a large scale of a plan of a monumental column, it was voted, that he be requested by the committee to draw a plan which might serve the purpose of public exhibition." "It was also voted that the same request be made to Mr. Alexander Parris, when he shall have exhibited a smaller plan to the committee." We have not found that Mr. Parris submitted any "smaller plan" to the committee, or any other plan until after the offer of a premium.

The idea respecting the proposed monument, entertained by

the committee at this time, may be considered as embodied in the following extract from the circular of October, 1824 :

" It is the design of the corporation to erect a column of two hundred and twenty feet in height ; of hewn granite, containing in its centre a circular stairway, by which it may be ascended to the top." . . . " As it will commemorate the greatest event in the history of civil liberty, it should be, and shall be, the grandest monument in the world."   This announcement, of course, would naturally lead artists who might be considering the subject, to suppose that the committee had determined upon the form of the monument — a column ; its height — two hundred and twenty feet ; the mode of ascent, by circular stairs, and the material — hewn granite, — and that the only matter undecided was its diameter.   But the committee had not yet called upon the artists of the country to offer designs for the work.

On the 4th of November, it was " Voted, that Mr. Willard be and he hereby is authorised to draw a plan of a monument, projected on a large scale, to be painted for the purpose of exhibition to the legislature and the citizens of Boston and vicinity." This plan was executed agreeably to the request of the committee, and proved to be satisfactory, as will be seen by the vote and correspondence which followed.

On the 17th of January, 1825, the Standing Committee accepted the form of an advertisement for a " plan," offering a premium of one hundred dollars for the best design which should be accepted.   The committee desired to avail itself of the artistic skill of the country, and received in response to their call about fifty designs of different styles and characteristics, a portion of which are yet preserved among the archives of the association, but no one of them was ever accepted by the Directors, nor was the premium offered ever awarded.

On the 16th of March, in the Standing Committee, it was " Voted, that the Secretary address a letter of thanks to Mr. Solomon Willard, soliciting permission to keep his plan and to compensate him for his trouble." Mr. Everett's letter to Mr. Willard is as follows :—

"Cambridge, March 22, 1825.

"Dear Sir, — I beg leave to inform you, that at a meeting of the Standing Committee of the Bunker Hill Monument Association, on the 16th instant, the following vote was unanimously passed :—

"That the thanks of the Committee be expressed to Mr. S. Willard for the preparation of a very beautiful plan of a monumental column at their request ; that, though the Committee have felt it their duty, at this stage of the business, in discharge of a public trust, to make a general advertisement to the artists of the country, yet nothing is farther from their purpose in so doing, than to undervalue the very beautiful plan prepared by Mr. Willard, whose services on this occasion, the Committee highly appreciate and desire to acknowledge by ample and honorable compensation.

"Permit me, dear sir, in communicating this vote, to offer you my private tribute of thanks for the display of talent, science and taste, in the plan prepared by you.

I am, very respectfully, yours,

EDWARD EVERETT,
Secretary of the Committee."

The following is Mr. Willard's reply :

"Boston, April 11th, 1825.

"Dear Sir, — I did not receive your note of the 22d of March until this evening. As I do not often call at the post office, it had remained there until sent to me by the post.

"I should be very sorry to have the Committee suppose that I question the propriety of their advertising for designs. On my own account merely, I should have preferred knowing their intentions at the outset, as I might thereby have avoided committing myself, and have chosen a course that might have been more successful. It requires some management to make and exhibit a design which will please the multitude. The purest design does not make the most catching picture, and an artist who intends to succeed in such a case should not draw what he thinks it proper to build, but that which he thinks will please. The design should be light and fanciful and the drawing deceptive and highly colored.

"I am not insensible to the honor that has been conferred on me by the Committee, and if my slender efforts have been of any service, they are entirely welcome. As respects the sketches, I think it due to myself to state that they were made under great disadvantages.

"Yours, respectfully,   SOLOMON WILLARD."

Up to this time, notwithstanding the many suggestions which had been made and the various designs offered, the impression appears to have been in favor of a monumental column, in preference to any other form. The subject had been for a long time and yet continued to be discussed in the Board of Directors, among the people, and in the public papers, and numerous plans were proposed. The Board of Directors was composed of distinguished gentlemen — lawyers, scholars and artists; and the discussion was so full and thorough that, if learning, ability and a desire to arrive at a wise conclusion could secure a wise result, it was scarcely possible that a mistake could be committed.

No less than three committees of the Board of Directors were appointed on this subject. On the 5th of April, it was resolved that a final decision " in regard to the kind of monument to be erected shall be made only at a meeting of the Directors warned by special notice to each individual and also by advertisement in two newspapers in Boston, twenty days before the time of such meeting." It was also resolved, " that whenever the Directors shall judge [it] expedient to take measures to come to a decision in regard to the kind of monument to be erected, they shall elect

10

a board to whom shall be submitted all plans and designs which
may be presented, in order that this board may give an opinion
as to the superiority of any plan or design thus presented; and
further that said board of artists be requested to give their
opinion in regard to any other plan which may occur to them,
besides those which may have been laid before them by the
Directors."

It was determined that this board should consist of seven
members, and the Standing Committee was requested to make
the nomination: This committee nominated the five following
gentlemen, viz. Daniel Webster, Gilbert Stuart, Washington
Allston, Loammi Baldwin and George Ticknor, — a constellation
of eminent men, statesmen, scholars and artists, equal to the full
discussion and final decision of any question that may be presented to a committee, in law, literature or art. The report of
the committee was accepted, " both as to the persons named and
the number of them."

To this " board of artists" fell the duty of examining the
designs offered for the premium, and on the 12th of April the
following proceedings took place:

" A report in part was made by the committee appointed at
the last meeting to examine plans for the monument, &c.

" Ordered that this report be laid on the table; that the further consideration thereof be postponed to the next meeting, and
that the committee have leave to make a further report.

" Ordered that the same committee be requested to report
which of the plans submitted be entitled to the premium of one
hundred dollars, as the best submitted plan." [The committee
were not previously instructed in this matter.]

At the next meeting, on the 26th of April, the following proceedings took place:

" A report was made by the committee on the subject of
awarding a premium to the author of the best plan or model. —

On motion and after discussion of the principles of the report, it was voted to lay this report on the table." [It does not appear that this report included a decision in regard to the premium, nor that the report itself was ever further considered.]

" Voted that a meeting of the Directors be notified for 19th of May, for the purpose of deciding on a plan of a monument."

SECOND COMMITTEE ON THE DESIGN.

On the 19th, "the proceedings of the last meeting having been read, a discussion arose upon the subject for which the present meeting was called, viz : the plan of a monument. After debate it was voted, that a committee of five be appointed to report the plan of an obelisk, and also of a column, with estimates of the expense of each. That this committee consist of the following gentlemen : II. A. S. Dearborn, Edward Everett, Seth Knowles, Samuel D. Harris, and Thomas II. Perkins."

On the 7th of June, ten days only before the great initiation-ceremony was to take place, the question had practically come to be between a monumental column and an obelisk : The following were the proceedings as recorded :

" The committee appointed to report a plan of an obelisk and of a column, with estimates of the expense of each, made a statement on the subject, by General Dearborn, their chairman. This statement is placed on the files of the association." [It is not now to be found ; but was no doubt in favor of a column, as the votes of a majority of the committee indicate.]

" A proposition was then made and supported, which was as follows : That the Directors of this Association do now decide on and adopt a column as the form of the object for the proposed monument.

" This proposal having been discussed at great length, the question was finally taken by yeas and nays, and each Director being called on in turn, answered as follows :

" Yeas : II. A. S. Dearborn, George Blake, Samuel D. Harris, Jesse Putnam, Seth Knowles, — 5.

"*Nays :* Daniel Webster, President, Joseph Story, Vice President, Nathan Appleton, Loammi Baldwin, Isaac P. Davis, Amos Lawrence, Samuel Swett, William Sullivan, David Sears, George Ticknor, John C. Warren, — 11.

" So, there being five in the affirmative and eleven in the negative, the proposition was rejected.

" It was then Voted, That the form of an obelisk shall be adopted for the proposed monument; or in other words, a pyramidal structure such as may hereafter be agreed on."

THIRD COMMITTEE ON THE DESIGN.

" A committee was then chosen by ballot to report a design of an obelisk, or pyramidal structure ; and to consider and report on the subject generally.

" This committee consisted of the following gentlemen, viz : Loammi Baldwin, George Ticknor, Jacob Bigelow, Washington Allston, and Samuel Swett."

While this committee had the subject in consideration, the ceremony of laying the corner-stone of the monument took place, on the fiftieth anniversary of the battle — arrangements having been hastened for the purpose of marking the half-century, and also to secure the august presence of General Lafayette, at the time the guest of the nation.

At the meeting on the 24th of June, " The chairman of the committee to present the design of an obelisk stated that he should be ready to report in about ten days."

July 1, 1825. " A report from the committee on the plan of the monument was, in the absence of Colonel Baldwin, chairman of the committee, read by Mr. Ticknor, and after a short discussion, the further consideration of the same was referred to the next meeting of the directors."

July 5. " After a short discussion, it was voted, *nem. con.* to accept the report of the committee on the plan of the monument."

These are the proceedings of the Directors as they stand upon the records. It having been determined, to the satisfaction of the whole board, " that the form of an obelisk shall be adopted, or in other words, a pyramidal structure, such as may hereafter be agreed on," the remaining questions relative to its proportions, height and accessories, (although settled, in a general way, by publications already made, and by plans prepared by Mr. Willard, to test the question of cost,) were finally determined by the acceptance of the

FINAL REPORT OF COLONEL BALDWIN.

We have obtained the original of Colonel Baldwin's report, — one of the few papers of importance which have been preserved among what are by courtesy called " the archives of the association." It recommends " an obelisk or frustum of a quadrangular pyramid, the base of which shall be a square of thirty feet on each side, to rise two hundred and twenty feet from the platform or ground on which it is to be erected, to be surmounted with an apex having its upper angle ninety degrees, and to be fifteen feet square at the top, agreeably to the plans and section herewith presented."

It further recommends, " that its four faces shall be respectively opposite the four cardinal points of the compass, and the north and south faces shall intersect at right angles, the plane of the meridian passing through the axis of the monument."

Also that the foundation shall be twelve feet in depth and fifty feet square, with offsets, and built of stones of large dimensions; and that in order to obtain a sufficient knowledge of the soil, &c. it is expedient to sink a well near the proposed site.

That the site shall be carefully examined, " to ascertain at what level, in relation to the surface of the hill about it, the platform should be fixed, so that in forming the *terre-plein*, or suitable and convenient area round the monument, an economical disposition of the earth shall be obtained. . . . Upon this point the committee consider it very essential to preserve as high a level for the platform as the nature of the land will admit, consistent with that easy approach to, and promenade round, a public monument of so much grandeur and importance."

That " the obelisk shall be erected of the dimensions and proportions and in the manner represented in the plan and section of the drawing herewith presented," — the general outlines of which are described and have been mainly followed in the structure as now completed.

The report also recommends that contracts be made for supplying the material, making the excavations, dressing and hammering the stones, &c., but that the erection of the obelisk shall be " entrusted to the care and superintendence of an experienced stone-mason, of known industry and integrity, and the work to be performed by hired workmen under his direction."

That "some skilful architect should be employed, in whom the public as well as the board may justly have confidence, who shall make and prepare the detailed and working plans, and who shall see that the execution of the monument shall be throughout, faithfully and substantially performed, agreeably to the plans and directions to be adopted and delivered by the board, or a committee by them appointed for that purpose."

The report further recommends the appointment of a Building Committee of three members, with full authority to employ an architect, make contracts, &c. By a vote of the Directors the number was increased to five.

After the completion of the monument, "and not before," the committee recommend around the obelisk, "a firm platform of broad, well-hammered stones, resting on foundation walls, and extending to the distance of twenty feet from each face of the building, having at the exterior boundary three steps, of not more than eight inches rise each, running round the whole platform." This *terre-plein*, it is suggested, should now be constructed according to the original design.

In concluding their report the committee state that " several other propositions have been examined, which presented dimensions and proportions varying from those of the plan they herein recommend. One scheme was to preserve the relative proportion of base and top, and to make the base a square of forty feet and the top twenty feet. Another was to enlarge the base to forty or fifty feet, and give the top a proportionally smaller area, so as to present an outline more distinctly pyramidal; but your committee having taken into consideration the funds already provided or probably attainable, as well as the practical compliance with the general wishes of the board and the public, had no hesitation in adopting the plan recommended, as the one most likely to be finally and satisfactorily accomplished."

The following copy of a letter shows that pending the discussion, an obelisk had been suggested by Mr. Ticknor, and also what Mr. Willard's views were upon the subject:

" Dear Sir, — I have made another slight sketch of the obelisk you suggested. I have supposed that the monument would be enclosed by an iron fence and have sketched the frustums of pyramids, in the Egyptian style, at the angles, which may serve as accompaniments and also for a lodge, watch house, &c. The obelisk and base is *as sketched before*, with the addition of a broad platform and a subterranean entrance.

" It has always seemed to me that any of the three figures which have been proposed, if well designed, would make a respectable monument. The obelisk I have always preferred for its severe cast and its nearer approach to the simplicity of nature. than the others. The column might be more splendid. The character of the obelisk, without a pedestal, seems to me to be strictly appropriate for the occasion and I think would rank first as a specimen of art and be highly creditable to the taste of the age.
                " Yours, respectfully,
" George Ticknor, Esq.   SOLOMON WILLARD."

In the report of the Building Committee, made the next year,
June 17, 1826, referring to the presentation to them of a plan
" of an edifice in the form of a Gothic church," it is said:

" While this committee were disposed to give their respectful
attention to the representation alluded to, they could not take a
measure of any description thereon.   Whatever the individual
opinions of this committee may have been, they are sensible that
the design had the sanction of two Boards of Directors in two
different years; that it underwent discussions perhaps without
example in this country, if the time and labor employed in them
are considered, and the talents of those who took part in them,
are estimated as they should be.   Moreover it has seemed to
them, so far as they have been able to judge, that the choice of
the Directors has been sanctioned by public opinion, as fully as
any design of this description ever was or can be."

During the whole period of discussion and action, on the subject of a design for the monument, Mr. Willard appears to have
been on the most intimate terms with the Standing Committee,
the Directors and the several committees of the association to
whose consideration it was successively referred.   He was freely and constantly consulted by them and not only sketched outlines of various designs but prepared one or more models of his
plans for their use.   His views of the matter are shown in the
following remarks:

" The general dimensions of the obelisk that was adopted were
thirty feet at the base, and two hundred and twenty feet high;
with stairs to the top; and a foundation twelve feet deep and
fifty feet in diameter at the bottom.   The directors would have
preferred a structure of greater magnitude, had the state of the
finances warranted it.

" In order to ascertain the size of the largest obelisk that could
be safely undertaken, estimates were made of the expense of

three, of different dimensions; all, however, of two hundred and twenty feet in height.

"An estimate was made for one of fifteen feet base, with a pedestal, in imitation of one of the Roman antiquities. Another estimate was made for one of the dimensions finally adopted; and a third for one of forty feet base. But after mature consideration, it was decided that one of thirty feet base was as large as could be safely undertaken with the means at disposal.

"It will be perceived, therefore, that the size of the obelisk had necessarily to conform to the means available; and it was so decided by the committee on the designs. But whatever related to the form and arrangement of the details — the construction, and mode of carrying the work into execution — was left entirely to the architect and superintendent of the work."*

---

* "Plans and Sections of the Obelisk on Bunker's Hill, with details of the Experiments made in quarrying the Granite. By S. Willard, Architect and Superintendent of the work." Boston, 1843. Quarto, pp. 31.

CHAPTER XI.

AUTHORSHIP OF THE DESIGN FOR THE MONUMENT.

WE have given in the preceding chapter as full an account of the proceedings of the Board of Directors, regarding the design or plan of the monument, as their records allow. It is incomplete and unsatisfactory, affording no decisive evidence as to the authorship of the design or of the part several persons are said to have had in its production — its suggestion or modification. We have never supposed that there was a great deal of credit due to any one person, or in fact to any number of persons, for the mere form of the monument, since it is entirely without any claim to originality of design, and if it is indicative of genius in this respect, it belongs to a remote antiquity. The form of a column is nature's own, exhibited in almost endless proportions in the vegetable kingdom; the form of an obelisk — simply making the column quadrangular — is so readily accomplished that, though not simultaneous, must have soon succeeded the column, wherever either was applicable in art or architecture. The only claim that can be set up in relation to the design of the Bunker Hill Monument is for the first suggestion, not for the copying of any particular form, or expanding the proportions of any particular structure. So far as the external form of the monument is concerned, the merit of that belongs not to the builders of the present age. Nevertheless there are those who claim the design, for themselves or others, and also the reward publicly offered by the Directors. And still there is no pretension of originality, unless it be in some additions or ornamentations, all of which were rejected.

The obelisk form, in contradistinction to a monumental column, was not the suggestion of a single mind, but was presented to the committee, from two or three sources, as appears from Mr. Willard's letter to Mr. Ticknor, already quoted, and the report of the Building Committee of 1826. In the course of the discussion in the Board of Directors, which was continued so long and sustained with so much ability, learning and investigation, the merits of the various forms were elaborately presented, and when the vote was proposed the minds of all were made up and the result showed a decision not again to be disturbed, — the friends of the obelisk form were more than two to one. Of the second committee, of which General Dearborn was the chairman, three members voted in favor of a monumental column and the two other members did not vote on the question.

We have seen that Mr. Willard made the earliest designs for the monument, before the offer of a premium, which were exhibited at the first meeting of the Standing Committee, and there is satisfactory evidence in the bound volume of designs and plans,* preserved by the association, that he made the last, which was adopted, and in strict conformity with which the monument has been constructed; and notwithstanding all that has been said and claimed on the subject, for modifications and improvements, is in wonderful conformity with the earliest ideas entertained and published by the friends of the enterprise.

We have no disposition to claim for Mr. Willard what he did not think it necessary to *claim* for himself; and what we, with-

---

* There is in this volume a large plan, drawn by Mr. Willard, which is undoubtedly the plan reported by Colonel Baldwin. It shows a section of the whole structure, from foundation to cap-stone, with the interior and exterior walls, the courses of the foundation, the circular steps, and also a ground plan of the foundation — precisely as delineated in Mr. Willard's printed volume.— In conformity wtih this design the working plans were made.

out any intention to underrate the importance of the question of a design, esteem of less moment than some others, on the score of merit. But it is very clear, we think, that the merit, whatever that may be, of the design as finally adopted and carried out, belongs chiefly to Mr. Willard, by whom it was reached through what was very nearly an experimental process. In the greater merit of the work, — the construction, — of which we shall speak hereafter, Mr. Willard's claims are beyond the reach of question or cavil.

The premium offered by the Directors for the best design submitted, was never awarded, and the action of the board in regard to it indicates that no one of the competitors was, in their judgment, entitled to receive it. The premium proposed was one hundred dollars, and the only money paid, (Mr. Willard declined to charge or receive anything for the various services rendered by him,) on account of the design, was the amount of fifty dollars paid to Captain Alexander Parris, " For plans and estimates made for the intended monument, made by direction of H. A. S. Dearborn."

The reader will not be surprised, after what has been said, to know that the question of the authorship of the design is by some parties smartly controverted, — though we know of no pretensions that can for a moment exclude those of Mr. Willard. The following letter to Mr. Ticknor, and the enclosure from Mr. Mills, on this subject, form a part of the history of the work and are deemed proper for insertion in this place :.

" Boston, October 4th, 1832.

" Sir, — The enclosed is a letter written by Mr. R. Mills, a respectable architect residing at the south, and will speak for itself. It was put into my hands some months ago, and I have sent it to you, presuming that you were better acquainted with the subject than any other person. I recollect seeing at the exhibition, the drawings in oil referred to ; but had always supposed they were the production of Mr. Allston or Mr. Morse.

I propose to publish a work in relation to the monument, showing the construction and giving to the public the results of our experiments, and should like to be able to give credit wherever it is due.   There has been something from the beginning in relation to the subject that I have nót been able to understand. On the plate that is deposited, Mr. Parris is said to be architect; in the North American Review for July, 1830,* Mr. Greenough is said to be the inventor, and Mr. Mills's letter shows that he considers himself the designer.   I was not aware that either of them had anything to do with the design that is in progress.— Indeed so far as relates to the accessories, and the height, I did not know that the design was yet determined on.†

" If you can give me any information where the design originated, or in relation to Mr. Mills's claims, or can refer to the paper containing the advertisement for the design, it would oblige much.   Mr. Mills evidently thinks there has been some unfairness — and I consider it due to myself to inform him that it does not attach to me.

    " Yours, respectfully, &c.,

                              SOLOMON WILLARD.
    " George Ticknor, Esq., Park street."

We have not been able to find any answer to this letter : it probably was not answered, as no reference is made to the subject in Mr. Willard's published " work."   Our inference from the letter, is that he was a little annoyed by the disputatious

---

* This must be a mistake : the North American Review does not contain any article on the subject between the years 1824 and 1832.

† In 1834, May 5th, the Directors on the report of the Executive Committee, discussed and passed the following vote, viz : "That the Monument be raised to the height of one hundred and fifty-nine feet six inches, and be considered as completed, when raised to that elevation, as to the effort to be made at this time."   Records of the Association.

This was long after Mr. Willard's letter was written.   He, of course, was opposed to the measure.   The " effort to be made" was that undertaken by the Massachusetts Charitable Mechanic Association.

character which the question had assumed and the "something in the beginning" that he could not understand. He had worked in good faith, and had made and modified several designs, to make them acceptable to the committee and within the probable means of the association. If suggestions were made to him, he could not know whether they were original or purloined, and was in no way responsible for their use — if any such were used, as Mr. Mills rather broadly insinuates.

In reference to the inscribing of Captain Parris's name on the plate, as architect, the only explanation to be given is, that it was his own act, authorized, (as he seems to have supposed,) by the circumstance that he was employed by Dr. Warren to "make preparations for the laying the corner-stone," and the fact that he was a prominent candidate for the office. Among other duties he procured the engraving of the plate. His bill for this service contains the following particulars (omitting the items,) : For expenses, labor, materials, &c., $336.48 ; For engraving plate, $131.00 ; Total, $467.48. On the face of this bill is the following memorandum : " My own services I will not at present make any account of." Subsequently, Captain Parris presented a bill, which was paid, containing two charges : the one above-mentioned for " plans and estimates," and another : " For services in making preparations for the laying the corner-stone, by order of Dr. John C. Warren, $50.00." The wrong done to Mr. Willard, inadvertently and certainly without any design on the part of Captain Parris, is almost irreparable; and so, doubtless, Mr. Willard felt it to be when, with his own hands, he placed the box containing the plate, under the true corner-stone, more than a year after the ceremony the professional part of which Captain Parris superintended.

The advertisement for a design, which appears not to have been seen by Mr. Willard, we judge had a very limited circulation. It was inserted only once in the Boston paper in which we found it, and was left to the voluntary action of other publishers, who might not see it, or might not choose to do the work at their own expense. As its statements and requirements are somewhat peculiar, we copy the principal portion of it :

" The Committee esteem it their duty on this occasion, to act altogether in conformity with the public taste and judgment. — For this reason, although there are some obvious recommendations of a Column as the best form for a monumental structure, on the spot in question, yet the committee are determined to propose no plan whatever to the association till they have had the means of comparing all the suggestions which may be offered by the architectural skill and genius of the country. They accordingly publish their invitation to artists, without any limitation ; and are desirous of receiving proposals and plans for a monumental structure of whatever character or design. But as a column is recommended, by various local circumstances, and appears to enjoy a general preference, the committee are particularly desirous to receive plans of a Monumental Column of about 220 feet in height, to be built of hewn granite.

" It is wished that proposals should contain two plans : one, the architectural plan and elevation of the work, with a suitable scale ; vertical and horizontal sections of the interior ; particular statements of the proportions and magnitudes of the members ; and if a column, drawings of the ornamental portions of the pedestal : and the other, a handsomely finished perspective view of the work. For the plan of this description, which shall appear to merit the preference, the committee offer a reward of one hundred dollars."

MR. ROBERT MILLS'S LETTER.

The following is the letter from Mr. Mills, addressed to his friend, Richard Wallack, Esq., which was handed to Mr. Willard, and by him sent to Mr. Ticknor : —

" City of Washington, July 1st, 1832.

" Dear Sir, — Understanding that you will remain in Boston some time, I would take the liberty of asking you to represent

me in a case in which I am professionally interested : When
the Bunker Hill Monument committee advertised for designs for
the monument, I took a good deal of pains to study one which
should do honor to the memory of those worthies it was intended
to commemorate, and prove an ornament to the city which it
was to overlook.   I went into some detail on the subject of
monuments generally, and in sending them two designs, I recommended in strong terms the adoption of the Obelisk design,
not only from its combining simplicity and economy with grandeur, but as there was already a column of massy proportions
erected in Baltimore, we ought not, therefore, to repeat this
figure, but construct one of equally imposing figure.   I was
then residing in South Carolina, and was at much trouble to
forward the roll of drawings to their place of destination.   I
never heard anything on the subject of these drawings until it
was announced that the committee had adopted the *Obelisk* form
for the Bunker Hill Monument, and I was left to conjecture
what part of my design was taken and what left, until some time
after, when I saw that all the decorations were omitted, and the
naked pillar preserved in all its original proportions.   (By the
way, I would observe that the committee have erred in omitting
the simple decorations proposed in my design ; the grand gallery
about one-third the height of the shaft would have been useful
as a lookout platform as well as presenting an appropriate decoration, as the outline of the gallery showed the monumental
character used by the Egyptians, from which nation originated
the obelisk form.)

" From the obelisk design being adopted, and my having recommended this form to them, I thought it was a courtesy due
from the gentlemen to have dropped me a line of thanks for the
trouble I had taken in the business, though they may have not
awarded me the premium, as they may have made a design
themselves, and simplified that sent, which however does not
obliterate the idea.   [Mr. Mills has just remarked that the idea
originated with the Egyptians, to which he certainly had no

personal or professional claim. As the Egyptian obelisks were erected before the Christian era, the idea had been public property for many centuries.]

"I would ask the favor of you, my dear sir, to see or inquire of any gentleman of the committee if there was any other design of the obelisk form presented for adoption to the committee with mine, and where this design came from, and if such design was offered, whether it was not made in Boston, or neighborhood, and if so, should not some credit be given to me at the distance I was, for suggesting the same idea? The design now carrying into execution bears all the proportions of that I sent them, and I ought reasonably to infer that some reference must have been had to my drawings. If the committee are not disposed to award me any credit for my design, I would thank you to procure my drawings, and when you have an opportunity forward them to me. The drawings were on a large scale and finished in oil colors, with a distant view of Boston in the back-ground.

"With sentiments of respect, and esteem, dear sir, I salute you,   ROBERT MILLS."

The following is that portion of the remarks of Mr. Mills, in his communication to the Standing Committee, in which he recommends the Obelisk form. Plans were to be received until the first of April, and this communication is dated at Columbia, S. C., March 20, 1825:

"In the designs for the monument which I now have the honor to lay before you, I would recommend the adoption of the *Obelisk* form in preference to the *Column*. The details I have affixed to this species of pillar will be found to give it a peculiarly interesting character, embracing originality of effect with simplicity of design, economy in execution, great solidity and capacity for decoration, reaching the highest degree of splendor consistent with good taste.

12

" The Obelisk form is, for monuments, of greater antiquity than the Column, as appears from history, being used as early as the days of Rameses, King of Egypt, in the time of the Trojan War. Kercher reckons up fourteen Obelisks, that were celebrated above the rest, namely, that of Alexander; that of the Barberines; those of Constantinople; of the Mons Esqulinus; of the Campus Flaminius; of Florence; of Heliopolis; of Ludovisco; of Saint Makut; of the Medici; of the Vatican; of M. Cœlius, and that of Pamphila. The highest on record mentioned is that of Ptolemy Philadelphus in memory of Arsinoe.

" The Obelisk form is peculiarly adapted to commemorate *great transactions*, for its lofty character, great strength, and furnishing a fine surface for inscriptions. There is a degree of lightness and beauty in it that affords a finer relief to the eye than can be obtained in the regular proportioned column."

———

We have given to Mr. Mills the benefit of his letter and his original recommendations of the Obelisk form. They present his case in its strongest light, and in a manner which seems to require either explanation or answer. This, perhaps, is not demanded here. Probably the committee regarded his design as a whole — not in parts — and as such, whatever they might have thought of its proportions, it was not accepted by them. They could not accept a part of it, or modify and then accept it as a whole. Besides, the decorative parts, which alone were truly his, were certainly not acceptable to the committee, and when stripped of these, only the " naked pillar" was left — which was an Egyptian obelisk, such as others had suggested and such as, under the circumstances, was not entitled to the offered reward. As to the " original proportions," claimed by Mr. Mills, the principal measurement, which more or less controlled the rest, — the height, — was determined by the committee in their advertisement; the diameters had also been mentioned and estimates made of others by Mr. Willard, and "after mature deliberation it was decided that one of thirty feet base was as large as could be safely undertaken." Evidently Mr. Mills relied much upon the "simple decorations proposed in his design," and thought the committee made a mistake in not adopting them; but they desired a structure which should be substantial and grand, not decorative. In short, they did not approve or accept Mr. Mills's design, and therefore could not give to him the reward. The intimation in Mr. Mills's letter, of any unfairness in the matter, Mr. Willard did well promptly to repudiate as not attaching to him. As against the committee or the Board of Directors, such an implication is not to be credited for a moment.

So far as Mr. Willard is concerned in the remarks of Mr. Mills, he has answered, with all the force of brevity and truth, in the letter to Mr. Ticknor, "I was not aware that either of them, [Messrs. Parris, Greenough, or Mills,] had anything to do with the design that is in progress." This was said by Mr. Willard after he had become aware of the claims of each of these parties. As he made the design that was in progress, he ought to have known whether either of them had anything to do with it or not. It is presumed that neither Mr. Mills or any other artist will claim a premium for the idea of the obelisk form, and as regards the proportions, we know that Mr. Willard made designs of three different diameters for the last committee. How many he had previously made, some of which he modelled also, we are not able to say; but we think he spent weeks in the service of the association in making designs and estimates, where Mr. Mills or any other artist, spent hours, — and at no time did he ask for or accept any compensation for his labor, his expenses or his time.

We conclude, if the premium offered by the committee for a design was justly to be claimed by any one it was Mr. Willard. He never claimed it, and if it had been awarded to him he would have placed it in the treasury of the association. Notwithstanding his untiring study and long labor upon it, he professed, honestly no doubt, not to know to whom the credit of the first suggestion belonged. If it did not belong to him, it is quite certain that in every other respect, he was the true and only architect of the work, the evidence of which, it is due to his public spirit and devoted patriotism, should be preserved, and the fact made distinctly manifest by the association.

CHAPTER XII.

CEREMONY OF LAYING THE CORNER-STONE.

THE corner-stone of the monument was laid, — rather figura-
tively than permanently, for it was a mere ceremony, — on the
17th of June, 1825, by the Grand Lodge of Freemasons in
Massachusetts, and strange as it may seem, Mr. Willard had no
part assigned to him in the arrangements.   It was one of
the most imposing spectacles ever witnessed in this country, or,
in some respects, in any other country.   It was not simply that
such a work — the spontaneous undertaking of a free and grateful people, — was to be inaugurated; there were other induce-
ments to a general observance of the day and the occasion, which
operated upon all classes.   The usual recurrence of this anniversary was heightened in interest by the circumstance that fifty
years had elapsed since this famous battle, and the fact that but
few of the undisciplined heroes of that day still survived to par-
ticipate in a work designed to commemorate the event in which
they alone, of all living, had taken an active part.   In addition
to this, the patriotic sentiments of the country had been stirred
and gratified by the presence as the Nation's Guest, of General
Lafayette, the early and devoted friend of the country and the
associate in arms of our venerated Washington.   The story of
his services to this country in the struggles which commenced on
Bunker Hill, and the trials and sufferings he had endured for the
establishment of the principles that inspired him, was patent to

the people; and the Directors of the monument association, for many reasons, desired his presence on the occasion. To these considerations, likely to be as highly appreciated by the public as by the Directors, may be added the name and reputation of the Orator, whose profound thought and massive eloquence were known to be so admirably adapted to the subject and the place; and which will preserve the remembrance of the occasion and its associations to the remotest posterity.

Inspired by the feeling of national pride and national fame, which in that memorable year filled the whole country; when prosperity·and abundance, peace and happiness crowned the land; when all the people lived in harmony, honoring and blessing the benignant government which blessed and protected them — the event of which we speak, local only geographically and belonging to the whole country, was everywhere hailed with joy by the people, and all hearts present or absent, beat in unison with the patriotic sentiments of the day. Then we were ONE PEOPLE — united, prosperous, happy — having no anxious moments about the future and never dreaming of those terrible disasters which have destroyed our peace and people, desolated our land and threatened our existence as a nation.

Such was the extent of popular interest and patriotic feeling on this anniversary, that the directors and architect, — whose joint labors had been employed, in conjunction with the public press, to interest and arouse the people, — beheld with wonder the spectacle presented to them, on the morning of the seventeenth; and felt a new impulse to effort in order that the contemplated work should be worthy of the purpose for which it was undertaken and the noble patriotism of a community so alive to the value of their inheritance — an inheritance which to-day is more estimable than ever before and which is to be preserved as it was obtained by sacrifice and blood.

The people had assembled in numbers almost too large to estimate, thronging not merely the streets of Charlestown and Boston, but covering the battle-field with a living mass as it never had been covered before. They came from all parts of New England, in societies and associations, with music and banners, arms, emblems and patriotic devices, and even from distant parts of the country — all as to the great National Altar of law and liberty. They came not as their fathers came, at the roll of the drum, to lay down their lives if need be, for their just rights; not as then, armed with fowling-piece and rifle; nor came they now for conflict of any kind, but rather as a people filled with gratitude, to manifest their sense of obligation to the fathers, to revive the fire of patriotism in their souls, and perform an act of justice to an ancestry such as no country had before seen ; and worthy of the renown which embalms their memories.

At the appointed hour there moved through the crowded streets of these cities, on the way to the battle-field, crossing the bridge which now spanned the "royal Charles," a procession of military, civic and social bodies, all existing in virtue of principles there baptized in blood and now emblazoned on the banners of a people absolutely revelling in their enjoyment. Such a sight as this moving mass afforded to the more numerous thousands that gazed upon it, its venerable men, and the august patriot whose fame is the just property of two great nations, has rarely been seen in this, and as a voluntary exhibition never in any other country. It was a spontaneous outpouring of the people and seemed to demonstrate, more than anything else, how correctly the movers in this enterprise had judged of their feelings in proposing the structure now to be commenced. Those venerable men who were so early called upon to defend their homes and maintain the rights they claimed, and who had alone survived their compatriots in arms to behold this glorious and grateful day, were everywhere greeted with enthusiastic cheers ; while the acknowledged Apostle of Liberty, whose presence connected a nation with the occasion, received from the gathered thousands that grateful homage of mind and heart which would have been the breath of life to Gesler, and was never before so rendered to any man.   It was a day well spent for the nation, and worthily by the people.

Judging from what we know of Mr. Willard's views of the purpose of this work and his sympathy with the undertaking, his heart must have swelled with emotion at the enthusiasm, and he realized more forcibly than ever, how inadequate were his powers to embody the sentiments of the occasion and give expression to the gushing gratitude of the people in the structure to be erected.

After the completion of the ceremony by the fraternity charged with its performance, Mr. Webster, in his admirable oration on the occasion, said, .

"The foundation of that monument we have now laid.   With solemnities suited to the occasion, with prayers to Almighty God for his blessing, and in the midst of this cloud of witnesses, we have begun the work.   We trust that it will be prosecuted, and that, springing from a broad foundation, rising high in massive solidity and unadorned grandeur, it may remain as long as Heaven permits the works of man to last, a fit emblem both of the events in memory of which it is raised, and of the gratitude of those who have reared it."

Another purpose of Bunker Hill Monument, suggested by the orator, in his muscular English, is peculiarly applicable at the present time and marks the profound thought of the statesman : "We wish that, in those days of disaster, which, as they come upon all nations, must be expected to come upon us also, desponding patriotism may turn its eyes hitherward, and be assured that the foundations of our national power are still strong."

After what has been said of Mr. Willard's interest in the proposed monument, his continued service and his intercourse with the directors, it must appear singular to the reader that he was not employed to superintend the laying of the corner-stone in preference to any other person.   We do not attempt to account for the omission, but presume it to have been inadvertent, — if that is to be considered a sufficient excuse for the neglect. Mr. Willard, as was to be expected of him, ·has not mentioned the circumstance even in his familiar correspondence ; and perhaps felt that he had no right to complain.   It is true that he had not then been elected architect ; but it is also true that no other person had been elected.   No other architect had been employed by the directors as he had been ; no other had been elected to membership as he had been : for these and other considerations, it seems to us now that he should have been selected instead of a less interested party.

Nevertheless, while the laying of this corner-stone was very properly regarded as the inauguration of the work, the true corner-stone of the monument, upon which the structure rests, was laid by Mr. Willard, in a workman-like manner, at a subsequent period.

13

CHAPTER XIII.

ELECTION AS ARCHITECT AND SUPERINTENDENT.

NEXT in importance to the selection of a design for the monument, if not in fact first in importance, was the election of an Architect and Superintendent of the work.   Great responsibility, — to the contributors and to posterity, — would rest upon this officer for the faithful and skilful performance of his work, and upon the Building Committee for his appointment.   They were not long, however, in making a selection, for at their first meeting, October 31st, 1825, Mr. Solomon Willard was chosen without a division.   It is not too much to say that, notwithstanding what had been done four months previously, the Board. of Directors and the public were prepared for this result : the skill and judgment, the fidelity and perseverance of Mr. Willard, and the final completion of the work under his careful superintendence, confirm the propriety of the choice and attest the faithfulness with which he discharged the trust.

On the 2d of November, Mr. Willard received the following notice of his appointment from the chairman :

" Mr. Solomon Willard, — Sir, I beg leave to inform you that you have been chosen Architect and Superintendent of the Monument to be erected on Bunker Hill.   You will please to inform me whether you would accept this office, and on what terms, for a year.   The duty will be to prepare the requisite plans, to make contracts, and to do such other duties as may be required for this construction under the direction of the Building Committee.

JOHN C. WARREN, Chairman."

To which Mr. Willard, on the succeeding day, sent the following reply :

"Dear Sir, — In reply to your note of the 2d instant, I should be willing to render any service in my power to forward the views of the committee; and as respects compensation, it must depend on the portion of time required. If my whole time should be thought necessary, the pay ought to be about three dollars per day. For many reasons, however, I think that the interests of the association would be best served by having the services gratuitous, and if it should be thought so by the committee, I will agree to it.

"I should like to have a few minutes' conversation with you, when other engagements will permit.

"Yours, respectfully,

SOLOMON WILLARD."

"John C. Warren, M. D., Chairman."

At the time of this appointment, Mr. Willard, by reason of his skill and connection with works already accomplished or in progress; from his acknowledged soundness of judgment and constructive talent ; his eminent reliability of character, originality of thought and mechanical ingenuity, in some respects, to say the least, was at the head of his profession, and had fairly earned his position. His appointment, therefore, as architect of the monument and superintendent of the work, was wise and judicious, and as the result has shown, a fortunate selection on the part of the Building Committee. We do not absolutely know the fact, but as no other architect seems to have competed with him for the office, we have reason to believe that his appointment was made with the concurrence of the ablest and best

artists and architects in Boston. All things considered no one
of them, had they been disposed to seek the position and responsibility, could have served the association more faithfully, more
successfully or more skilfully, than did Mr. Willard.

That Mr. Willard had an honorable ambition to do this work is
undoubtedly true, and he thought the honor of the office a sufficient reward for the services required. It was national in its
character and in its purposes.   It was an undertaking which,
at this time in his experience, he would desire, on account of its
novelty and for the reason that it might make new and profound
demands upon his mechanical as well as artistic skill.   It was
the kind of excitement that he wanted, germane to his taste and
genius, consonant with his ambition, and afforded an opportunity
for that experience in the use of a building material, which he
desired to possess.   If ever a man entered upon such a piece of
work, *con amore*, with his time, money and heart in it, it was
Mr. Willard upon this work — and he pursued it with a quiet
greatness of skill and interest worthy of a noble record and the
remembrance of every patriotic and generous heart.   His soul
was in the work : it lived in his thoughts, journeyed with him,
and tarried wherever he tarried.   During the progress of it,
he was at the quarry, the railway, the site of the monument,
ready with hand to help or word to direct ; and while working
without pay and employing the best mechanics at liberal wages,
he exerted himself to avoid every unnecessary expense.   The
reader of his letters, estimates and calculations, would infer that
his leading purpose was to see how cheaply stone could be got
out and worked, and with how little expense the monument
could be built.

On the 9th instant, the following contract was drawn up and
signed by the parties, and by an understanding between them,
was to continue in force for one year :

" Memorandum of an agreement made by Solomon Willard,
on the one part, and John C. Warren, in the capacity of Chair-

man of the Building Committee of the Bunker Hill Monument, on the other part, — Witnesseth, That the said Willard agrees to prepare the requisite models and drawings for an Obelisk, to be erected on Bunker Hill ; to aid in making the contracts, and to superintend the completion of the same ; and also to do such other duties as may be required — In consideration of five hundred dollars per year, to be paid for such services by the said Warren.

" In testimony whereof, the parties have hereunto set their hands this ninth day of November, eighteen hundred and twenty-five.

JOHN C. WARREN.
SOLOMON WILLARD."

Previously to his election, in June, 1825, after the committee had decided upon the form of the monument, Mr. Willard addressed a letter of which the following is the substance,* to Mr. Ticknor, giving his views as to the best manner of carrying forward the work :

" I have seen by the papers that the committee have adopted the obelisk for the monument, and as I have more than a common interest in its being carried into effect in a spirited and economical manner, I hope that a few hints, respecting the best course, will not be considered impertinent.

" A Building Committee should be chosen, who are favorably disposed to the design, and who will unite heartily in carrying it into execution. An agent may be employed to assist in making the contracts, and an architect, if his services are considered necessary. The services of the committee and agents should be gratuitous, as the honor of the employment will be a sufficient compensation. The committee should mature the designs in all

---

* This is the letter referred to on page 59, ante.

their details.   The form, dimension and tonnage of every block
of stone in the structure, should be known, and the management of the contracts should be the same as would be employed
in an individual concern.

" After the dimensions, the quantity and quality of the stock
wanted, is known, it might be well to advertise for proposals for
supplying it.   I do not apprehend much difficulty in procuring
any of the stone at a fair price, except the blocks for the outside,
which being of considerable dimensions, and required to be of
stock which is very valuable to those who have it, will probably be held very high.   Should this be the case, it might be
better for the association to buy the quarry and to employ a
skilful superintendent to see the stone quarried.   An experiment
might also be made to ascertain the cost of dressing the stone
per foot, that the committee may judge of the economy of having
them done at the Prison — and also to determine the probable
cost of the work.

" It is estimated that the stock quarried would be worth
twelve and a half cents per foot cubic measure, at the quarry ;
dressing for twenty-five cents per foot superficial, including cost
of tools, and twelve and a half cents for the beds.   The transportation may cost two dollars per ton, delivered at the Hill or
State Prison.

" Taking a block of stone of mean dimensions, of ten feet long,
three feet wide, and one foot six inches thick, it will contain
forty-five cubic feet, which at twelve and a half cents per foot,
will amount to $5 62½
    30 feet of face dressing, at 25 cents,   7 50
    30 feet of beds, at 12½ cents,   3 75
    Transportation of 3¼ tons, at $2,   6 50
                                                                           ———
              Total cost per block, $23 37½

" A stone of the given dimensions, according to the foregoing
estimate, will cost twenty-three dollars thirty-seven and a half

cents, if it be transported in the usual way; but should a railway be constructed, as has been suggested, it may save much expense in so large an undertaking.

" I should like to have the work commenced skilfully and in a spirited manner, and to see it finishéd before the public become tired and disgusted as is usually the case. I feel some solicitation for the good management, having given estimates and knowing from experience that false steps at the outset are with difficulty corrected, and not generally perceived until too late for a remedy.

" The quarry which I mentioned the other day, has been purchased expressly for the work; but if on examination, the Directors should not think it the most eligible, it will be no loss.

       .   .   .   .

Yours, respectfully, &c.

SOLOMON WILLARD.

These suggestions were favorably considered and acted upon in each distinct particular by the Directors, but they were not permitted to see the work finished as speedily as desired by Mr. Willard. Of his election the Building Committee, in their first report, June 17th, 1826, speak as follows :—

" No sooner was the Building Committee organized than they proceeded to the election of an architect and superintendent, and chose Mr. Solomon Willard, a gentleman whose talents and perseverance had already called forth in his favor a distinct expression of the opinion that he was well qualified to execute a new and difficult structure. Mr. Willard readily undertook the office, but he was desirous of making it a condition of his acceptance that his services should be gratuitously rendered to a work originating from sentiments of patriotism. To this proposal, however, the committee did not feel justified in acceding. They knew that the Superintendent would be called upon to devote a large part of his time to the objects connected with so great a work. They therefore, felt bound to provide him with a proper salary

for his support, and with this, though much less than what his
merits might have demanded, Mr. Willard declared himself
perfectly satisfied."

Notwithstanding these remarks of the committee, readers of
the present day will be inclined to the opinion that they did, in
point of fact, accede to Mr. Willard's proposition, for in no just
sense, either then or now, can a compensation of five hundred
dollars per annum, be regarded as a "proper salary for his support." A really proper salary for such services as were to be
rendered by Mr. Willard, would be as many thousands as the
committee adjudged him hundreds; and from first to last, his
services were gratuitously rendered, he receiving, as Mr. Amos
Lawrence says, "merely his necessary expenses, which were
very small."

It seems fitting to pause here for a moment, to consider the
position which Mr. Willard had gained to himself and the means
and appliances by which he had gained it. The honorable character of the position will readily be admitted. As to the means,
they were such, and such only, as every young man, in our
favored country, has within himself. His advantages of reading
and education, adequate as these have proved to be in so many
instances, by prompting to higher efforts, were quite inferior to
those enjoyed by the young men of the present day. In the
latter he had no other opportunities than those afforded by the
public schools of his native town, probably open only a portion
of each year, and his attendance was doubtless interrupted by
his labors in the field and the shop. Without public libraries,
few books were to be obtained in a country town seventy or
eighty years ago; and these few most likely unsuited to his taste
or desires, and not the best calculated to engage his attention or
develope his mind. As in the case of Dr. Franklin, whose first
books were on matters of "polemic divinity," they answered the
purpose of the moment and created the desire for more congenial
reading and study. Men in humble life, who have shown any

remarkable qualities or become celebrated in the world's history, have generally been devourers of books, reading all which they were able to obtain, almost without regard to their contents.

Mr. Willard's mind in youth, turned naturally to mechanics, and probably there were not half a dozen books in his native town, on any branch of science or art, of a character calculated to afford him any instruction which he could make available to his taste or inclinations. It was not, therefore, until he came to Boston, master of his own time and thereafter to be the "architect of his own fortunes," that he could reach higher and better means of self-culture, then and now open to young men of studious and exemplary habits in the metropolitan city. How he availed himself of these — economized his earnings and improved his time — is shown by his life and the position to which he had now been chosen. Wisely spending his money for books and such instruction as he desired, he acquired information very rapidly, and in one of his favorite pursuits, soon ceased to be a pupil, though always a learner, and became a teacher. Not only did he seek his own improvement, but took an interest in affording the means of improvement to others. He was early interested in the "Social Architectural Library of Boston," (November, 1809,) the "Associated Housewrights' Society," the "Boston Mechanics' Institution," the "Scientific Library," and other similar associations, and for a number of years was a subscriber to the Athenæum. In his efforts to educate himself and popularize knowledge, he was associated with such men as Bowditch, Claxton, Moody, Treadwell and others, — men who were willing to assist in a good cause and contribute their share to the mutual improvement and social elevation of the community. Especially did the mechanic interests of Boston profit by their generous efforts.

With means of his own and the appliances of his industry, Mr. Willard became preëminently qualified for the position to which he was elected. So well known was this that the public judgment pointed him out as the man to be entrusted with such

14

an enterprise. In the commencement of the work, he entered at once into plans for its speedy and economical accomplishment; made suggestions to the Directors and Building Committee, and responded readily to any suggestions they had to make to him. He felt at all times the responsibility of his position and the necessity there was for certainty and accuracy in his calculations, — and he looked forward with ardent desire for the accomplishment of his designs and the attainment of a just reward for his labors.

At the time of his election, Mr. Willard was forty-two years of age, having been twenty-one years, almost to a day, in the city, (with the exception of his visits to the south,) working and pursuing his education.

CHAPTER XIV.

PURCHASE OF THE BUNKER HILL QUARRY.

WHILE the Board of Directors was engaged in devising plans to obtain the means wherewith to build the monument, Mr. Willard was seeking for a suitable material of which to construct it. He took care to inform himself on the subject of monuments generally, and especially of their peculiar characteristics, the nature of the material used and the manner of construction. — His idea, — though not at all peculiar to himself, but held in common with the whole community, — was that the work should be of extraordinary magnitude and built of durable and massive materials. His taste and experience were opposed to outside-show as a quality in architecture, and especially against everything of that nature in construction. No brick-and-mortar work, however grand the proportions, would have met his views, not even were the outside to be of a durable and unexceptionable material. An occasion so well worthy of a monument, commended itself to all as worthy of one which should be massive, solid and durable; something bolder, nobler and grander, than art had yet furnished: something more adequate to the commemoration — not of a man, or a battle-field merely, but of a code of great principles, and of the gratitude of a whole people. Everybody felt what was wanted, but time and labor were required for its attainment — much more of each, before the end, than was contemplated, or peradventure the work would hardly have been undertaken.

Interesting as this question of material was to the community, it was much more so to Mr. Willard and called forth exertions as extraordinary as they were necessary and successful. As already intimated, before the design of the monument had been decided, he had been actively occupied in exploring the country in pursuit of a quarry from which could be obtained blocks of sufficient size for the purpose, and in a location to be made available with existing means of transportation. This was one of the most laborious undertakings of Mr. Willard in connection with the monument, and he was indefatigable in its accomplishment. We have no means, from any record of his own, of ascertaining the extent or cost of these explorations, but they were in both respects very considerable. The only reference to them which we have found is the following note, in the hand-writing of Mr. Lawrence, on a blank leaf preceding the records of the Building Committee, of which he was for three years, (from June, 1827, to June, 1830,) the Secretary :

" Solomon Willard walked three hundred miles to examine " granite quarries, (Hallowell and other places,) gave a thous- " and dollars to the monument association, and worked like a " dog for the association for years, for merely his necessary ex- " penses, (which were very small,) and is now at work at " Quincy.   Boston, August, 1849.

    (Signed,)   AMOS LAWRENCE."

The result of these journeyings was the selection of what was subsequently known as the " Bunker Hill Quarry," in Quincy, — a most fortunate selection and one manifestly made with a wise judgment. A quarry was also purchased by a member of the Building Committee, (Mr. Lawrence,) at Rockport, Cape Ann, where it was supposed peculiar facilities would be secured in shipping the blocks to Charlestown ; but this was not considered as desirable as the quarry at Quincy, and was never owned by the association.

The quarry discovered by Mr. Willard, was purchased in June, 1825, by Mr. Gridley Bryant, of Frederick Hardwick, and conveyed to him by deed, dated the 9th of that month. The conveyance was of " all the rocks or stones, on and in a certain piece of woodland, lying in the town of Quincy aforesaid, in the — lot, so called, and was part of the estate of Nathaniel Savil, containing four acres, more or less, and is bounded and butted as follows, viz : southerly on woodland formerly owned by Captain John Hall, deceased, now owned by said Hardwick, Ebenezer Crane and George Nightingale ; westerly, northwardly and eastwardly, on woodland of Hon. John Quincy Adams, and however bounded, or reputed to be bounded, together with the privilege of taking away or removing said rocks or stones, at any time hereafter, to suit said Bryant's convenience — and further it being understood by the parties, that the said Bryant shall have a right to cut, clear off any of the wood, or remove any other obstacle that may hinder or prevent the said Bryant from taking and carting off the rocks or stone, whenever he pleases, on or in said lot — and it is hereby agreed between said parties, that all the wood that said Bryant shall cut on said lot, shall belong to said Frederick Hardwick." The consideration paid by Mr. Bryant was two hundred and fifty dollars. [This is the quarry referred to in the letter to Mr. Ticknor in the preceding chapter.]

In November, immediately after the election of Mr. Willard, and upon his recommendation, the quarry was purchased, and Mr. Bryant conveyed to the Bunker Hill Monument Association " the privilege of quarrying any quantity of stone which may be wanted in erecting said monument, from a quarry which said Bryant purchased of Frederick Hardwick, in June last, the same lying in Quincy — in consideration of the sum of three hundred and twenty-five dollars," Mr. Bryant, like most other men, regarding it as an ordinary business transaction and taking a handsome profit.

On the sixteenth of this month, the committee published an advertisement for proposals for furnishing the stone required for the monument; but it is presumed, from what had already been suggested by Mr. Willard, that no proposals which the committee could accept, were looked for, — at any rate, however this might be, the committee deemed it prudent to secure the ledge while it was at their option.

The location of the "Bunker Hill Ledge" is described above in the words of the deed of conveyance ; its distance from the site of the monument, by the land route through Boston, was measured under the direction of Mr. Alexander Wadsworth, who reported as follows :—

"Boston, November 10th, 1834.

"Solomon Willard, Esq., — Sir, The measures reported by my chainman, who measured for me the distance by the road, from the Bunker Hill Ledge, in Quincy, to the monument on Bunker Hill, are as follows, to wit:

FROM BUNKER HILL LEDGE TO—	MILES.	QRS.	RODS.
Howard's Corner, . .	0	3	40
Railway House, . . .	2	2	58
Stone marked "8 M. to Boston," .	2	3	0
Commencement of lower road, at mills,	4	2	0
Road leading to Neponset Bridge, .	5	2	40
Turnpike, . . .	6	0	44
Glover's Corner, ...	7	1	40
Draw of Free Bridge [to South Boston,]	10	0	16
Church, head of Sea street, . .	10	2	4
Hanover st., through Federal and Marshall,	11	0	72
Bunker Hill Monument, . . .	12	1	29

"Very truly, yours,

ALEXANDER WADSWORTH."

The Building Committee, in their first report, speak of the purchase of this quarry as follows :—

" On the recommendation of the Superintendent, they then proceeded to examine a ledge of rocks 'discovered by him in the town of Quincy, and found there a magnificent range of granite containing materials inexhaustible, the use of which they immediately, for a trifling sum, secured for the benefit of this corporation.

" The design of the committee in making this purchase was to quarry the stone on account of the corporation, instead of buying it ; and this mode they have the strongest reason to believe, will put it in their power to make a great saving of expense. Their intention at the time of the purchase was to have begun the cutting of the stone immediately ; and they expected to have been able to convey it by land, a distance of two miles only, with greatest economy in the winter season, so that by spring a sufficient quantity might be ready at the water's edge, in Quincy, to be transported by water to Charlestown, and afford materials for beginning the work and carrying it forward with rapidity. The quarry was accordingly opened, and its excellence fully answered the expectations which had been formed."*

It appears by later records and papers that Mr. Willard still retained an interest in this quarry. When it was proposed to take the stone wanted, from Pine Hill Ledge, in order to save distance and expense in the building of the railway, one of the conditions of the change required by Mr. Willard, was the following : " 1st, It will be requisite that the railway company should refund the money which has been expended at the

---

* Report of Building Committee, June, 1826.

Bunker Hill Ledge, and pay me the fair value of my right in that ledge."

The change was not made. The quarry was opened and worked, and at the end of six months, with all the preliminary preparations, the committee say, " Under the eye of the indefatigable Superintendent, more than three thousand tons of stone have been split from the beds in form, and lie ready to roll down the railway as soon as it is opened to them." A little reflection will suggest to the intelligent reader how much labor, in preparation, opening and working the ledge, is included in this statement.

Mr. Willard's estimate of the importance of a good quarry for the work to be done, may be seen in the following sentence from a report written by him in November, 1827 : " The most important object of attention in erecting a work of the magnitude and construction of the one in progress, is a good quarry — as the getting out of the stone required is an arduous and expensive undertaking, and indeed, I consider a good ledge in such a case as not only the first requisite to success, but (as has been said in another case,) the second and the third also."

The Directors, however, seem to have had a different view of this matter, for in their address to the public, in 1830, they express themselves as follows : " The Directors thought that the chief precaution to be observed was to engage the services of an architect of acknowledged taste and skill, (and such an one they were so fortunate as to find in Mr. Willard,) and to take all practicable means to ensure economy in the expenditures made necessary in the progress of the work."

The purchase of this quarry, according to Mr. Willard's calculation, fixed the cost of the material for the monument in the ledge, at about a quarter of a cent per cubic foot.

CHAPTER XV.

THE RAILWAY ENTERPRISE AND CONTRACT.

THE circumstance has been noticed that the proposition to build the Bunker Hill Monument was the immediate suggestion and reason for introducing the Railroad into this country ; and it is true that the first work of the kind on this continent was built and used for the transportation of the material to erect that monument.   Insignificant as this now seems, it was an enterprise of considerable importance, and probably would not have been undertaken, at the time, but for the patriotic motive connected with it in the minds of the builders : it is therefore right to say we should not as early as 1825, have adopted this species of " internal improvements," regarded even at a later period as an experiment, excepting for the intention of building Bunker Hill Monument — and might have had to-day, instead of that magnificent line of railroads which crosses the State, Colonel Baldwin's gigantic canal flowing through the " Hoosac tunnel" and meandering along the vallies either side of it, between the Hudson River and Boston Harbor.

Tramways and Railways had been in operation in England, at the coal mines, for several years — the result of a gradual progress towards the great achievements of the present day. — The success which had attended the use of these in the transportation of heavy burdens to tide-water, naturally led to the belief that they would be found equally advantageous and economical

15

at the granite quarries in Quincy, and a considerable saving of expense was expected by the monument association from their introduction. It was therefore determined to await the construction of the railway before the removal of the stone for the work should be commenced.

In January, 1826,* a petition was presented to the Massachusetts Legislature for an act of incorporation to construct a railway, in the following form :—

" The undersigned petitioners represent that it would be of great public utility to establish a Railway from certain quarries in the town of Quincy to the tide-waters, for the carrying of stone to be used in building; that your petitioners are disposed to establish the same, or to aid in effecting it ; but that it will require a voluntary subscription and employment of a large sum of money, and that such sum can only be obtained by extending the subscription among many persons, and that it would greatly facilitate the enterprise if those who engage in it should act under corporate powers."

This petition was signed by Thomas H. Perkins, William Sullivan, Amos Lawrence, Solomon Willard, David Moody and Gridley Bryant. An act of incorporation was granted by the legislature, and was approved on the fourth of March, 1826. — The company was immediately organized and Colonel Thomas H. Perkins chosen President. The route was surveyed and the railway built during the year, but not without the most tedious

---

* The " Report of the Commissioners of the State of Massachusetts, on the routes of Canals from Boston Harbor to Connecticut and Hudson Rivers," (including Colonel Baldwin's various surveys,) was sent to the Legislature, by Governor Lincoln, on the 11th of January 1826, the very day on which an " order of notice" was issued on the petition for the railway. It is understood that Colonel Baldwin declined to serve on the Building Committee of the Monument Association, partly for the reason that he was engaged on these surveys and expected to be occupied in carrying forward the great public work then contemplated.

delays ; and on the twenty-seventh of March, 1827, a contract was made with the Building Committee for the transportation of the stone from the quarry to the wharf in Charlestown. By this contract the railway company, agrees "to receive on the said company's railway, during the year eighteen hundred and twenty-seven, three thousand tons of hewn stone, to be used in building the monument aforesaid, at such times during the said year as the said John C. Warren, or the Superintendent, shall offer to be carried, and not exceeding thirty tons in any one day — and that said company will carry the same hewn stone from the place where the same shall be delivered on the railway to the wharf of the said company, and thence by water to Devens's wharf in the town of Charlestown, and there deliver the same, ... and the said company hereby promise to do the said carrying with all reasonable care and fidelity and without doing any injury to the stone which can be avoided with due care and reasonable diligence."

Like those in England, until the successful experiments of Blackett and Stephenson, in the invention of the locomotive and the application of steam, this railway was operated by horse-power, and as it has not been extended, has required no other motor. The first proposition of the railway company was to transport the stone from the quarry to the tide-water, at fifty cents per ton, and from thence by lighters to the wharf at Charlestown, at forty cents ; but the contract, which was negotiated by General Dearborn and Mr. Lawrence, on the part of the association, fixed the price at seventy-five cents per ton for the whole distance. For some reason not now apparent, Mr. Willard, a part of whose duty it was to assist in making contracts for the work, declined to take part in this negotiation, and seems to have become early dissatisfied with the contract and the " delinquencies," as he calls them, of the company.

Two months after the completion of the contract, in May, 1827, Mr. Willard had become impatient of the delays which

annoyed him, asked for a copy of the contract, and suggested
to the Building Committee the propriety of discharging the
workmen at the hill.   He wrote to the chairman, Dr. Warren,
as follows :—

"The Railway Company, through mismanagement, have been
rather unfortunate, and there is little prospect of our stone which
are first wanted, being carried very soon.   Mr. Savage called on
me at Quincy for direction, and suggested the idea of discharging
the men at the hill for the present. . . .   We have been in
readiness to commence the mason work for a month and have
been waiting ever since for the stone to be carried.   As I never
had any confidence in the contract being fulfilled, on the part of
the railway company, and as the agreement was made by the
committee contrary to my wishes, I consider myself free from
responsibility for any hindrance or loss which may be sustained
in consequence of this contract."

Mr. Willard, however, had recommended that a contract with
the railway company should be made, only a month before it
was completed, and the ground of his complaint seems to have
been that it was "unskilfully made."   On the fifteenth of May,
Mr. Lawrence informed Mr. Willard of a modification of the
contract, by which Mr. Gridley Bryant, the agent of the railway
company, had agreed "for you to load the stone upon the railway carriages at five cents per ton."   But the trouble was a
continuous annoyance; and on the twenty-third of September,
Mr. Willard writes sharply to Mr. Bryant, "As we have nearly
a hundred tons of stone ready to move, we wish to see your
carriages at our shed to-morrow morning.   Our work will close
for the season in about eight weeks, and we shall prepare a
freight of seventy tons each week, if no accident occurs.   It
will be important that we shall be kept clear."

In a letter of the next year addressed to General Dearborn,
as one of the committee on accounts, Mr. Willard explains this

matter and endeavors to show that as a means of facilitating or cheapening the work on the monument, the railway had failed of its purpose :—

"Quincy, [date left blank,] 1828.

"Dear Sir, — I have enclosed a copy of the instructions which I received from the Building Committee a year ago. It will be seen by these instructions that the committee had authorized me to make all the contracts which were required in the prosecution of the work of erecting the monument for the season past. In one case, however, courtesy induced me to refer back the power given me, and I allowed the committee to make a contract which I considered injurious to the interests of our employers. I refer to that made with the Railway Company. This appeared to me unskilfully made in two respects : the Railway Company were neither accountable for the fracture of the stone, nor bound to fulfil their agreement. And this contract has not only proved an expensive thing to the association, but a source of infinite trouble to me.

"There has been a strange misapprehension respecting the importance of the railway to us. The following statement, I think, will illustrate this point : The whole quantity of stone carried from our ledge to the water, is 2287 tons, which at 35 cents per ton, comes to $800 45. The price offered by a respectable company for hauling in the common way, was 50 cents per ton, — so that, all the gain that was ever expected, provided they had fulfilled their agreement, was only the difference between 35 and 50 cents, on 2287 tons, $343 05, in a work where $28,000 had been expended.

"On the other side of the account we must reckon the loss of two years in waiting for this company to perform a job which amounts to little more than $800. For loss in time no estimate in money can be made. It has been, however, an injury which is irreparable. The loss in cash paid to men with their hands tied in consequence of the delinquency of the railway company.

(I should say, to speak within bounds,) was ten times the whole cost of carrying 2287 tons to the water, to which must be added the sacrifice of an invaluable quarry.

" It would have been much better for my own interest and reputation, had I paid the $343 and carried the stone in the common way, and it would also have saved thousands to the association.

" It will be seen by the above statements that the railway has been of little consequence to us, nor can it be, provided the company were well disposed, as it costs them to carry our stone twice what we give them for it."

This last statement, repeated on the authority of Mr. Bry-- ant, probably accounts for, if it does not excuse, some portion of the neglect or mismanagement alleged against the railway company, which appears to have been so vexatious and trouble- some to Mr. Willard, who undoubtedly, we think, is somewhat to blame in this matter : he encouraged the building of the road and making of the contract, and while he asserts that "the agreement was made by the committee contrary to his wishes," he also says " I allowed the committee to make a contract which I considered injurious to the interests of our employers." On this statement he was blamable — though possibly he "allowed" what he could not prevent in the hope that his apprehensions might prove groundless. Mr. Willard was probably wrong also in supposing the railway company not well disposed towards the monument association, as the President was one of its earliest and firmest friends.

As the use of this railway was continued for many years after the date of these transactions, by Mr. Willard himself, and is still used, it is probable that its services were found to be valuable and its earnings remunerative to the proprietors, especially after they became the owners of the quarry.

CHAPTER XVI.

PRELIMINARY WORK ON THE MONUMENT.

THE first year of Mr. Willard's service, from November, 1825, to November, 1826, was mostly devoted to preliminary matters, under a general vote of the committee, "authorising and empowering the chairman to take measures for proceeding in the construction of the monument, with all expedition, and that whenever he may think necessary he call a meeting of this committee." The purchase of the quarry had been effected, as already stated, and the supply of stone secured. The railway act had been obtained and the work began. The old foundation of the monument had been taken up and preparations for the new foundation made. It was soon after practically decided to do the hammering of the stone at the ledge, and a boarding-house and other buildings were erected there to accommodate the workmen. A contract was also made for the transportation of the stone.

In reporting upon the work done in thirteen months, Mr. Willard says, " From a recent examination of the accounts kept at the ledge, it is ascertained that the whole sum paid out of the funds of the association, from the 15th of November, 1825, to the 15th of December, 1826, little exceeds ten thousand dollars, of which $348 has been paid for digging out the foundation on Bunker Hill ; $195 for four acres of land near the quarry, and $712 for building a boarding-house for the workmen. The quarrying apparatus has cost $2000, and is now on hand, partly

worn, but is probably worth two-thirds its first cost.   It consists
of machinery, lumber, iron, steel, hammers, bars, wedges, &c.
The house and land are probably worth what they cost.   If we
deduct the above from the sum stated, there would be left $6,-
745, total expended in opening the quarry, making roads, quarrying and rough dressing 20,000 feet of foundation stone and
10,000 feet of fine hammering — to which must be added the
cost of transporting 125 tons of stone to Charlestown.

" Much time has been necessarily spent in clearing and opening the ledge, making roads, and much unnecessarily wasted by
the delinquency of the railway company.   The 20,000 feet of
foundation, although but a small part of the work executed within the thirteen months, would come to more, at the prices charged
for similar work at the prison, than the whole sum paid out."

The experiments instituted by Mr. Willard at this time, to
ascertain the cost of dressing the different blocks of stone, net
measure, whether circular or straight, and allowing two feet of
coarse dressing for one of fine dressing, resulted as follows :—
433 feet quoins and hollow cone, 36 cents per foot ; 81 feet
platform and steps, 39 cents ; steps jobbed out in winter, 26
cents ; large quantity of hollow cone by sundry persons, 30
cents — average 32¾ cents per foot, to which six cents per foot
may be added for tools.

In view of the work which had been done and the plans to be
pursued for the coming year, Mr. Willard addressed to the
chairman the following letter :—   ·

" Quincy, November 6th, 1826.
" Dear Sir : — As my engagement expires on the 9th of
November, a new agreement becomes necessary.   I should like
to engage for another year, if past services have met the approbation of the committee ; and as a compensation, I would engage
on the condition that the necessary expenses of living should be
paid by the association.

" The past month having been an important one to us, it has

been thought expedient to employ an extra number of workmen, and the monthly expenditure has increased proportionately. — On the 4th of November, there was due from the association to various persons, the sum of nineteen hundred dollars. It might be well to have these bills all paid before the ninth of the present month.

" If the committee should consider it for their interest to give me charge of the work another year, I should like to have the plan in all its details for prosecuting the work agreed on by them, with written instructions to me. The experience of the last year induces me to suggest the following for their consideration :—

" I should not think it for the interest of the association to attempt the transportation of any of the stock to Bunker Hill this fall, as it is late and the carriages for transporting on the railway and machinery for loading, are not in readiness at Quincy.

" For unloading in Charlestown it will require an apparatus of considerable expense, which would be exposed through the winter, and the loss would over-balance any advantage which could be derived from it. I would rather spend the time, between this and March, in making the necessary preparations for a rapid movement in the spring. Should the hammering be done at the ledge, a shed should be erected to shelter the workmen. A large space should be levelled in and about the shed. The rough and the hammered stone should be removed out of the way, and the ledge should also be cleared of every incumbrance.

" The timber-run from the ledge should be repaired and all the quarrying apparatus put in the best order. The winter would be a favorable time to finish the drawings and models which are requisite, and experiments may be made in order to ascertain the exact value [cost] of hammering each of the blocks of the stone used in the construction of the monument. This is indispensable whether the stone are hammered at the prison or not, as the experiment will enable us to detect any overcharge in their bills, and if the work is done at the ledge, the fair value per foot will be determined.

" For the above service a small number of men will be sufficient. For the building of the sheds, clearing and levelling, it might require six men, including the master quarryman. The experiment might require four hammerers, and it would be necessary to have two blacksmiths to make new hammers, sledges, jacks and other quarrying apparatus wanted. The winter months are profitable for doing the blacksmith's work, and the only loss in doing it at this season is the interest of the money on the stock for a few months, which would be greatly over-balanced by the convenience of having the tools ready.

" In commencing the work next season, I suppose the railway company will deliver the stone at the wharf and furnish apparatus for loading, and they intend to furnish vessels to transport the stone, which are to be towed by a steamboat. Should these vessels not be ready by the time the ice leaves the river, we can employ lighters.

" At the landing in Charlestown, (at Devens's wharf,) it may become necessary to erect a kind of crane to unload the stone. From the wharf the stone will be carried to the hill on a wagon already constructed, and by the persons who have agreed to do it. I should recommend that a rigger should be employed by the day to fit up the machinery, and to do the hoisting, and a good mason, to see to the laying of the stone under my direction. The lime, sand, and iron for cramps, may be bought by the quantity as they are wanted.

" Bunker Hill, on the south side, where the road will pass, is rather steep and springy, and it has been suggested that it might be economy for us to lay flags of granite for the wheels to run on in the manner of an Italian railway, [?] which would probably make a difference in the draft of a common load of one yoke of oxen. These flags may be got out this winter, and laid in the spring, and when the work is completed, may be taken up and sold.

"The work requires the aid of all its friends, to forward it with the desired expedition, and if I should be engaged another year, I should like to have the Chairman of the Committee give more attention to it than in the past, or if this is inconvenient, to authorize some other person. If it becomes a necessary part of my duty to receive and pay out money, I should like to have such an arrangement made as that I could receive it by calling on a single individual.

"Yours, respectfully.

SOLOMON WILLARD."

"John C. Warren, Chairman of Committee."

On the 7th of September, 1826, the Building Committee held a meeting at Quincy, when there were present, the Chairman, (Dr. Warren,) George Blake, H. A. S. Dearborn, and Amos Lawrence. There were present also Edward Everett, Nathaniel P. Russell, and Nathan Appleton, of the Board of Directors.— After examining the Railway, which was then in progress, "the Committee next examined the Bunker Hill Ledge, and were fully satisfied with the progress made in getting out stone, and at the economy and dexterity of the processes employed for the purpose."*

---

* Records of the Building Committee, 1826.

CHAPTER XVII.

In November, 1826, the contract with Mr. Willard expired, of course with an understanding that it would be renewed; and on the 7th of December, the Chairman forwarded to him copies of a new contract, which were signed and executed as follows:

" Contract between John C. Warren, as chairman, etc., on the one part, and Solomon Willard, architect, on the other part, Witnesseth, The said Willard having been appointed Architect and Superintendent of the Bunker Hill Monument, doth agree to prepare the requisite models and drawings; to aid in making the contracts: to superintend the completion of the same; and to do such other duties as may be required to facilitate the erection of said monument: In consideration of five hundred dollars a year, so long as he may perform the above duties, to be paid by said Warren in behalf of the above-named corporation.

" And this contract is to remain in force until the monument is erected; or the funds of the corporation are exhausted; unless revoked by consent of the two contracting parties.

JOHN C. WARREN.
SOLOMON WILLARD."

" Boston, December 7, 1826."

This contract differed materially from the former one but was still not what Mr. Willard wanted.   It made the appointment

permanent, but continued a fixed nominal salary which was dis-
agreeable to him.   The original copy of this contract, found
among Mr. Lawrence's papers, bears the following endorsement,
in his hand-writing : " *Mem.* Mr. Willard's intention was not
to have a salary, but a support, which up to the period of January, 1829, has not exceeded the sum named as a salary."

The instructions given to Mr. Willard, in accordance with his
own request, were the following :

" The Building Committee of the Bunker Hill Monument Association, in the name and behalf of the corporation for erecting
a monument on Bunker Hill, to Solomon Willard, Esq.,
" Whereas this Committee, having special confidence in your
abilities and integrity, do hereby appoint you Architect for the
construction of said monument, and furthermore they do also
appoint you Superintendent of the execution of the same, in all
its details ; and also commit these important trusts to your
charge in full confidence that you will employ your best ability
to complete the same with all the economy and despatch so
great a work will permit.

" In the execution of the monument, you will take for your
guide a plan drawn by yourself and accepted by the Directors of
the Bunker Hill Monument Association, which plan is now in
your hands — and all the models and plans are to be formed on
the ground of the above plan, and you are requested to have all
plans, models and all parts of the work under your care, so arranged that in case of any accident befalling to you, (which may
a good Providence avert,) the plans, models and other works
may be delivered over to your successor, so that the great work
which you have conducted thus far, may be continued without
impediment.

" As a considerable quantity of material for the construction
of the monument is already got out, and as your experience on
this subject will guide you as to the quantities and times of

preparing them, it is not necessary to give any instructions on this head. Our wish is that a sufficient quantity of stone should be got ready to begin the construction of the monument as early in the spring as the weather will allow ; and to carry it on without delay through the following season.

" We do not consider it best to transport any stone to Charlestown this season, except a small quantity, as an experiment made to gratify the public curiosity. But we should wish that contracts should be made for the transportation of the stone to Charlestown, in season to open the spring without delay. It would be best also to make all other contracts in season to prevent loss of time ; and therefore we authorize you to make such contracts for the sand, lime and other materials, and also for masons' and carpenters' and blacksmiths' work, as far forward as you can see the necessity of employing such workmen.

" In order to determine whether it will be best to have the stone hammered at the quarry, or in Charlestown, we wish you to make an experiment of the cost of hammering stone of the various forms you may require ; and this being done, to apply to the Superintendent of the State Prison to ascertain what the hammering of similar stones would cost at the prison. In case we should decide to have the hammering done at the quarry, we authorize you to erect the necessary buildings, procure the requisite apparatus, and to employ as many hands as may be required for such work — and the sooner this is done after the principal point is settled the better.

" You will no doubt employ this winter in making such plans and models as may be wanted ; in getting all machinery in good order, and placing it in the most convenient situation, and for these purposes you are authorized to employ suitable artificers. It will be best to see that a proper wharf or place for landing the stone at Charlestown, is secured for the benefit of our operations, as long as may be required, provided the expense thereof be not great. Also that the wharf thus procured be in a proper condition to receive the material, and all necessary works be

erected there in good time.   We also authorize you to lay flag-
stones of granite on that part of Bunker Hill where you determine to carry up the stone.

" In case of any deficiency in your instructions or the occurrence of any new question, you will refer to the committee
through the Chairman, and whenever the case is important this
should be done in writing.

" You will be provided with such monies as you may require
by applying to the Chairman, giving him sufficient notice, so
that he may have time to draw the money from the Treasury ;
and you will exhibit the state of your accounts monthly, or as
nearly so as your duties permit, to Amos Lawrence, Esq., who
with the Chairman, constitute the Committee of Accounts.

" Should you find it necessary, in order that you may devote
your time to more important objects, officers will be appointed
under you, for writing, payment of monies, and the performance
of other duties which might interfere with higher concerns.

" By order of the Building Committee of the Bunker Hill
Monument Association.

JOHN C. WARREN, Chairman."

" Boston, December 1, 1826."

CHAPTER XVIII.

MISUNDERSTANDING AND RECONCILIATION.

IT is no purpose of this memoir to revive or publish any personal misunderstandings, which may, perhaps very naturally, have arisen between the parties having a duty to perform or an interest in the progress of the work on the monument. Nor must it be inferred from this remark that anything of a serious character as to persons, or of importance as regards the public, ever occurred to disturb the harmony which existed in the Board of Directors and the Building Committee, and characterized the relations between these bodies and the Superintendent. On the contrary, in all the discussions in relation to the adoption of a design for the monument, in the selection of an architect, in the initiation of measures for the advancement of the enterprise, in the suggestion of a lottery for the same purpose, in the proposition for the sale of the land comprising the battle-field, and in other matters, where there might arise differences of opinion, all feelings were consulted, the great interests of the work considered, and unity of action as of purpose, generally obtained. In some of these cases, personal opinions and preferences were readily yielded to promote the paramount purposes of the association.

In the early part of 1827, there grew up from various causes and influences, some dissatisfaction on the part of the Superintendent; which, as soon as expressed by him, was promptly explained and adjusted in a manner especially honorable to the Building Committee, the Railway Company and the Architect. Annoyed as Mr. Willard had been by the delays in the progress of the railway and the operations of the company, and probably a little restless under the suggestion made to change the design of the monument, to which he refers in a letter of February, 1827, as follows : " A vote of the Directors at the last meeting to adhere to the plan first adopted, settles the question as respects any change in the form," — he was perhaps too sensitive to some action of the Directors or the Building Committee, which he alleges took place on the 17th of June. The following note suddenly opened the correspondence and the difficulty :

"Wednesday morning, June 20th, 1827.

"Dear Sir, — The vote of the Association [?] on the 17th, leaves me but one course to pursue : I shall remove whatever belongs to me in Quincy, this day, and shall give no farther direction to the workmen. Your interests there may require attention. I should have given you earlier notice had you called on me yesterday.

"Yours, respectfully,

SOLOMON WILLARD.

"Amos Lawrence, Esq."

How far this letter was censurable or justifiable, — and it certainly seems to have been somewhat hasty, — we have now no means of deciding, as both mystery and confusion envelop the subject. We have two copies of Mr. Willard's note, each in his hand-writing and precisely alike, — yet, according to its own date, the 17th must have been Sunday, on which day a meeting of the Association, or of the Directors, would not have been held. Nor are there any proceedings on record, at this time, having a particular or even a general reference to Mr. Willard. The only action recorded that might be displeasing to him, was the choice at a meeting of the Building Committee, on the 18th, of the President of the Railway company, Colonel

17

Perkins, to be chairman of the Committee, in the place of Dr. Warren, who had declined a reëlection. Mr. Willard's displeasure with the Railway company would very naturally extend to its President.

Mr. Lawrence's reply to Mr. Willard is as follows :—

"June 23d, 1827.

" My Dear Sir, — I called at your office this morning, and not finding you, wish you to inform me what your wishes are, that will obviate your objections to remaining in the superintendence of the great work thus far so favorably prosecuted by you. The inference you gathered from the late doings of the Directors, having in them anything intended to be disrespectful to yourself, I do most solemnly assure you is without foundation. I need not again assure you how much I desire the work to go on under your care.

AMOS LAWRENCE.

" Solomon Willard, Superintendent."

The reply of Mr. Willard to this assurance of respect and to the personal desire of his friend, — who, from the beginning of the enterprise to the end, had manifested the highest appreciation of his services, his disinterested patriotism and his devotion to the work, — is out-spoken, characteristic and decided. He calls it " Copy of a letter from the *ex*-Superintendent to Amos Lawrence, Esq., in answer to the foregoing," and it is dated on the same day :—

" Dear Sir, — The thought of returning to take charge of the work in Quincy, never occurred to me until this morning, and although *money* will not induce me to return, there are other considerations which might have some weight, were certain objections removed, which may be easily done by the committee if they choose.

" First. I should want a new agreement with the association, wherein the condition shall read thus : and the said Superintendent shall have for his services the necessary expenses of living paid by the Association, — this being one of the original terms of the agreement, but altered to the specific sum of five hundred dollars per year, by the Chairman, when the contract was executed, which sum is something more than is required for the purpose.

" Without reflection this may seem trifling. As it stands, I perform the service without money or credit; altered, I should have due credit for what I do, viz: of rendering my services gratuitously. The practice of the [late] Chairman, [Dr. Warren,] in certain cases, will illustrate the case, who frequently performs his services gratis rather than degrade his profession by accepting a low charge.

" Second. I should also wish the Committee to agree to furnish the means requisite to finish the work as speedily as a due regard to economy will permit, as the sum wanted is trifling and it is for the credit of all concerned to terminate the work in a rapid and masterly manner.

" Yours, respectfully,

SOLOMON WILLARD.

" Amos Lawrence, Esq., one of the Committee."

On the 25th, General Dearborn addressed to Mr. Willard a note, which he transcribed under this heading — " Copy of a letter from General Dearborn, one of the Building Committee, to the *ex*-Superintendent," — as follows : —

" My Dear Sir, — At a meeting of the Building Committee of the Bunker Hill Monument Association, I was appointed a committee to wait on you to state the results of their deliberations; but not finding you in your room, must communicate by letter.

" The Railway company will appropriate to your use, or to the Bunker Hill Monument Association, as you may think proper, one thousand dollars, for the right you had in the

quarry.   Colonel Perkins entertains the highest opinion of your
integrity, talents and uniform efforts for the accomplishment of
the great undertaking which you have so zealously undertaken,
and you can rely upon his harmonious support in the prosecution of the work.   You will go on pleasantly beyond all doubt.*

"As to your compensation, a vote was taken as you desired,
altering the former vote so that it now stands that your expenses
are to be paid instead of an annual compensation of five hundred dollars.   Thus, I trust, every difficulty is removed, and
that you will return to the works as soon as possible, as much
depends on your presence there.

"If you can call out to my house, [in Roxbury,] this evening, I shall be glad to see you.   As I am obliged to leave town
in the morning, in the steamboat, at 5 o'clock, for Maine, and
shall be absent eight or ten days, I have no other means of
communicating with you than this, unless you can spare time
to call at my house this evening.

"But, at all events, let me entreat you to return to the
works, which we all most ardently desire.

"With great esteem, your obedient servant,

H. A. S. DEARBORN.

"Solomon Willard, Architect."

The arrangement proposed, it appears, was deemed or made
satisfactory, and was immediately carried into effect, to the honor
of all the parties.   The thousand dollars was justly due to Mr.
Willard, who had probably expended nearly as large a sum in
his explorations for a quarry; but, regarding it from his stand-
point as a profit gained by reason of his connection with the
monument, he promptly rejected the idea — suggested by friends
who knew what sacrifices he had made — of appropriating the

---

* A note from Colonel Perkins to Mr. Lawrence, three days after the date
of this note, June 28th, says, "I was at Bunker Hill Quarry yesterday, and
found Willard very pleasant."

amount to his own use,* and in the same month prepared and signed the following subscription paper. Mr. Lawrence thought the pleasure of contributing this large sum to the great patriotic enterprise of the day, was the chief inducement with Mr. Willard to return to the work. He also induced most of his workmen to make themselves members of the association by contributing the requisite sum to its funds : —

" Copy of a subscription paper originated at the Bunker Hill Quarry, in Quincy, June, 1827 :—

" The subscribers, having been engaged in the executive department of the work of erecting a Monument on Bunker Hill, and wishing to contribute our share towards the means for prosecuting a work so successfully begun, and also wishing to become proprietors in the work, and sharers in the honor of erecting an appropriate monument to commemorate an important event, will cheerfully pay for this purpose the sums annexed to our several names. The aid also of every citizen is respectfully requested, that means sufficient may be obtained to terminate the work in a spirit and manner worthy of the heroic deeds which it is intended to commemorate.

" NOTE. The whole sum expended on the work to the seventeenth of June, 1827, is $15,000. The work has been in progress nineteen months, in which time a new quarry has been opened, the foundation of the monument quarried, dressed and laid. The quantity in the foundation has been estimated at 1500 tons, (1167 measured on the work,) on which there has been more than 30,000 feet of rough dressing. There is also a

---

* " A friend proposed to him to lay aside that sum for a time of need ; but he decisively rejected the proposal with the remark : ' Do you suppose I would soil my hands by making money out of the Bunker Hill Monument.' Had other men, with much larger means, possessed the same spirit, the monument would have been completed at a much earlier period, and without the embarrassments and delays which caused the best friends of the project so much mortification and discomfort." History of the Bunker Hill Monument, by Professor Packard, of Bowdoin College.

quantity of stone finely dressed for quoins, steps and hollow
cone, to the amount of 6,000 feet, and every preparation has
been made for prosecuting the work with facility and economy.

NAMES SUBSCRIBED.	AMOUNTS.
Solomon Willard,	$1,000 00
Ezra Badger,	20 00
Hazen Abbott, .	5 00
Theodore Rogers,	5 00
John White,	5 00
Joseph French,	5 00
Daniel Leonard,	5 00
Jacob B. Collins,	5 00
William Frederic,	5 00
D. M. C. Knox, . . .	5 00
Samuel Ames, .	5 00
Andrew Bunten,	5 00
John Adams,	5 00
John C. Knox,	5 00
John Frederic, . . .	5 00
George Frederic, jr. .	5 00
John Robertson, .	5 00
Samuel Ela, . .	5 00
Eli Stebbins,	5 00
Eleazer Frederic,	5 00
Daniel Ela, .	5 00
Almoran Holmes,	50 00
Total,	$1,165 00*

The receipt of the above amount is properly acknowledged by
N. P. Russell, Treasurer of the Monument Association, under
date of December 13th, 1827.

* A copy of this document among Mr. Lawrence's papers, contains several
other names, as follows : Luther Marble, John Devanny, and Thomas Pike, jr.
five dollars each, and James S. Savage, fifty dollars, making the aggregate
$1,230 ; but Mr. Russell's receipt is for $1,165, as above.

CHAPTER XIX.

LEGISLATIVE AID TO THE MONUMENT.

Two years after the incorporation of the association, in January, 1825, the attention of the legislature was called to the contemplated monument, by Governor Eustis, in his annual message of that year. He suggested that the model should be submitted for approval to the legislature — a body much less competent at any time to decide upon the merits of such a work than the then Board of Directors — and commended the undertaking in the following language : —

" Should the funds prove insufficient for the completion of such a work as is worthy of the occasion and becoming the character of the State, I do not permit myself to doubt, that aid will be afforded by an enlightened legislature.

" To commemorate one of the principal events of the Revolution, to consecrate the field in Massachusetts on which in the first stages of the war, our heroes and statesmen sealed with their blood the principles they had sworn to maintain, when a disciplined enemy received from untutored yeomanry a lesson which produced the most beneficial consequences through the whole of the revolutionary war. is worthy of the care of the patriot and statesman. The splendid column on Bunker Hill will unite principle with history, and patriotism with glory. It will be read by all ; its moral will strike deep into the heart. and leave an indelible impression on the mind."

136 MEMOIR OF SOLOMON WILLARD.

With a liberal disposition to assist in the erection of the proposed monument, the legislature passed a law, which was approved on the 20th of February, 1825, authorizing the association " to have the stone of which their intended monument may be constructed, hammered and prepared to be used, at the State Prison, in Charlestown," . . . " Provided, that the hammering of stone under the provisions of this section, shall never exceed in value the sum of ten thousand dollars," and also that no existing contract shall be interfered with or retarded. The same act authorized the association to receive " the two cannon called the Hancock and Adams, to adorn the intended monument, and to be preserved, as the earliest of the relics of the revolutionary struggle, and also for the same purpose two other cannon. used in the revolutionary war, and now belonging to the State, as to the Governor and Council may seem proper."*

The same act gave to the Directors authority to " take and appropriate to the legal uses of said association any land on Breed's hill, in Charlestown. which said Directors may find to be necessary in the design of erecting a monument and laying out the surrounding ground in the appropriate manner, not exceeding five acres." The necessity which called for the grant of this high prerogative of government — the right of eminent domain — affords a remarkable contrast to the conduct of Mr. Willard and an instance of cupidity and avariciousness almost too gross to be believed. While Mr. Willard declined to accept the slightest profit or commission for any service rendered to the association, or any compensation for his many years of labor, from high patriotic considerations, there was found a man willing to sacrifice his integrity, degrade his very nature and

* The two cannons here mentioned as the " Hancock" and " Adams," are now in the chamber in the top of the Monument. The inscriptions upon them say they originally belonged " to a number of citizens of Boston, and were used in many engagements during the war." No others have ever been received by the Association.

soil his own conscience, to gain by a trick,* an advance in the price of his land beyond that at which he had agreed to dispose of it to the association. Although he succeeded in this instance, it is a satisfaction to be able to believe that, if men who act from as high motives as those which governed Mr. Willard, are rare, those who act from such sordid and unmanly impulses are still more rare.

There had always been some doubt as to the availability of this grant by the legislature : Mr. Willard certainly never had much confidence in it : and in 1827, the Directors petitioned the legislature, praying that "the ten thousand dollars granted by a law of this Commonwealth to said association, to be paid in the labor of hammering stone at the State Prison, may be paid to said association in money." A hearing of the parties was had before a committee of the legislature, in January, when it was made apparent that the proposed change would be advantageous to both parties, and especially to the Commonwealth.

For the purpose of this hearing Mr. Willard estimated the rough blocks to weigh twenty-five per cent. more than when dressed ; the delay in passing the draws of two bridges at five per cent. ; allowed considerable expense for extra apparatus for handling and loading the large blocks at the prison, and concluded his statement with the following " Recapitulation" :—

" The first and second items make the extra expense of transportation thirty per cent. and the third, fourth and fifth, cannot amount to less than five, making the aggregate extra expense of

---

* The proprietors of the lands on Breed's Hill had consented to have their valuation fixed by appraisers and entered into bonds to abide by their decision. One of the owners, after the other proprietors had conveyed their portions, "deliberately paid over the forfeiture agreed upon, five hundred dollars, and demanded five thousand dollars for his land. The Committee were struck dumb, ... but, reflecting that a contention at that time might delay the whole enterprise for an indefinite period, they reluctantly paid the ungenerous and exorbitant exaction." Prof. Packard.
We are sorry to say we have never heard this story contradicted.

18

transportation at least thirty-five per cent. ; besides the great
delay in the prosecution of the work which must inevitably
ensue from this mode of carrying it on.   From items six and
seven it appears that the difference of cost in hammering the
blocks at the quarry and at the State Prison, taking thirty
cents as the mean price per square foot at the former, is as 30
to 210. or as 1 to 7."

The results of Mr. Willard's experiments and his calculation
of the extra cost of transportation, were so clear a demonstration
that the work of dressing the blocks at the ledge could be done
much more economically than at the State Prison as to put
at rest that question in the minds of the directors.   But the
testimony of Mr. Harris, Warden of the State Prison, was much
more to the purpose, so far as the Commonwealth was concerned, for he testified that the work could not be done at the State
Prison, irrespective of the price, without great pecuniary disadvantages to the institution : The work of its regular customers
would be delayed and finally lost ; the convicts " could earn
thirteen thousand dollars, in the usual mode of doing business,
with less inconvenience, than they could hammer ten thousand
dollars' worth of stone for the monument," and in addition to
these conclusions, the Warden testified that if they did the work
they would have to draw from the Treasury ten thousand
dollars extra for the work on the new prison.   In short, Mr.
Willard's evidence decided the question of economy as regarded
the association, and Mr. Harris's testimony decided the question
of profit as regarded the Commonwealth.

With such evidence presented to them, the committee could
do no otherwise than report a resolve according to the wishes of
the petitioners.   Good policy, prudence and economy, on the
part of the State, demanded the measure, and good taste — vio-
lated in the original act — approved of it.   It was shown quite
conclusively that a loss of not less than three thousand dollars,
— not to mention the cost of various alterations and additions

at the prison, and the probable injury to its business — would accrue to the Commonwealth, in the effort to fulfil the contract with the association.   But the legislature — at the suggestion of some member more prudent and less patriotic than the rest — did not think ten thousand dollars' worth of convict labor quite equal to that sum in money, notwithstanding it was shown that it would bring thirteen thousand in the market.   Ready to make a saving for the Commonwealth, in what no doubt was supposed to be an honorable way, the legislature readily adopted the suggestion of its prudent member and amended the resolution of the committee by reducing the sum named in it to seven thousand dollars, as the equivalent of the grant of their predecessors — thus effecting an actual saving to the Commonwealth of six thousand dollars and a probable saving of a much larger sum.   The proceeding was no doubt regarded at the time as advantageous to the Commonwealth, and was a better arrangement for the association than that for which it was substituted : which would have proved troublesome and unsatisfactory, if not absolutely impracticable.   It would have been almost impossible to adjust the prices to be charged for the work in a way which would have been satisfactory to both parties, as Mr. Willard, in the example quoted by him, made the charges at the prison six or seven times greater than the cost of similar work at the quarry.   Besides the objection to having the work done by convicts. in which Mr. Willard participated. (for he wished all his workmen to be members of the association,) the cost would have been greater and the actual result less advantageous than the reduced grant in money.

The " Resolve," as finally passed by the legislature, on the second of March, authorized the payment of seven thousand dollars in money, in annual payments in three years.   This was accepted by the directors, and the stone used in the construction of the monument was hammered at the ledge in Quincy. — It is a satisfaction to every member of the association be able to say that none of it was done at the State Prison.

This seven thousand dollars is the whole amount of aid ever received from the public authorities towards the monument — a sum probably not equal to the interest-account against the association — and, with this exception, it may be said that the entire cost of the monument, the land, fences, &c. was raised by voluntary contributions and efforts. Subsequently, in 1829, a petition was prepared for presentation to the legislature, at the instance of a majority of the directors, praying for the grant of a "Lottery" to raise fifty thousand dollars for the completion of the monument; but it was ascertained that the general sentiment of the members was opposed to such a grant and it was abandoned — notwithstanding only four years before, Lottery Tickets were allowed to be sold in aid of the monument.[*]   A later application for State aid was ineffectual.

---

[*] Some amusement was indulged in among the dealers in Lottery Tickets, in Boston, in 1825, (when the subject of suppressing their sale engaged the public attention,) in connection with the proposed monument. Mr. John Jay Jerome had advertised to sell lottery tickets for the benefit of the Bunker Hill Monument Association, whereupon Messrs. Gilbert & Sons made the following announcement : "For our own Benefit ! Several of our brother venders have set apart particular days to sell lottery tickets for the benefit of a particular institution, &c. such as ' for the benefit of the Bunker Hill Monument ;' ' in aid of the Greeks,' &c. &c. Now we frankly confess that we cannot afford to sell tickets except for our own benefit," &c.

To this gentle innuendo Mr. Jerome replied : "My neighbors in Exchange street are very facetious in their advertisement of yesterday relative to the Bunker Hill Monument, &c. They say they cannot afford to sell tickets for the benefit of the Monument, in aid of the Greeks, &c. Fie on such patriotism ! Gentlemen Sirs, would ye not afford the members of the Legislature another opportunity of contributing something towards so praiseworthy an object as the Bunker Hill Monument ! N. B. On the 22d inst. [Washington's Birth-day,] the profits on the sale of Lottery Tickets will be appropriated towards the erection of a monument on Bunker Hill."

Messrs. Dean & Hooper, referring to these cross-firings of their neighbors, concluded their announcement as follows : "Now we are willing to sell them for the benefit of the purchaser ; and those who wish to be benefitted are requested to call at the Old Stand and obtain some of the following prizes."

We think the monument was not benefitted much by any of these propositions.

CHAPTER XX.

CONTRACTS AND WORK ON THE MONUMENT — 1827 — 1828.

THE making of the contracts for carrying forward the work on the monument was a part of the duty of the Superintendent; but these were not necessary until the actual commencement of the construction in 1827.   It seems but justice to the contractors that their connection with the work under Mr. Willard should be mentioned.   Besides the contract with the Railway company already mentioned, there were three others, made by Mr. Willard in the name of the chairman : 1. Contract with James Sullivan Savage, of Boston, in which he agreed to take charge of the Mason's Department and " perform any other duty which the interest of the association may require, and to do the same as if it were his individual concern."   2. Contract with Almoran Holmes, of Boston, " to take the charge and duty of hoisting the stone to build the said monument," and to " superintend this department in all its details and employ competent and faithful men to perform the service, without profit on their work."   3. Contract with Thomas O. Nichols and John Peirce, of Charlestown, to " take at Devens's wharf, . . and carry thence to the site of the intended monument, three thousand tons of stone, at forty three cents per ton," &c.

These contracts completed Mr. Willard's arrangements for the progress of the work.   He was to prepare every block of stone according to the position it was to occupy. ready to be laid when delivered upon the hill. The machinery, mechanical and human agencies, were arranged and only required to be put in operation and kept in operation by the oversight of one master mind, for the regular, systematic and rapid advancement of the work. — All the operations were designed and all the forces directed to this end, and they were so nicely adjusted as to constitute a single machine, by which had the means been supplied, the stone would have been quarried and the monument erected without delay or impediment. This was Mr. Willard's hope and expectation, and it is not possible to estimate the disappointment and chagrin he suffered in consequence of its failure. He knew the means were not in possession of the association, but he believed they would be furnished. The failure had an effect upon his whole after life, affecting his spirits and ambition, changing his plans, purposes and hopes.

PROGRESS ON THE MONUMENT IN 1827.

The contracts were performed in a satisfactory and exemplary manner by the parties named, during the years the work was in progress, though before the monument was completed an entire change in the methods of proceeding took place.

When they were made, Mr. Willard expected to go on with the work, as he expressed it, " in a spirited and masterly manner." He had long waited for the opportunity to show to the people, and to the "combination" which hoped to see his plan of construction fail, what could really be done with that comparatively new building material, the "gray Quincy granite," in massive structures. In February, he spoke of the "difficulties which had so long hindered the work," as likely to be soon removed; but in May, he complained that he "had been in readiness to commence the mason work for a month, waiting for stone to be carried." The work, however, was began at this time, and up to the seventeenth of June, twenty-four thousand two hundred and sixty-three dollars had been expended by the association — only fifteen thousand dollars of which was considered as directly for the monument. The committee appointed to audit the accounts of the Superintendent, on the eighteenth of July reported as follows :—

" The work is now in a favorable course of prosecution : the daily expenses at the quarry are for twenty-seven men, $42 98 ; for tools, including the steel, coal and time of the blacksmith, $8 33 ; together $51 31. This gang of men will get out one course of the monument in twelve days. The first course of stone will contain one hundred and twenty-four tons four feet and four inches, in which are sixteen hundred and nineteen feet three inches of hammering, including the hollow cone. The average contents of the first eight courses is one hundred and twenty tons, and the expense of a course may be calculated thus :

Say for twelve days' work at the quarry,
    at $51 31, per day, is .   .   . $615 72
Transportation to Devens's wharf, at 75 cts. 90 00
   Do. from wharf to the hill, at 48 cents,* 57 60
Expense of laying including everything, at
   66 and 2-3ds cents per ton, . . 80 00

                                $843 32

" But we suppose it may amount to near nine hundred dollars. . . . . Mr. Willard, our disinterested Superintendent, has been paid his expenses from the ninth of November, 1825, to the seventeenth of June last, eight hundred and two dollars, in full satisfaction of his services, and has also subscribed to the funds of the association one thousand dollars in addition to his time thus given." Signed by H. A. S. Dearborn and Amos Lawrence, as a sub-committee, July 18th, 1827.

In November, 1827, at the close of the work for that year,

---

* The contract price was forty-three cents per ton.

which appears not to have equalled the desires of the Directors, Mr. Willard made a report to the committee in which he gives an account of one of his "experiments," from which we extract the following paragraphs :—

"It may be seen by the roll, which I wish the committee to examine, that the number of working days, from the 16th of July to the 17th of November, inclusive, amounts to 108. The whole number of days' labor, done in the hammerers' department at the ledge, during that time, is 2257 — equal to 20 and 97-108 days' work each day. If the time spent in fitting the stone on Bunker Hill, viz. 181 days be taken into the account, it will increase the average per day to 22 and 62-108.

"By the roll also it will be seen that the average labor on the ledge, during the same period of time has been only 6 and 38-108 days' work, having been performed by three splitters and three capstan men. In the one hundred and eight days referred to, these six men have split and run down one hundred and eleven blocks of stone, which will average over six tons each after being dressed ; and they have also split and run down one hundred and eighty blocks for skirting and hollow cone, which will average two-thirds of a ton each, besides clearing away the cellar and wharf stone, which though valuable to those who come after, is waste to us. In the description of work which has been quarried at our ledge, there is much greater difference in the tonnage, before and after being dressed, than usual : I should think that the difference, including the cellar stone, would amount to one-third of the whole.

"The large and small blocks together amount to seven hundred and eighty-seven tons, to which if we add three hundred and ninety-three for loss of tonnage in dressing and for cellar stone, the whole number of tons will be eleven hundred and ninety, quarried and delivered by six men in one hundred and eight days : equal to eleven tons per day for one hundred and eight days in succession. The expenses of the six men to the association were $10 45 per day, which sum divided by eleven, the number of tons got out daily, gives ninety-five cents per ton. Then the cost per ton divided by thirteen, the number of cubic feet in a ton, gives seven cents and three mills for the cost per cubic foot for the rough stone."

" Our stock, according to the last experiment, costs us ten cents per cubic foot, measured after it is dressed. Then, if we add nine and a half cents for carrying, it will amount to nineteen and a half cents per cubic foot delivered on Bunker Hill. — I do not believe that stock as good could now be obtained at any other place, within twenty miles of Boston, for four times this sum. The original estimate was sixteen and a quarter cents, and with the facilities anticipated, I have no doubt the actual expense would have corresponded with the first estimate."

The following extracts from the same report will exhibit in their proper light the high spirit and patriotic feeling which influenced Mr. Willard in undertaking and conducting this great work :—

" For executing the work I have thought it the best policy to hire good men, to pay them fair wages, and to see that their labor is well directed. In this way you can obtain good men and keep them, and by using the proper means to excite emulation, they will not only be faithful but the work will go on with a spirit and economy which cannot be attained in any other way. No graduate from our penitentiary or foreigner has been employed. The workmen are Americans ; natives of neighboring States ; some are relatives of those who fought on Bunker Hill and inherit a genuine spirit for the work. Thus far there has been an uncommon degree of harmony among them. In a few instances I have discovered a disposition in some to tyrannize which I have thought proper to discountenance. It seems to me an improper place to act the Bashaw, the slave or the sycophant. The work which we are engaged in is a work of patriotism, where all should be on equal terms.

19

" In the prosecution of the work there is nothing required, (as I conceive,) but to follow the original plan. Provision should be made immediately for the carrying of the stone. This although a trifling part of the expense, is important, as a failure subjects us to hindrance and heavy loss.   I do not see any propriety in having it in the power of any evil disposed person to stop our work at his pleasure.   If my written instructions from the Building Committee, given a year ago, do not authorize me to provide for the carrying of the stone, I wish them to make such amendments as to make *that* a part of my duty.

" It is now two years since we commenced quarrying at our ledge.   Time has already elapsed sufficient to have built two such monuments, if the work had been prosecuted with a spirit worthy the occasion.   What has been done thus far, has been done with our hands tied, and the way we are going on it will require another year to finish the work.   To me the sacrifice of three years of my life, together with the labor and vexation which has attended every movement since the commencement of the work, is trifling compared with the mortification occasioned by its tardy progress."

This was Mr. Willard's feeling at the end of two year's labor, "under difficulties," if not with his "hands tied."   He little dreamed that fifteen years more would elapse before he should see the work fully completed.

PROGRESS ON THE MONUMENT IN 1828.

The work for the season of 1827, having closed, the committee to audit Mr. Willard's accounts reported the amount of expenditures through him, from June 17th to December 17th, at thirteen thousand four hundred and forty-two dollars.   Now that the monument was rising above the surface, the committee looked forward to a more rapid progress in the coming season. At a meeting on the 10th of December, it was " Voted, that the committee entertain and think it due to Mr. Solomon Willard, to express to him their very high sense and respect for his able and faithful services and unwearied assiduity in accomplishing the patriotic object of the association, and that a copy of this vote be presented to him." Another vote was passed authorizing him " to employ a suitable number of hands, at such times as he thinks best, to complete twenty courses of the monument."

In communicating the above vote, Mr. Lawrence, Secretary of the committee, wrote to Mr. Willard as follows :—

"January 9th, 1828.

" Dear Sir, — Permit me to hand you a vote of the Building Committee of the Bunker Hill Monument, passed at their last meeting, (which gives me the more pleasure in communicating, as the expression of every individual of the committee,) with the assurance of the ardent wish I feel that the great work you have so long been so faithfully and earnestly engaged in accomplishing, may be completed in a style worthy the conception of its author, and that your name and fame may go down with the Bunker Hill Monument to the latest posterity, which I deem next in honor to sharing the glory of the event this monument is intended to commemorate.

" With great sincerity, yours. &c.

AMOS LAWRENCE."

The committee were very anxious to complete twenty courses of the monument, as expressed in their vote, the present season : and the chairman, General Dearborn, addressed a letter with interrogatories to Mr. Willard directly upon this point : In reply to the fifth question, — " What will be the expense of completing twenty courses, and what will be the daily expenses ?" — Mr. Willard stated the cost at about one hundred dollars per day, or ten thousand dollars to accomplish the work by the 4th of July, in one hundred days ; but, taught by the experience of the past, he added in a note, " No allowance is made in the above estimate for unnecessary hindrance which may be occa-

sioned by the stone remaining in our way after they are dressed."
—The work was commenced at Charlestown, about the middle
of April. Mr. Lawrence previously wrote to Mr. Willard,
" I have come to the conclusion that you had better have enough
stone on the ground for five or six courses before beginning, as
the stone can be laid up faster than they can be got out with
our fifty men ; and we have the advantage of making an impression at once upon the public mind, which last thing is
essential to our obtaining the needful for carrying it on."

The directors and architect were zealous and active — the
former giving the work much of their attention and encouraging
by their frequent visits the labors of the latter. During the
two years, Mr. Lawrence was almost a daily visiter to the
hill, and has left the remark that however early in the morning
he arrived there, he was sure to find Mr. Willard on the ground.
He was devoted to the work, and the success of his plan for
carrying it on seems to have been complete and satisfactory. —
It could not have been otherwise with the system which he had
inaugurated. Superior workmanship was obtained at the cost
of half the price of ordinary material and work, and had the
means not failed, the whole would have been accomplished
on the same terms.

With respect to the work done up to this time, the amount of
stone quarried and required, together with the cost of the same
per foot, the committee placed on record the following :—

" By a statement furnished by the architect, it appears that
the quantity of stone actually laid, is, in the foundation eleven
hundred and sixty-seven tons ; in the fourteen courses completed, fifteen hundred and eighty-two tons ; and that there is now
lying on Bunker Hill, hammered, four hundred and ninety-four
tons, (and one hundred tons of flag-stone not wanted for the
monument,) together for the monument, three thousand two
hundred and forty-three tons. The whole quantity required

[dressed] is six thousand six hundred and eighty-six tons :—
There is quarried at Quincy, twelve hundred and thirty-two
tons ; a very small part of this is also hammered ; and to complete the monument, twenty-two hundred and ten tons more are
required to be quarried. The south-eastern section of the ledge
is now prepared and in the best possible order to take out this
whole quantity, the expense of which, at the rate we have paid,
will fall a little short of three thousand dollars. The price paid
for quarrying is seven and a half cents per cubic foot, in the
rough state, which is equal to ten cents in a finished state, or
one dollar and thirty cents per ton finished."

The following "account of the original plan of carrying on
the work, with the success which has attended it," was prepared
by Mr. Willard, for the Committee in 1828, and is a history of
the commencement and progress of the work almost wholly
unknown to the public :—

" Gentlemen — In consequence of the state of the finances
of the Bunker Hill Monument Association, being such as to
require the best possible management in the future prosecution
of the work, Mr. Lawrence has been induced to suggest some
improvements in the mode of conducting it, which may be worthy of consideration by the committee : but previously to acting
on them, it might be well for the committee to take a brief
review of the original plan which occurred to me more than
three years ago, on my first discovery of the quarry, and which
plan has been followed, so far as circumstances would permit.

" The outline of the plan may be seen in a correspondence with
a member of the Committee on the Design, before the Building
Committee were chosen. It was there recommended to choose a
,Building Committee of members who were friendly to the design
adopted ; to employ agents to conduct the work, who would
manage it with the economy of an individual concern, and the

services of the committee and agents to be gratuitous. It was
also recommended that the design should be matured, the form
and construction determined, and after the dimensions, quantity
and quality of the stock required were settled, to advertise for
proposals for furnishing it. In case of the proposals coming too
high, it was recommended to the association to purchase a quarry
and to employ men by the day to get out the stock, and also to
make experiments to ascertain the cost of dressing it.

"A quarry had been purchased and kept in reserve expressly
for the work, for a year previous to this time, and all the
estimates for the different designs were based on the supposition
that the stock might be obtained there with great facility and
economy. This may be seen by the following estimate made at
the time :. the whole quantity required was estimated at about
nine thousand tons, equal to 117,000 cubic feet. The right to
quarry the stock required for the monument cost $325, equal
to one-quarter of a cent per foot, - - ¼
Cost of quarrying, - - - - 6
Cost of transportation to the hill, - 10
———
Total cost per foot, - - 16¼ cents.

"The Building Committee were chosen — the agent appointed — the Plan matured, and the following advertisement was
inserted in the Columbian Centinel, of November 16, 1825, by
the Chairman : —

"'Proposals will be received for furnishing the granite for an
obelisk to be erected on Bunker Hill. The quantity required
will be about 9000 tons, and must be delivered at the prison in
Charlestown, or at a wharf near the navy yard, as may be required. The dimensions of the blocks to be about two feet six
inches wide and twelve feet long. The granite for the foundation may be of a coarse kind, and it will require about 1400
tons. The outside courses of the obelisk must be of the best
Quincy granite, of uniform color, of which about 2600 tons

will be required.   Proposals will be received for Chelmsford granite for the outer courses.   Those who estimate may furnish any quantity to suit their convenience.

" ' Proposals are to be handed to S. Willard, Architect and Superintendent of the Monument, next to St. Paul's Church, Boston.   Mr. Willard will furnish all necessary information on the subject.   As the work will begin immediately, it is desirable that the proposals should be sent in as soon as possible.'

" Most of the persons who furnish stone in this vicinty examined the designs accordingly, but offered no proposals.   All wished to have the construction so altered as to use small stones. One offered verbally to furnish a part at sixty-two cents per cubic foot.   The majority, however, entered into a combination to compel the association to change the construction, and to come to their terms, as respects the price, (as I was informed at the time, by one who had been initiated into the mysteries of the combination.)

" The object of advertising was to give every one an opportunity to furnish the stock, and had their proposals been lower than the estimates according to our original plan, the association would have accepted their terms, and abandoned the project of quarrying their own stock. [There was no possibility of this, for as we have already seen, Mr. Willard found his own estimate less than the actual cost.]

" We commenced opening the quarry on the 16th November. 1825.   A wharf was hired in Quincy, and it was intended that a part of the foundation should have been transported on sleds during the winter.   Severe weather, however, put a stop to our quarrying in a few weeks, and the remainder of the winter was spent in clearing the earth and rubbish from the ledge, and digging out the foundation on Bunker Hill.

[During the winter. Mr. Willard states, the Railway company was projected, but it " was of no service to us until the last of September. 1826."]

" According to the general plan referred to, the work was divided into five departments, viz : the Quarrying, Hammering, Carrying, Hoisting and Masons' Departments.   The number and cost of the men, who filled the various departments, were as follows :—

" *Quarrymen's Department*.   1 master at $2 ; 5 common hands at – : 3 capstan men at – : 1 blacksmith at 1.67.

" *Hammerer's Department*.   30 hammerers at $1.73 : 2 blacksmiths at 1.67 : 1 pattern maker at 1.19.

" *Hoister's Department*.   1 rigger – ; 1 master at $2 : 1 foreman at 1.67 : 3 common hands, 4.50.

" *Mason's Department*.   1 master mason at $2.50 ; 3 journeymen at 1.67 : 1 apprentice 1.00 : 1 blacksmith : 1 tender.

" The whole was intended to move with the regularity of a time-piece.   A due proportion of strength was assigned to each department and provision made by a reserve in case of a deficiency in any particular part.   The number of men to be employed to vary as circumstances might require.   The agent of the association was to be authorized to make all the contracts, to keep the roll, and to receive and pay out the money.   It was to be his duty to employ the masters in the quarrying, hoisting and mason's departments, who were to have the liberty to choose their own assistants, in order to insure unity of effort.   The variety of form required for the stone, and number of men employed in the hammerer's department, rendered it necessary that it should be under the immediate direction of the agent, and means were proposed to excite a proper emulation among those employed. and also to insure a faithful performance of duty.

" The value of the quarry has exceeded our highest expectations, and although the stone delivered in the hammerer's shed costs us more than was first estimated, viz. $7\frac{1}{2}$ cents per foot, [instead of $6\frac{1}{4}$,] it must be recollected that in the experiments made in order to ascertain the cost, the quarrymen labored under disadvantages, which are not likely to occur again.   In the course of the 108-days experiment, the timber run gave way, and it became necessary to rebuild it. The run was first constructed to carry from five to six tons weight — this being the heaviest required for the foundation, or for the obelisk on the original construction; but the blocks being doubled in size, the run was found to be insufficient to carry them, although it had answered its first intention for more than a year. There was also an unusual share of rainy weather during the experiment when nothing could be done on the ledge. The quarrymen suffered also in common with the rest, for want of room, in consequence of the delinquency of the railway company.

"The dressing of the stock in the hammerer's department, has been executed in a superior style of workmanship to what was first intended, and has consequently cost more per foot. — The rough dressing of the beds of the foundation, about twenty thousand feet, was contracted for at ten cents per foot, and would have been profitable to the undertakers, if there had been sufficient room, or had the railway company fulfilled their agreement. By four experiments of some hundred days, on blocks of stone of every form required, the cost of fine dressing has been ascertained to be about forty-three cents per foot superficial, net measure. A considerable proportion of our work, however, is circular which has commonly been measured double : this mode of measuring would reduce the price per foot about one-third, or say to thirty cents."

.   .   .   .   .   .

"The economy with which our stock has been dressed, I think, must give satisfaction. Notwithstanding the superiority of the workmanship, and disadvantages under which we have labored, it costs but about half what has been given by others for inferior work the season past.

"The first course of the Tremont Theatre cost, as I have been informed by the architect, $1 25 per foot. If we deduct twenty cents per foot for the stock, it will leave $1 05 for the dressing. Mr. Webster's underpinning cost one dollar per foot. deducting twenty cents leaves eighty cents for the dressing. —

This is gratifying to me, as some of our particular friends have been very industrious in attempting to impress on the public mind, (and I think probably on the minds of the committee,) that work so well done, and done by the day, (an expensive mode,) by high-priced hands, must necessarily be very expensive.   Further on many circumstances will unite to make it come lower.   The workmen will become more experienced and the fineness of the execution may graduate as the monument rises.   And if the proper room is given to the workmen by removing the stone when finished, I think it will make a difference of half in the expense of dressing."

CHAPTER XXI.

SUSPENSION OF THE WORK — DISCHARGE OF MR. WILLARD —
PROPOSED SALE OF THE LAND — 1829.

FOURTEEN courses of the monument above the foundation, —
or about forty feet in height, — were completed with the close
of the season of 1828 ; and the result clearly demonstrated
the fact that a work of this magnitude and character could
not be put forward as rapidly as the committee and the architect
desired, nor yet as cheaply as they had calculated, the quality
of the work considered. No dissatisfaction is anywhere expressed at the result, nor is any explanation of it recorded : but
it seems certain that the expenditure was larger and the progress of the work less than the committee expected at the end
of the season. Yet there was no ground of complaint : Colonel
Perkins had frequently visited the quarry, and Mr. Lawrence,
as we have said, was a daily visiter at Bunker Hill. Of Mr.
Willard and his workmen, Mr. Lawrence wrote : "Mr. Willard
is engaged in the work with all his soul, . . . and the
quarrymen have as much zeal in performing their duty as their
fathers had in seventy-five." In such hands as these the work
had gone steadily on ; but the committee had worked under
the disadvantage of inadequate means, and were very early
compelled to borrow money to continue their labors. Mr.
Willard had exerted himself to meet the expressed wishes
of the directors and so far succeeded as to have the stone for

twenty courses nearly completed and on the ground before the close of the season, as will be seen by the following statement : The fourteen courses laid required 4582 tons: the six next courses required 580 tons: there were upon the hill ready for use 494 tons and more at the quarry.

As early as the 16th of June, 1828, the Building Committee appear to have become disheartened and passed an order '·that as the means of the corporation are so nearly exhausted, no further expense be incurred beyond present engagements ;" and on the next day another order "that the work going on at the Bunker Hill quarry be forthwith suspended." The Secretary, Mr. Lawrence, appends a note to this last order : " It is expected that all the stone to complete sixteen courses of the monument will be made ready first." It was stated at a meeting of the committee, on the sixteenth of September, '· that the monument had now attained a height of about forty feet ; that the quantity of stone prepared and on Bunker Hill is equal to carrying the monument about fifty-eight feet, and that the quarrying is still continued at Quincy, the committee feeling unwilling to relinquish that part of the work so long as there appears strong expectations of raising more funds."

In partial explanation of the above result, Mr. Lawrence, in an incidental letter to Dr. Warren, made the following statements : " The committtee caused the stone for forty feet of the monument to be completed ; in getting which, owing to former arrangements at the quarry, there has been a quantity equal to fifty-eight feet prepared, although not in the regular order in which it will be laid. . . . The outlay of money has been greater than was contemplated, owing to the increased quantity of stone which it was necessary to prepare to complete the forty feet. The only loss to the association is the advance of the money for work that cannot be immediately completed."

But the inevitable moment had come and could no longer be postponed. The funds of the association were exhausted and its landed property, as well as the balance of the seven thousand

dollars due from the Commonwealth, had been hypothecated, —
there was no possibility, therefore, of being able to continue the
work. The directors thought they had done all that the public
could require of them. The mortgaging of the land they had
most unwillingly consented to, under the belief that it would
soon be redeemed. The feeling of the committee on this subject
is very well shown in a note appended to the record of the
meeting, (July the 10th, 1828,) at which the loan of sixteen
thousand dollars was authorized : " *Mem :* It is contemplated
making an appeal to the public after the monument shall have
been raised forty three feet, for the means to pay off this loan,
and to preserve the land, (to be conveyed as security for the
above loan,) forever from occupation for buildings ; that the
Battle-field of Bunker Hill may remain to posterity a stimulant
to patriotism, a corrective to anarchy." With this loan the
sum of five thousand dollars previously borrowed, was paid off,
and there " now was no lien upon the land excepting this one
of sixteen thousand dollars." Subsequently, however, October
third, a further loan of five thousand dollars was made ; and
again on the twenty-third of January, 1829, another loan of
fourteen hundred dollars was required, making altogether a lien
of twenty-two thousand four hundred dollars upon the land. —
This amount was further increased by the accruing interest.

At the meeting of the Building Committee, on the twenty-
third of January, 1829, " after considerable conversation was
had upon the present condition and prospects of the association,"
the following vote was passed :—

" Voted, That all the work at Quincy, or elsewhere, attended
with any expense to the association, be wholly suspended, the
committee having in their opinion gone to the full extent of the
value of all the disposable property of the association, and as
far as public opinion would require of them, until further means
are provided for carrying on the work ; and this committee give
it as their unanimous opinion, that a subscription in some form,

should be immediately circulated for obtaining the requisite funds for carrying forward the work."

The work had all been suspended previously to this vote : at the hill on the first of September, and at the quarry on the seventeenth of January following, — as stated in an "address" prepared by a committee appointed in September and printed in February. This address was "never circulated on account of the depression of the times."

At the annual meeting of the association, June 17th, 1829, an almost entirely new government was chosen, with ex-Governor Levi Lincoln as President. At this meeting, after considering the condition and prospects of the association and referring to what had been done, it was formally declared that a sale of the land had become necessary, and a resolution was passed, authorizing the President, with the consent and approbation of the Directors, " to make and sign any deed or deeds to convey all or any part of the land, except an area of six hundred feet by four hundred feet around the monument, now owned by this association, and situate in Charlestown, in fee simple, and to acknowledge any deed or deeds by him executed, and to cause the seal of this corporation to be thereunto affixed — whenever and so soon as it shall be deemed expedient and proper by him, with consent and approbation aforesaid, so to do."

At the next director's meeting, a new Building Committee was chosen, General Dearborn chairman, and at their first meeting, August 8th, 1829, the subject of laying off the land of the association into lots, was considered, and the record proceeds — " The prospect of Mr. Willard's services being further required, (in the present state of the affairs,) being so distant, it was voted, that the chairman give Mr. Willard his discharge from the service of the association, with such expressions of respect for his services as their nature and character require : the committee only regret that they have not the control of means sufficient to authorize him to go on and finish the great work for which he has sacrificed so much."

The following is the note sent to Mr. Willard in accordance with the above proceedings :—

"Brinley Place, August 18, 1829.

"My Dear Sir, — It having been found necessary to suspend our labors on the Bunker Hill Monument until the funds have been augmented, your valuable services in the meantime will not be required; but we shall rely upon them the moment it may be in our power to prosecute that glorious work.

"It affords me sincere pleasure to assure you, that the arduous and very responsible duties which devolved upon you as Superintendent and Architect, have been discharged in the most faithful and efficient manner, giving unqualified satisfaction to the Building Committee, and entitling you to the gratitude of the Association. Science, genius and taste have been so conspicuously evinced in the plan and execution of the whole work, as cannot fail to exalt your reputation as an artist, and secure for you the confidence and patronage of your fellow-citizens.

"With the best wishes for your prosperity and happiness and assurances of my great respect and esteem, I am, dear sir, your most obedient servant,

H. A. S. DEARBORN, Chairman, &c.

"S. Willard, Esquire, Architect."

Notwithstanding these proceedings, Mr. Willard was immediately employed in accordance with the vote of the association in relation to a sale of the land, in laying it out into streets and lots, with the reserved square around the monument; and on the 28th of November, the whole committee being present, it was determined to recommend to the directors the adoption of the following vote : "That the plan herewith submitted, drawn by Solomon Willard, the architect, for laying off the land, be adopted, and secondly, that it is inexpedient to sell any part of the land owned by the association at present." These votes were reported to and adopted by the directors, and together with another relative to a lottery, concluded the proceedings of the directors for the year 1829.

There was great reluctance on the part of some of the directors to disposing of any portion of the land, and they were very unwilling to do anything with that end in view. They were encouraged at this time by the lottery scheme, and subsequently by the hope of gaining the aid of the Commonwealth. Mr. Willard was probably willing to dispose of the land with a view to the completion of the monument, but Mr. Lawrence was earnestly opposed to the lottery and as earnestly desirous of preserving the battle-field intact. The following views on this subject are from his pen* :—

" It is probable that Boston and the country around, taking in a distance of three miles from the State House, will contain a population of more than two hundred thousand within thirty years, which will of course fill up the most eligible building lots within that distance; among the best is the land on and about Bunker Hill; all that part of Charlestown within the neck will either be joined to Boston, or will be so intimately connected with it as to be practically nearly the same thing to the city. When our present worthy Mayor†, built his house on Beacon street, he was as much out of town as he would be now on Bunker Hill, and the land on and around Beacon Hill to Charles street, was of little more value then, than the land on and around Bunker Hill is now. Fifty years ago [i. e. eighty years ago,] Boston Common could not have been sold for a thousand dollars an acre; at this time it is above price; and had our fathers allowed it to be sold for what seemed then a great sum, we should now say they were not so provident for

<hr>

* "March, 1846. I find this among my Bunker Hill papers, which I prepared, and the substance was issued in 1832 or '33, without a name. Amos Lawrence."

† Hon. Harrison Gray Otis, Mayor in 1829, 1830 and 1831 ; but the house was built some years before.

us as they ought to have been. The whole Bunker Hill field is perhaps the most beautiful open space in Charlestown; and besides the interest in it, growing out of its connection with a new era in the history of man, it will have the charm of adding directly to the comfort of the people who reside in its neighborhood, or who use it for a promenade. This beautiful field, (except a space of six hundred by four hundred feet,) is mortgaged and must be sold unless the means can be raised to save it. The Bunker Hill Monument Association owe about twenty-five thousand dollars. It may be said perhaps that six hundred by four hundred feet is space enough for a Monument Square. It would be enough, if you had no more, and could get no more; but would one fourth part of Boston Common be enough for the citizens if they could sell the other three-fourths for enough to pay the city debt, and save two millions of dollars besides? The Bunker Hill field is above price; the time will come if it is left open, when it will be the most interesting spot in this country, perhaps the most interesting in any country, and will exert a high moral and political influence upon posterity. Can we of the present day in any other way appropriate twenty-five thousand dollars so much to their advantage? What man in this city, who received an inheritance from his fathers, wishes his money had been increased by the sale fifty years ago of our beautiful Common? Is not his inheritance increased in value by its being left open a hundred times the amount it would have sold for? . . . Whatever adds to the comforts of our city, adds to its property; and every citizen has an interest in making the residence of every other citizen as comfortable as possible. In this way we secure the best population and keep alive a home attachment, a self-respect, of more worth than all the coin of this Union.''

21

CHAPTER XXII.

DIFFICULTIES IN ENTERPRISES — PLANS FOR THE PROSECUTION

OF THE WORK — 1830.

It has often been remarked that if the difficulties and obstacles, to say nothing of disasters and accidents, which are sure to attend the progress of every considerable enterprise, public or private, could be fore-known, very few of those successfully accomplished would be undertaken, unless prompted by some imperative necessity. Fortunately it is not so — fortunately, perhaps, the reverse is more nearly true : the best view of contingencies, the easy side of obstacles, the plausibility of theories, the friendly circumstances, the ease with which difficulties are to be surmounted and means to be commanded — all these are contemplated and weighed, — and with an assured reliance upon our own judgment and energies, no undertaking within the scope of man's capacity to plan is supposed to be beyond his ability to execute ; and reasoning from what has been accomplished, in ancient time and in our own time, the conclusion is neither illogical or without substantial basis.

The Directors of the Bunker Hill Monument Association were too intelligent to be misled by any mere plausibility ; but were liable, from the warmth of their own patriotic and generous impulses, to over-estimate the weight of these upon the public mind and the readiness with which they would be responded to by the people at large. This mistake, it is thought, they did make — honorable to them as showing their confidence in the patriotism and ability of the people, — but productive of the result which ensued. They believed that all the means, however considerable, required for the work which they proposed to do, would be ready for their asking: ·In the address of August, 1830, the Directors say, " The funds on hand were adequate to a considerable progress in the structure, and reliance was placed on the public spirit, liberality and patriotism of the community to furnish the means which should be eventually wanting to complete it :" and Mr. Willard, whose interest and ardor were equal to their own, placed entire confidence in their judgment in this matter, and in their ability in any event to forward the noble work which they had undertaken. — He was very much averse to " begging," as he called it, and hoped as the directors did, that the worthiness of the object would command the means. They appear to have thought, in the first place, that the contributions would be so general that a small sum from each individual would be sufficient to accomplish the object ; but it was a mistake to suppose that all would or could give the same sum : the least able in hundreds of instances, gave the amount apparently desired, and the wealthy, in other hundreds of instances, contented themselves with subscribing the same amount. The records of the association show that in the towns and cities of the Commonwealth, the sums subscribed by the rich were almost invariably of the small amount required for membership, — as if membership and a diploma and not the monument were the object ; — those who could not give that sum did not give at all — so that the lowest amount was obtained from the rich, and the same or nothing, from all other classes.

The work having been suspended, the directors earnestly engaged in plans and efforts to provide means for its prosecution, when the next season opened. The proposed lottery scheme having been abandoned, the committee charged with the prosecution of that measure were instructed to petition the legislature

for " a grant in money or land, or aid in such other manner as
the general court might deem most expedient." But the general court had no idea of aiding the work, and never did so excepting as already stated. Mr. Willard was opposed to these repeated applications and preferred to rely on the people. Upon
being repulsed again at the door of the State House, the committee on the sixth of April, reported as follows : " We are thus
thrown back upon public patronage for obtaining the requisite
funds for completing the monument; and have no doubt of
ultimate success; for the cause is honorable, patriotic and
sacred, and the people will assuredly go on with a work which
they have commenced with ardor, and will glory in prosecuting
until it towers aloft in completed magnificence." This was
entirely in accordance with Mr. Willard's hopes and feelings.

The proposition of Mrs. Sarah J. Hale to inaugurate an effort
to raise funds to complete the monument by an appeal to the
Ladies of New England, made to the Building Committee in
January, was laid before the Directors in April, 1830. It was
accepted with avidity, and it was voted " that this commendable
effort . . . . merits the grateful acknowledgments of the
Directors, . . . and that whatever sum of money may be
obtained shall be considered sacred and applied for the sole
purpose of completing the monument." This effort produced
something over twenty-two hundred dollars, which was deposited
with the Massachusetts Hospital Life Insurance Company, and
when applied to the work amounted to about three thousand
dollars.

Notwithstanding the confident language of the committee
above quoted, at the annual meeting in June, the Directors
were instructed to petition the legislature again for a grant of
money from the amount at that time expected from the general
government " on account of the militia services rendered by the
State during the last war." They were also instructed to prepare an address to the people explanatory of the views of the
association, of its operations and condition, and to distribute the

same in every town in the Commonwealth.   The address, from
the pen of Mr. Everett, was submitted on the thirteenth day of
August, and was an earnest, argumentative and eloquent appeal
to the people and the legislature for aid in the completion of
their patriotic undertaking.   In confirmation, as it would seem,
of the remarks in the opening of this chapter, the committee
speak of their labors as follows :   " In short, the Directors ask
permission to observe that their labors have been arduous beyond what would be thought by those unacquainted from experience with similar undertakings ; that they are conscious of
having been actuated by no motives but those of public duty ;
that with a single eye to the completion of this great public
work, many of them have bestowed more time, attention and
labor upon it, than can often be spared from private avocations ;
and that they have done this without the hope of any other reward than that of being regarded as faithful agents of an important public trust."

Referring to the history of the debt due to the State and assumed by the general government, the address says, " In the
debate on the assumption [of this debt] in the first Congress, it
was particularly stated (as we are informed by Chief Justice
Marshall,) 'that the ammunition which repulsed the enemy at
Bunker Hill was purchased by Massachusetts and formed a part
of the debt of that State.'   In the war. of 1812, this fund was
again expended by Massachusetts in active preparation to repel
an anticipated invasion.   Being a second time returned by the
general government to the coffers of the State, what more appropriate use could be made of a small portion of it than to
grant it for the completion of this grand and interesting memorial of that ever memorable achievement of the militia of Massachusetts and her sister New England States which will render
this portion of our soil sacred and famous to the end of time. —
. . . The fund originally bestowed in providing warlike supplies of the seventeenth of June, 1775, will then, as it were, be
visibly embodied and preserved upon the field of that day's un-

dying glory.   There it will exist for the admiration of posterity,
ages after every vestigo of the ordinary disbursements of the
State shall have passed away; teaching the children of America,
who from every portion of the Republic will make their pilgrim-
age to this sacred spot, while they behold the majestic structure
that crowns it, that the people of Massachusetts of this generation are resolved that the gallant deeds of their fathers shall not
pass uncommemorated."

   This appeal of reason and eloquence was lost upon the legislature, the petition never receiving its attention.

   Mr. Willard thought to aid these efforts of the directors by
preparing a pamphlet for the press, containing the act of incorporation and by-laws, a list of contributors and the amount
subscribed by each, a statement showing the magnitude and
purpose of the work and the original estimate of its cost.   The
manuscript copy of this pamphlet, now among the papers in
possession of the association, is an evidence of the industry and
application of Mr. Willard in whatever he undertook.   It com-
prises nearly one hundred pages of copying, including several
thousand names, arranged under the headings of the counties
and towns in which the contributors resided.   At the meeting
on the seventeenth of June, the association voted to pay the cost
of printing the pamphlet and ordered copies to be distributed
among the members.

   The last meeting of the Building Committee was held on the
the sixteenth of June, 1830.   The report of the Treasurer, at
this time, shew a balance of $2025 34, in his hands, nearly one
half of which had been received from the ladies.

⋆ ⋆⋆

CHAPTER XXIII.

INTERRUPTION IN THE GOVERNMENT — EFFORTS OF THE

MECHANICS' ASSOCIATION — 1831 — 1833.

THE application to the legislature and the appeal to the people, eloquent and forcible as these were, and sustained in the one case by a most respectable committee and in the other by the entire government of the association, may have made an impression on the public mind, but produced no direct results in the prosecution of the work. Other measures, inaugurated towards the end of the last year, were not prosecuted during the winter, and the recurrence of the annual meeting in June, 1831, found the monument covered in, and all the work in *statu quo*. Only forty persons attended the meeting of the association, and a majority of these were prominent among the leaders of a newly-formed· political party,* who were violently opposed to those proceedings of the association which admitted the Masonic fraternity to a participation in the service of laying the corner-stone in 1825 ; and they succeeded in electing themselves and their friends to office — a measure preliminary, it was said but since denied, to changes of a more objectionable character on the work itself. At this meeting the President was elected by *twenty-eight* votes, being a majority of seven. The offices, heretofore filled by the projectors and early friends of the mon-

---

* This party was known as the " Anti-Masonic party "

ument, were thus taken possession of by those who had other
purposes to subserve than the completion of the work which they
proposed to assume. The designs of this party, however, whatever they were, were thwarted by their failure to elect a full
board of directors and by measures which were adopted at an
adjournment of the meeting when the existing vacancies were
filled. The meeting for this purpose was held in Faneuil Hall,
when *five hundred and eighty-two* members of the association
were present and voted. The remainder of the directors were
elected by a nearly unanimous vote, no one of them having less
than five hundred and seventy-nine votes. Not only the members of the association but the whole community condemned
the proceedings which rendered a second meeting necessary.

The new party held numerous meetings, — generally without
a quorum, — during their year of service, but did not attempt
to organize a Building Committee, nor succeed in inaugurating
any measures to forward the work. In a "report," printed but
never presented to the association, the President and his *con-
freres* attempted to justify their proceedings, establish the hon-
esty and disinterestedness of their motives, and throw blame and
odium upon the honorable, patriotic and devoted gentlemen who
both preceded and succeeded them in office. The conclusion,
however, to which they came very early in their "report," was
that "They found the monument incompleted, . . . and
they left as they found it." This was precisely what it was
feared they would not do ; but they were held in subjection by
their associates and the still stronger bias of public sentiment.
It may be said of their "report" that "what there is true in it
is not new, and what is new is not true." The true portions
are admitted ; the untrue it has never been deemed necessary
to answer. Among the truths which form the exceptions to its
general character, are the words bestowed upon the patriotic
architect, whom they accurately describe as "the indefatigable
and extraordinarily disinterested architect." The argument
intended to demonstrate the fact that Mr. Willard was the true

architect of the monument, was wholly uncalled-for from them and only necessary for a sinister purpose, — that of casting odium upon the masonic fraternity and the proceedings in which they took part.

At the annual meeting in June, 1832, the association redeemed itself and restored the government to those to whom it rightfully belonged. Mr. William Prescott, who had been so unceremoniously displaced, was again elected President by over four hundred votes. Nothing was done towards the completion of the monument during the year. In December a committee was appointed " to consider what measures it will be expedient to adopt with reference to raising funds for the completion of the work ;" but its services were never made available.

In May, 1833, the Massachusetts Charitable Mechanic Association, " not less in accordance with their own feelings than in compliance with the desire of others," undertook the inauguration of measures for the immediate completion of the monument. They adopted resolutions, published an address to the people, held a great public meeting in Faneuil Hall, and in other ways entered earnestly upon the undertaking. In all their measures they had the consent, the sympathy and the cooperation of the Monument Association, the Directors having promptly voted, "That this Board are highly gratified by this manifestation of interest in a great national work on the part of the Massachusetts Charitable Mechanic Association ; that this Board respectfully recommend to all the members of the Bunker Hill Monument Association to render all the aid and support in their power in this highly acceptable and praiseworthy interposition to do honor to the past and to the present age, and to deserve the gratitude of ages to come."

The public meeting in Faneuil Hall, was held on the 28th of May ; the Directors determined to attend in a body and invited the members of the association to be present " in testimony of their accordance in the honorable and patriotic feelings which have influenced the Mechanic Association to take these meas-

22

ures."   The principal address on this occasion was by Mr.
Edward Everett, whose heart had been interested in the subject
from the first suggestion of the work.   This speech, Mr. Lawrence wrote, was "the most eloquent he ever made."   It was
"touching and beautiful, and was considered at the time as decisive and that the money would be subscribed for finishing the
monument and saving the whole field, at once."   Mr. Lawrence
was sick, could do nothing himself and became impressed with
the idea that the mechanics had failed in this instance, "to
strike while the iron was hot."   "If I had been in health," he
wrote on a copy of this address, "I would have had the whole
thing done, so far as collecting fifty thousand dollars would have
done it, in forty-eight hours after the adjournment of this meeting."   We feel justified in quoting a brief passage from the
address of Mr. Everett, as the argument may be almost as necessary with some persons today as when first delivered :—

"But I am met with the great objection, *What good will
the Monument do?*   I beg leave, sir, to exercise my birth-
right as a Yankee, and answer this question by asking two or
three more, to which I believe it will be quite as difficult to
furnish a satisfactory reply.   I am asked, What good will the
Monument do ?   And I ask, What good does anything do ?
What is good ?   Does anything do any good ?   The persons who
suggest this objection, of course, think that there are some projects and undertakings that do good ; and I should therefore
like to have the idea of *good* explained and analyzed, and run
out to its elements.   When this is done, if I do not demonstrate
in about two minutes, that the Monument does the same kind of
good that anything else does, I will consent that the huge blocks
of granite already laid, should be reduced to gravel, and carted
off to fill up the mill-pond : for that I suppose is one of the
good things.   Does a railroad or canal do good ?   Answer, Yes.
And how ?   It facilitates intercourse, opens markets and in-
creases the wealth of the country.   But what is this good for ?

Why, individuals prosper and get rich. And what good does that do? Is mere wealth, as an ultimate end, — gold and silver without an inquiry as to their use, — are these a good? Certainly not. I should insult this audience by attempting to prove that a rich man, as such, was neither better nor happier, than a poor one. But as men grow rich, they live better. Is there any good in this, stopping here? Is mere animal life, — feeding, working, and sleeping like an ox, entitled to be called good? Certainly not. But these improvements increase the population. And what good does that do? Where is the good in counting twelve millions instead of six of mere feeding, working, sleeping animals? There is then no good in the mere animal life, except that it is the basis of that higher moral existence which resides in the soul, the heart, the mind, the conscience ; in good principles, good feelings, and the good actions, (and the more disinterested, the better entitled to be called good,) which flow from them. Now, sir, I say that generous and patriotic sentiments; sentiments which prepare us to serve our country, to live for our country, to die for our country, — feelings like those which carried Prescott, and Warren, and Putnam, to the battlefield, are good ; — good, humanly speaking, of the highest order. It is good to have them, good to encourage them, good to honor them, good to commemorate them; and whatever tends to cherish, animate and strengthen such feelings, does as much right down practical good as filling up flats and building railroads. This is my demonstration."

This eloquent and beautiful address, and especially the ennobling lesson we have quoted, as well as the celebrated orations by Mr. Webster, is to be counted among the " good things" which the erection of the monument has produced.

That the Directors of the Monument Association fully appreciated the " interposition" of the Mechanic Association has already been shown. As a further acknowledgment of the interest manifested and the service proposed to be rendered, the byaws were altered so as to enlarge the Board of Directors, and the office of first Vice President was made inherent in the person holding the office of President of the Mechanic Association. At the annual meeting in June, in accordance with these purposes, Mr. J. T. Buckingham was elected first Vice President, and a number of gentlemen in the same interest chosen on the Board of Directors.

Thus were the different classes of society, as represented by the various occupations and professions, again united as in revolutionary times, in a common object of public interest. Then, the merchants, the lawyers, the doctors and the clergy, united with the mechanics; now, the mechanics had come to the aid of the professions, in a cause of much less magnitude, but one entirely worthy of an united effort.

As a means of promoting subscriptions, a new certificate of membership was prepared in the name of the two associations; and this, while it afforded a slight encouragement to art, required the expenditure of a thousand dollars, which of course, was added to the amount to be raised for the monument. The design of this diploma included a view of the battle-field, and one of the completed monument with the city in the back ground.

In July, at a meeting of the Directors, an Executive Committee of nine was appointed, with Mr. Buckingham as chairman. They were instructed to inquire into various matters pertaining to the progress and completion of the work and state of the subscriptions, and to report their opinion as to the best mode of future proceedings. Two other meetings were held this year, but the committee were not then prepared to report.

CHAPTER XXIV.

REPORT OF THE COMMITTEE — MR. WILLARD'S REVIEW OF IT.

THE year 1834, it was hoped and believed, would see the monument re-commenced and completed. It had been for ten years before the public, and nearly nine years had elapsed since the ceremony of laying the corner-stone was performed — at which time no one supposed it would require more than a year or two to complete the work. When the Mechanic Association inaugurated the present movement, public confidence revived and there was a general desire to see the roofing removed from the monument and the work begun.

In January, Mr. Buckingham reported that the Mechanic Association had obtained subscriptions to the amount of about thirty thousand dollars, mostly on the condition that fifty thousand dollars should be subscribed. In May, the same gentleman presented the report of the Executive Committee in detail. — The following extract is from this report : —

" The report [of a sub-committee] is herewith submitted, and it will be seen therefrom that the work already done under the direction of the architect, Mr. Solomon Willard, is well and faithfully done, and at less cost than it could have been done by any person but Solomon Willard, who has devoted himself to the monument with extraordinary enthusiasm.

" The sub-committee estimate the future work at one dollar and thirty cents per cubic foot. Mr. Willard estimates it at eighty-nine and a half cents. The former estimate is assumed for the present purpose as the safest, and on that basis the sub-committee report that it will cost —

"To raise the monument 121 feet, $28,967 36
"   "   "   159 feet 6 inches,   42,922 40
"   "   . "   220 feet,   55,576 40

"The Committee are of opinion that the present effort should be limited to raising the monument [to the height of] one hundred and fifty-nine feet six inches.

"The corporation owes $30,000. This debt arose from the purchase of the battle-ground in the hope that it might be kept open and sacred forever. . . . . Assuming two things for the present purpose, viz: 1st, That the battle-ground must go to common uses. 2d, That the monument shall be considered completed, as to the present effort, when raised to the elevation of one hundred and fifty-nine feet six inches,—Can means be found to complete it ?

"The Massachusetts Charitable Mechanic Association have subscriptions for about thirty thousand dollars, on condition that the whole amount subscribed rise to fifty thousand dollars by the first of June, 1834. Supposing that this condition can be complied with, then the case would stand thus : —

"Cost of building 159 feet 6 in.,   -   - $42,922 40
"Present debt,   -   -   -   -   -   30,000 00
                                              _____
        Total,   -   -   -   - $72,922 40

"It is hoped that a company can be formed to take the land of the corporation in shares of five hundred dollars each, leaving a four hundred feet Square and streets on each side fifty feet wide. If so, there would be raised —

"Towards the debt,   -   -   - $25,000
"Present subscriptions,   -   -   -   30,000
"Expected subscriptions,   -   -   20,000
"Sale of machinery, (cost $10,000)   -   2,000
"Ladies' fund,   -   -   -   -   3,000
                                          _____
        "Total,   -   -   -   - $80,000 "

In view of this state of affairs, the Monument Association consented that the Mechanic Association should "forthwith proceed with what means they have and can collect, to raise the monument one hundred and fifty-nine feet six inches," and that the "Ladies' Fund" and the new Certificates of Membership, should be placed at their disposal — and votes were passed accordingly at the same meeting, on the 5th of May.

Mr. Willard was a member of the Mechanic Association, and of course was cognizant of all these proceedings. Although discharged from the work, he was constantly consulted by the Executive Committee, both in relation to the laying out and sale of the land and the work on the monument, done and to be done. Mr. Peres Loring was employed by the committee to make a survey of the whole work and estimates of the amount of stone already in the monument or prepared for use, and of the amount required to complete the work.

The condition of things at this time, as now briefly stated, and especially the report of the sub-committee, drew from Mr. Willard the following characteristic letter :

"Boston, May, 1834.

"Dear Sir,—After reviewing the report of the committee, which was the subject of a conversation at your office the other day, I still think that there are parts of it which may be considered by some as wanting in accuracy. I apprehend that there are those who may be disposed to question the truth of the assertion that the work has been done "at a less cost than it could have been done by any" other. Indeed it is quite obvious that this could not have been known to be true ; and, admitting it to be so, it gives no definite idea of the value of the services rendered by the one who conducted the work, which appears to have been the principal object in making the statement. The services referred to had undoubtedly a value of a substantial kind, — a value in dollars and cents, — a mode of estimating things with which Bostonians are known to be competent judges.

And the exact sum might have been shown by merely stating the market value of the work done and deducting therefrom the sum expended.

" I have always felt solicitous to have this point settled, and it appears now to be a favorable time : One of the principal objects of my engaging in the enterprize was to ascertain by actual experiment the *prime* cost of a building material which was much wanted, and the design of erecting the monument presented a favorable opportunity.

" The plan for prosecuting the work was suggested by myself, and adopted by the Building Committee who then had charge of the work, and who are about to resign the trust into other hands. I think, therefore, at the conclusion of their labors, it would be satisfactory to all concerned to know the result of the experiment which has been made, whether favorably or not, and I think also that it is a duty which the committee owe to themselves to make a proper statement, as those who are about to take their places will not be backward in assuming whatever credit may fairly belong to them. I think also that a true and faithful account of their stewardship is due from the committee to those who have contributed to the funds, as by satisfying them that their money has been well expended is the most likely way to obtain more. A clamor has been kept up from the commencement of the work to the present time, in relation to the expenditure of the funds, and should it be found on examination that the work has actually cost more than has been paid for corresponding work at other places, it will undoubtedly be a proof of injudicious planning, and show conclusively that the services of their committee and agent have been of no advantage to the association, whatever their endeavor may have been to render them so. On the contrary, if it be found that the work has cost less than others have paid for similar work, there will be a credit due for skilful management, and its exact value will be indicated by the balance found.

" The quantities of stone and dressing that have been delivered are already known by actual survey. According to Loring's measurement, there are 57,802 feet of stone, cubic measure, already split out and a larger part delivered on Breed's Hill. The market value of such a lot of stone, I shall estimate at 75 cents per cubic foot, and the whole would amount to $43,351.50 at that price. The number of feet of dressing, according to the same survey and measured in the customary way, is 52,569 feet, superficial measure. The average price of first rate work, for fifteen years past, is assumed to be 50 cents, and the whole will amount at that price to $26,284 50. The number of cubic feet laid up, according to the same survey, is 35,878, and the market price per foot, is assumed to be 30 cents, including the fitting, hoisting, laying, mortar, iron cramps, and scaffolding, with the wear on the machinery, and every other expense connected, and would amount at the above price to $10,763 40,— and the total amount of the three items at the assumed prices, would be $80,399 40.

" The question to be settled is whether the assumed prices are an average of those paid for similar work for the last fifteen years, or whether they are above or below the current prices.

" In order to ascertain this it will be necessary to refer to the bills paid for similar work at different places. And in relation to the cost of the stone, of the dimensions of those used at the monument, we may refer to the bills paid at the General Hospital, for the blocks which compose the columns, and to those paid at the Branch Bank for the architrave pieces, and the blocks for the columns which were originally intended to have been in five pieces, and for which contracts were made. We may also refer to the bills paid at the Tremont House, for the blocks for the columns to the portico and in the cornice ; and to those paid at the Washington Bank for the footings to the columns, and at the Arcade in Providence, for similar pieces. We may also refer to the bills paid at the Dry Docks in Charlestown and Norfolk, for a large number of blocks of a corresponding size ; and to those paid at the new Bank now erecting in

23

State street, for the piers that support the columns. And also to those that are to be paid at the New Court House for a large quantity of work about to be contracted for, and to any bills which may have been paid for blocks of four tons weight, sold in the market within the time specified.

" In order to ascertain the value of the dressing, of first rate work, we have only to refer to the prices paid at some of the principal buildings that have been erected, viz : to those paid at Mr. Sears's house, for straight and circular work ; to those paid at the Tremont House, at the Theatre, at Mr. Webster's house, at Mr. Cushing's house, at the New Court House, at the new Bank, at Astor's Hotel, &c. The market value of the mason work may be found in a similar manner, and a bill in the form of an account current, including the three items above-named at the prices found, would probably stand as follows :

[We omit the form of account mentioned as being simply a recapitulation of the above statements.]

" Allowing the prices assumed to be the market prices, the above bill shows that the work already done would have cost the association the sum of eighty thousand three hundred and ninety-nine dollars, had they paid the current price, — a sum far exceeding the one actually paid out.

" But the advantages already derived are not all that are possessed by the association, in consequence of the labors and good planning of those who commenced the work. There are still nearly thirty-four thousand feet of stone required to carry the monument to the height proposed, for which the association would have to pay the market price were they excluded from the quarry they now possess, and from other advantages derived from the exertions of those who have been early engaged.

" The current prices may be found as in other cases, namely, by collecting an account of sales for the time specified. With respect to ascertaining the prices which have been paid for the dressing and mason's work, there will be little difficulty. The prices paid for blocks of granite, of the dimensions used at the monument, will not be so easily ascertained, as care has generally been taken to conceal the amount paid. This has been accomplished either by a secret contract or evasive answers, or by "lumping" the high and low priced stone together. The prices which have been paid per cubic foot at the different places referred to, are supposed to be nearly as follows :

Per Cubic foot.

At the General Hospital, for columns, . .	1 00
At the Branch Bank, for architrave, . .	2 00
Which were to have been paid for columns, .	1 00
At the Tremont House, for columns, . .	1 00
" " " blocks for cornice, .	60
At the Washington Bank, for footing, . .	1 00
At the Arcade in Providence, for do., .	1 00
At the Dry Dock in Charlestown, . . .	60
At Norfolk for Dry Dock, ...	70
At the New Bank in State street, for piers, .	1 00
For the New Court House, ...	1 00

Average price of these sales, 99 cents.

" It will be observed that the average of the above sales is higher than the one assumed in the account.

" Nothing appears to be necessary in order to show the value of the plan that has been pursued, and the credit due to the managers than to settle the market value per foot of the three items of the foregoing bill. . . . . .

" In relation to the estimate made by the sub-committee of the expense of the work to be done, there is something that I do not understand. It is stated in the report that ' the sub-committee estimate the future work at one dollar and thirty cents the cubic foot; Mr. Willard estimates it at eighty-nine and a half cents. The former price is assumed for the present purpose as the safest, and on that basis the committee report.' That one hundred and thirty cents per foot would be considered more safe than eighty-nine and a half cents, I think is quite probable ; and that two dollars per foot would be considered still more safe; but it strikes me that it would have been much more ingenuous for the sub-committee to have stated the exact sum that the work had cost per foot, and if they perceived any reason why the work to be done should cost more, to have given their reasons and the estimated amount. An actual experiment is a practical demonstration, and to oppose the opinion of any one who never saw a stone quarried to the best possible wisdom, is exceedingly absurd. I think also that it is presuming quite too much on the gullibility of the public to present so loose an estimate.

"The expenses connected with any great enterprise, it is well known, consist of the outlay required in making the necessary preparations for commencing it; and the cost of the labor and wear of apparatus in prosecuting the work. The preparations for commencing the work of building the monument required a considerable expenditure. At Breed's Hill, the preparation consisted in sinking a foundation nearly fifty feet square and twelve feet deep, and laying an inclined plane of flag-stone from the road to the monument, to facilitate the drawing up of the large blocks of granite which it would have been difficult to do on the soft ground. The prosecution of the work required also an expensive hoisting apparatus, with substantial guy-posts, planted deep in the earth and ballasted. A capstan-house was also necessary, with sheds and blacksmiths' shops, and various sets of tools, jacks and other apparatus. A hoisting apparatus was also found necessary at the wharf where the stone was landed.

"The preparations at Quincy consisted in clearing and opening the quarry; making roads, erecting a boarding-house, blacksmiths' shop, stone cutters' sheds and other buildings; a timber run and machinery for lowering the stone, &c. And there was also a large quantity of quarrying apparatus wanted, consisting of jacks, iron bars, sledges, hammers, &c., the greater part of which are now on hand.

" The expense of all this apparatus, with the time lost; cost of superintendence, and various other expenses, have been carried to the contingent account, where they properly belong. The total amount of this contingent bill is about $17,400, and this sum being divided by the whole number of feet of stone required at the outset, namely, 87,000, would give twenty cents, as the cost per foot for the contingent expenses in making the necessary preparation for commencing the work, &c.

" The cost of labor and wear of apparatus per foot, for the work already performed, have been found by experiment to be seventy-three cents, namely, cost of quarrying per foot measured after the blocks are brought to form, ten cents ; cost of transporting from the quarry to the site of the monument, nine and a half cents per foot ; the cost of dressing one foot and one-fiftieth of a foot, (being the quantity on each foot cubic measure,) was about thirty-seven cents ; and the cost of fitting, hoisting, mason work, mortar, iron cramps, scaffolding, &c., per foot, has been sixteen and a half cents. This has been ascertained by dividing the whole sum paid out by the whole number of cubic feet laid up, according to Loring's survey. And all the details of the expense of a foot will be as follows, viz :

Cost of quarrying, per foot, . . .	10
Cost of dressing one and one-fiftieth at 36, .	37
Cost of transportation, . . .	09.5
Cost of fitting, hoisting, masonry, &c.	16.5
Total for labor and wear, . . .	73
Contingent expense per foot paid, . .	20
Total expense laid in the work, . .	93 cents.

" It must be obvious that had the work been completed without interruption, there would have been but little further occasion for the kind of expense which has been carried to the contingent account, as all the necessary preparation had been made. The quarry was considered in perfect order for finishing the work without any further expense in clearing. The roads were all made and in good repair, and most of the apparatus was in perfect order, and consequently all the expense that could have attended the completion of the work, was the cost of the labor and the wear on the apparatus, which has been proved by actual experiment to have amounted to only seventy-three cents per cubic foot, laid in the work. And the thirty-two thousand feet required to carry the work to the height proposed at seventy-three cents per foot, would amount to only twenty-three thousand three hundred and sixty dollars, ($23,360.)

" But in consequence of the suspension of the work for several ‚years, and the decay of various parts of the apparatus, and other circumstances connected, there are parts of the work which I think will cost more than similar parts that have been already done. The quantity of dressing in proportion to the cubic foot, is found to increase as we rise in height. The average of the part which remains to be done is about one and a quarter feet of dressing to each cubic foot of stone ; whereas in that which has been already finished there is only one and one-fiftieth to each cubic foot. But having in view all the important bearings, I shall estimate the cost of the work to be done at the following rates, provided it be under the direction of competent managers : [This estimate differs from the preceding in putting the transportation at 12 cents per foot, making the cost for labor and wear of machinery 76 cents ; and reducing the contingent expenses to 6 cents, making the total cost per foot laid in the work, 82 cents.] 32,000 feet, the quantity required to carry the work one hundred and sixty feet high, at 82 cents, $26,240 ; deduct for the value of the apparatus to be sold at the end, estimated by the sub-committee, $2,500 ; balance required to be raised, $23,740. Balance required to be raised as estimated by sub-committee, ' in order to be safe,' $42,922 40.

" The committee appear to have made quite a mistake in saying that ' Mr. Willard estimates [the future work] at eighty-nine and a half cents.' If the committee will turn to the pamphlet published some years ago, they will see that eighty-nine and a half cents is estimated as the mean average cost of the whole work, and consequently it should have been inferred that part of the work had cost more than that sum and that a part would cost less. This sum of eighty-nine and a half cents covers the expense not only of the labor and wear on the apparatus, but also a contingent expense which has already been paid on the work to be done as well as on that finished. If the committee will examine my last estimate, they will see that the whole work was estimated at eighty-five thousand seven hundred and five dollars thirty-four cents. This sum divided by eighty-seven thousand and thirty-five, the whole number of feet, gives ninety-seven cents and seven mills, as the estimated cost laid in the work. This estimate they will observe, is accompanied by a proviso, namely, that ' the above sum is undoubtedly greater than would have been required to have completed the work with the advantages possessed at the time the work was suspended, and will probably effect it now, provided men are employed who possess equal tact and zeal with those who commenced the work, and who will render their service for the same compensation.'

" The ninety-seven cents seven mills includes the contingent expense of twenty cents per foot, which is already paid and should be deducted, which will leave seventy-seven cents seven mills for the cost of labor and wear of apparatus per foot, in the future work according to that estimate ; but since that estimate was made I have examined the state of things and think it expedient to estimate the cost per foot as high as eighty-two cents per foot for reasons before stated.

" I have not been able to satisfy myself what the true motives of the committee were in estimating the cost of the work so high. It has already been shown that the expense of the work to be done, at the cost of that which is already executed, would amount to less than $24,000. The committee estimate the sum required to do the same work at $42,922, without giving any reasons, except that they consider it a more safe estimate.—

Now if these gentlemen-mechanics consider it dangerous to attempt to execute a piece of work as low as it has already been done, by ' lawyers and doctors,' they had better let the old committee finish the work, as it would be an immense saving to the public of whom they beg the money.

" If the committee want the money for any other purpose than the one assigned, it discovers a duplicity which, I apprehend, will not be wholly agreeable to the public. For my own part I dislike the appearance of trick and deception anywhere, and in the present case in particular, I think a strait forward and manly course would be the best policy. To represent that more money is wanted than is actually required to finish the work, I think is bad policy, as it has a tendency to discourage the people from contributing, — and to leave them in ignorance of the merits of the transaction is still worse. I apprehend that not one in ten thousand of the subscribers to the funds is acquainted with the merits of the case. It is generally thought that much has been spent and little done. The reverse is actually the truth, and ought to have been explained to the people before they were solicited a second time for money. Had this been done, I have not a shadow of doubt they would have contributed freely and to any amount which might have been wanted to complete the work.

The people should have been shown what is actually true, that little had been expended and much performed, and that little more was required; that the proposed monument was comparatively a small work; that the association possessed at the outset every natural advantage for conducting the work with economy which the world ever afforded and that these advantages had been improved; that the executive parts had been in the hands of competent managers, who were zealous, a fact which is further shown by their performing the service gratuitously, and by the value of the work delivered for the sum expended.

" I have always disliked the plan of sending to foreign places to beg subscriptions. Everybody knows that we are abundantly able to complete the work without their aid were we so disposed. To send to France, to England, and to the Southern cities, when so little is wanted, seems to be making a great parade about a comparatively small matter, and appears to me to be boring our friends in those places unnecessarily.; "exposing our own meanness and disgracing the work on which we are engaged."*

Anxious as Mr. Willard was to have the monument completed, he was averse to anything which might be distorted or exaggerated into the appearance of deception, and was equally unwilling to have the reputation of the people compromised by asking for assistance in a work that ought to have been promptly and ungrudgingly done,—as he had done his share,—by a truly grateful people. Some of the free remarks in the preceding letter may appear to need the extenuation of Mr. Willard's peculiar views and feelings on the subject to justify the utterance of them. They are so indicative of his character for independence, self-reliance. and confidence in the justice of the people, that we have not thought it expedient to omit or modify them.

---

* This letter was addressed to Mr. William Sullivan, who was a member of the Executive Committee, first appointed on the movement of the Mechanic Association, in July, 1833. The Executive Committee was the lineal descendant of the Building Committee, as that was of the Standing Committee of 1824.

24

CHAPTER XXV.

EFFORT OF THE MECHANIC ASSOCIATION — SALE OF THE LAND:

1834 TO 1839.

THE vote of the Directors of the 5th of May, 1834, already mentioned, authorized the Mechanic Association "to proceed, under the supervision of the Executive Committee of this corporation, to apply any money which they have collected, or may collect, to the completion of the monument, by raising the same to the elevation of 159 feet 6 inches; and that they commence the work on the seventeenth of June next, and proceed therewith as speedily as may be done." In accordance with this specific authority, the work both at the quarry and on the hill, was commenced without any public formality, under the direction of Mr. Willard, as Superintendent.*

---

* The anniversary was observed as customary in Charlestown ; but on the previous year,— notwithstanding the unfinished state of the structure,— on the 24th of June, 1833, a Military Review took place on the hill, intended in honor of the visit of Gen. Jackson, President of the United States, who was expected on the 17th. The Review took place in presence of Governor Lincoln, Secretary Woodbury and other official personages. The distinguished gentlemen present ascended to the top of the monument, which was decorated with the flags of different nations, and enjoyed a fine view of town and city and the surrounding country. The President did not arrive in season for the seventeenth and was not able to be present on the twenty-fourth on account of indisposition. On Wednesday, 26th, the expected visit of the President, accompanied by Secretary Cass and other distinguished gentlemen, was made, and they were

At the annual meeting of the Monument Association, 17th of June, after the presentation of the usual reports, the subject of the sale of the land was introduced, and as all measures for its preservation for the purposes of the corporation had failed, the Directors were again authorized "to convey in fee simple so much of the land under and near the monument, on Bunker Hill, in Charlestown, as a majority of them shall deem expedient." The land had already been partially plotted out by Mr. Willard, with the streets as then proposed.

Mr. William Prescott was re-elected President; J. T. Buckingham, President of the Mechanic Association, first Vice President; and at the first meeting of the Board, thereafter, the following gentlemen were named as the Executive Committee : J. T. Buckingham, William Sullivan, Geo. Darracott, Nathaniel Hammond, John Skinner, Ebenezer Breed, William W. Stone, J. P. Thorndike, and Joseph Jenkins. Votes were passed empowering this Committee to sell and convey the land with or without conditions of reconveyance, and to mortgage "all the machinery, tools, implements and personal property belonging to this corporation," in security for the payment of a note or notes to be signed by the Treasurer, for $5,133 68, being the amount of interest due on the debt of the corporation, — provided that

---

received in an enthusiastic manner by the people and the military of the town. A brief and beautiful address of welcome was made to him by Mr. Edward Everett, then a resident of Charlestown, who referred to the monument in the following language : " To designate in all coming time, the place of the first of these eventful contests, the gratitude of this generation is raising a majestic monument on the sacred spot. We invite you, sir, to ascend it, and behold from its elevation, a lovely scene of town and country, — a specimen not unfavorable of this portion of the great Republic whose interests have been confided to your care, as Chief Magistrate of the United States." The accounts in the papers of the day say " The President expressed a desire to ascend the monument and could not but be dissuaded from the gratification of his wish."

In November, the same year, Henry Clay, the distinguished Statesman of Kentucky, visited the monument, which had already become an object of public interest, and it fell happily to the fortune of Mr. Everett to welcome him also to the " sacred spot."

the Mechanic Association shall have the free use of said property so long as they continue in the building of the monument.
This was a distasteful proceeding to Mr. Willard; but it should
be stated that the debt was paid without any resort to the
power contained in the mortgage.

On the 11th of June, the Mechanic Association appointed as
a Building Committee, the following gentlemen, viz.: Charles
Wells, John P. Thorndike, George Darracott, Charles Leighton and ———— ————. This blank is left by Mr. Buckingham. *
On the 4th of November, 1840, when the contract for finishing
the monument was made, the above-named gentlemen were appointed the Building Committee on the part of the Monument
Association, and they were continued in office until the whole
work was completed in 1845.

"The Building Committee, immediately after their appointment, engaged Solomon Willard, whose devotedness to the monument for several years, had been well known, to superintend
the work. Under his direction workmen were engaged in quarrying and dressing stone. The amount drawn from the treasury
for quarrying, hammering and transporting stone from Quincy
to the monument, for new implements and repair of old ones,
for lumber, and for the superintendent's salary, from June 17,
when the work was begun, to December 31, was $4,379."†

The whole amount collected at the end of this year, by the
Mechanic Association, was $13,978 04. The amount of fifty
thousand dollars not having been subscribed, a large portion
of the subscriptions failed by reason of non-performance of that
condition. As some additions were afterwards made to the
fund, the whole amount contributed was $19,073 03 ; to
which the "Ladies' Fund" was added, making the aggregate,
$22,010 93. According to Mr. Willard's statement the sum of

---

* Annals of the Massachusetts Charitable Mechanic Association.   † Ibid.

$20,421 77, was expended upon the work, up to January, 1836 — of the balance the sum of $852 66 was applied to contingent expenses, and $786 50 invested in stocks. The result, like the preceding effort of the ladies, was declared to be " not equal to justifiable expectation." , ᵛ

In 1835, Mr. Prescott was re-elected President; Stephen Fairbanks, President of the Mechanic Association, first Vice President ; and the Executive Committee of the last year, with only one change, was re-appointed. In 1836 and the following years to 1839, J. T. Buckingham was elected President, and various proceedings were had relative to the land and the debt, and various suggestions made for raising the money to complete the monument, but nothing was accomplished, in respect to either matter, until September of the last named year, when the land was finally sold.

In September, 1838, on motion of Mr. Nathan Hale, a committee was appointed " to visit Bunker Hill and after an examination of the ground, to report to the Directors whether in their opinion it is expedient to attempt to raise the money for the re-purchase of the whole of the land formerly belonging to the association, or any part thereof, and in case they should recommend a re-purchase of the whole, or any part of said land, to propose what measures shall be adopted by the Directors for raising the money for the purpose and for completing the building of the monument."

Quite promptly, on the 24th of the same month, Mr. Hale made his report to the Directors. After rehearsing the statement of the original purchase of the land, its hypothecation and sale, the reservation of the square and streets, the committee " recommend that the proprietors of the land be notified that no further effort will be made to re-purchase it. .   .   . They further recommend that an effort be made without delay to raise by subscription a sufficient sum to complete the monument. — .   .   . The charge of the work still remains entrusted to the Mechanic Association, who are ready again to lend their efficient aid to its advancement; the attention of the public has been frequently called to the importance of putting a finishing hand to the undertaking; a comparatively small portion of the work remains to be completed; the massive foundations of the stately obelisk are laid and it is already raised to the height of eighty-two feet from the surface of the ground — its size and consequently its cost diminishes as its height advances. It is computed by the architect that, exclusive of the cost of the land and of other preparatory expenses, the part of the work already completed, including stone quarried and not laid, is equal to two-thirds of the building the whole monument to the height originally proposed of two hundred and twenty feet. One third therefore of the monument remains to be completed, supposing it to be carried to the greatest proposed height."

This report having been accepted by the Directors, at their meeting on the twenty-fourth of September, settled the question of the disposition of the land. It also fixed definitely the height to which the monument had been carried by the architect, with the aid of the Mechanic Association. The Directors immediately determined to make a new effort to complete the monument, by soliciting subscriptions from individuals and societies for the purpose — but nothing was accomplished. The plan of the square and streets, suggested by Mr. Willard, was adopted:— One hundred and fifteen building lots were laid out around the square, on a reduced grade, comprising 317,054 feet, and the following year, September 25, 1839, were sold by public auction, producing in the aggregate the sum of $48,435 06. The Trustees,* under whose direction the land was sold, subsequently contributed five hundred dollars each towards the completion of the monument.

---

* Thomas B. Wales, William W. Stone, and N. I. Bowditch.

CHAPTER XXVI.

NEW EFFORTS FOR COMPLETING THE MONUMENT — THE

LADIES' FAIR — 1840 TO 1843.

FIVE years had elapsed since the solicitations of the Mechanic Association in behalf of the monument, and it began to be *felt* that the unfinished condition of the work might compromise the character of the people who had commenced it, fifteen years before, with such an outburst of popular enthusiasm. Their sincerity, their sense of justice and their appreciation of the services of the fathers of the revolution, might be called in question ; and the gratitude which had been professed, the expression of which it was proposed to make permanent, was almost sure to be misunderstood. The whole community was in a false position, and it became absolutely necessary that the work should be finished. The delays which had occurred, — erroneously explained or injuriously accounted for, — had given rise to a prejudice against the work or the managers, and had cooled the interest and checked the zeal of some of its friends. Appeals that were made in its behalf, however eloquent or forcible, seemed to fall unheeded to the ground.

Mr. Willard, — who was personally as well as publicly interested in the completion of the monument, — some years before made an attempt to disabuse the general mind in regard to the cost of the work, in the hope of promoting subscriptions to it, — but the public at this time were not to be moved by reason or rhetoric, and his effort was unavailing. During the delay, Mr. Willard had engaged in other work, and one of the objects long had in view by him, — the introduction of granite as a building material, — was partially accomplished ; but he was ready to make any sacrifice, or give up any other thing, in order to the completion of that which had occupied so much of his attention and for which he had labored so assiduously, always in the hope of seeing it finished. He promptly answered all inquiries made of him and furnished estimates of cost on various plans, favoring with his own approval only those which looked to a completion of the obelisk according to his original design. As an artist, and especially as architect, he could favor no other plan, and would not regard the work as finished until that was accomplished.

Mr. Amos Lawrence, who was always so desirous to retain the whole field, and at one time provided for it in his Will, was very anxious that an effort should be made to complete the monument, and offered ten thousand dollars to the association towards that purpose. A similar sum was also offered by Mr. Judah Touro, of New Orleans.

At the annual meeting, seventeenth of June, 1840, a vote was passed authorizing the President, J. T. Buckingham, and the Secretary, G. Washington Warren, "with such other members of the corporation as may be willing to coöperate with them in the effort, . . . to solicit and receive subscriptions and obtain sums by Fairs or other projects, in aid of the completion of the great object of the corporation, and that these gentlemen have power to adopt such measures as they may deem expedient in making this final appeal to the public."

In five weeks from this time, on the twenty-fifth of July, the President "reported to the Board that under the authority of the vote passed at the last meeting of the Board, a large committee had associated themselves with him and the Secretary, and that extensive arrangements were made to hold a 'FAIR' during the second week in September next, and to adopt other necessary measures for the completion of the monument."

At this meeting also, a vote was passed ignoring the proposition brought forward by the Mechanic Association, of reducing the height of the monument to 159 feet 6 inches, as follows : — "That Messrs. Charles Wells, George Darracott and John P. Thorndike, be a committee authorized to receive proposals for finishing the Monument on Bunker Hill, agreeably to the plan adopted by the corporation." Subsequently the vote of the 5th of May, 1834, on this subject, was formally reconsidered, in order that the original vote might be restored, and Mr. Charles Leighton was added to the above committee.

On the seventh of September, Mr. Wells reported several propositions for the completion of the monument, but upon opening them it appeared that they " were given on different bases and data," and it was thereupon voted, " that the several proposals for finishing the monument be again referred to the same committee, who are hereby requested to obtain of Mr. Solomon Willard a plan for finishing the top of the monument, and to receive estimates for finishing the top according to the plan which may be adopted by them." On the ninth of October, Mr. Wells submitted the plan of the top of the monument, as drawn by Mr. Willard and approved by the committee. The proposals were then opened and read, and it was found that the offer made by Mr. James S. Savage, was by far the lowest. He proposed to complete the monument according to the original design, to cover it according to the plan presented, to protect it with suitable lightning conductors, and to pay Mr. Willard for superintending the work, for the sum of forty-three thousand eight hundred dollars. Mr. Savage, who was first employed by Mr. Willard, under a special contract, had been engaged on the work all the time during its progress, and was altogether the most suitable person, next to Mr. Willard, to continue and complete it. The same committee were thereupon authorized "to contract with Mr. Savage on the basis of his offer, .

25

whenever they shall have ascertained that the corporation have
the means to enable them to fulfil the contract." A vote was
also passed in reference to an iron fence around the monument
and the grading of the square, under the direction of the architect. On the fourth of November, the contract with Mr. Savage was completed, although the Directors were not officially
informed of the result of the Fair which had been held.

It is known that Mr. Willard was not in favor of this method
of completing the work on the monument, but preferred that
which had been pursued under his superintendence, and which
as the result showed, would have cost much less money. In this,
however, as in matters similarly situated, Mr. Willard contented himself with the expression of his opinion when it was requested. After the contract was made with Mr. Savage he had
nothing further to say, whatever his feelings may have been :
his great desire was to have the monument completed, and no
objections to any particular plan which he might have, would
induce him to throw any obstacles in the way of that paramount
object. Mr. Willard was urged by some of his most influential
friends to contract for the work himself, as a profitable enterprise, (and so it proved to be,) but with his views and feelings
as to the character of the work, no such considerations could
ever have induced him to undertake it, — and we believe he did
not appropriate to his own use any portion of the pay received
from Mr. Savage, beyond his personal expenses. The truth
unquestionably is that Mr. Willard should have been allowed to
complete his work in his own way, when that way had proved
undeniably advantageous. He felt this but would not ask it —
he was mistaken in supposing that Right would be done without any effort on his part.

On the nineteenth of November, at a meeting of the Board
of Directors, the report of Catharine G. Prescott, Sarah J.
Hale, Lucinda Chapman, Susan P. Warren, Sarah Darracott,
and Abby L. Wales, Executive Committee of the Ladies' Fair,
and the report of Mary Otis, Treasurer, were received and read.

The net proceeds of the Fair amounted to $30,035 53. In concluding their report the ladies say, " Having done what we could, it only remains for us to hope that our days may yet see the completion of the monument which shall stand to tell of our fathers to coming generations." ͋ Suitable resolutions of acknowledgment and thanks to the ladies were passed by the Directors, one of which we copy, as a comprehensive and well-deserved compliment to the sex :

" Resolved, That while as Directors of a corporate body we thus in a formal manner express our gratitude, we cannot with-hold the declaration that in our opinion all those who are living in the enjoyment of the blessings of a free government, and of its civil, literary and religious institutions ; all who cherish the sentiments of the heroes and patriots of the revolution ; all who reverence the memories of those that suffered in defence of the principles of liberty ; all, in fine, who admire patriotism in its most attractive form, and love virtue in its holiest and most beautiful manifestation, — will admire, will applaud, and will reverence the deed herein recorded, the motive by which it was dictated and the agents by whom it was accomplished."

At the meeting of the Directors, on the fourteenth of Janu-ary, 1841, suitable resolutions of thanks and respect were passed to Messrs. Amos Lawrence and Judah Touro, for their liberal donations for the completion of the monument.   During the progress of the work, in July, 1842, a meeting of the Directors was called "at the suggestion of several members, in conse-quence of a desire expressed by many individuals that an alter-ation should be made in the mode of finishing the top of the monument, so that visitors might ascend to the top of the roof, or covering, by means of a balustrade.   After a full discussion it was voted unanimously, as the sense of this Board, that the monument be finished in accordance with the plan of Mr. Willard, the architect."   One of the most satisfactory features in the history of this great work is the consistent adherence of the Building Committee and Directors to the design made by Mr. Willard and deliberately adopted.

On the twenty-third day of the same month, the cap-stone was placed upon the monument. The occasion is mentioned in the records briefly as follows : " On Saturday, July 23d, 1842, at six o'clock in the morning, pursuant to public notice, the Directors and several hundred citizens assembled on Bunker Hill to witness the laying on of the top stone upon the monument. As the clock struck six, a signal-gun was fired by the members of the Charlestown Artillery, and the cap-stone, which had been previously adjusted to the hoisting apparatus connected with the steam-engine, began to ascend. It was surmounted by the American flag. In sixteen minutes the cap-stone reached the place of its destination on the top of the monument. At half past six it was embedded in cement and a national salute, fired by the Charlestown Artillery, announced the complete erection of the monument." The weight of this single stone was stated to be about two and a half tons.

CHAPTER XXVII.

CELEBRATION OF THE COMPLETION OF THE MONUMENT — 1843.

THE celebration of the completion of the monument was deferred to the anniversary of the battle in 1843, when Mr. Webster delivered his second great oration on the same inspiring spot, and to some extent before the same audience. It was eighteen years from the commencement of the work, and sixty-eight years from the day of the battle and the burning of the town. A new town had arisen from the ashes of the old, and the majestic monument now towered over a compact, thriving and intelligent population. Many of the heroes of that dark day, who had lived to see the commencement of the monument, had since then paid the debt of nature and fallen into peaceful and honored graves. There was no Lafayette now to call forth, by his living presence, the gratitude and patriotism of the people. He had died in May, 1834; but a few of his compatriots in arms still lived as the connecting link between the past and present times, and were again at the national altar of liberty to dignify and honor the occasion. The patriotic feelings of the people were awakened anew, and as a mere display, the occasion excelled the great demonstration of 1825. Owing to the facilities afforded for travel by the recent introduction of railroads, many thousands of people were present, some of whom came long distances. The newspapers of New York urged the patriotic sons of New England, in that city, to attend the celebration by informing them that they could leave the city on the evening of the sixteenth, attend the celebration on the seventeenth, and be in that city again the next morning, — thus losing only one day from business.   The same facilities were afforded in other directions.

Among the many distinguished persons present by invitation of the government of the Monument Association, were the President of the United States, John Tyler, and his Secretaries and Post Master General.*   The Military Escort consisted of four brigades of the volunteer militia, (including four companies of the New York National Guards,) under Major General Appleton Howe, and the Civic Procession was formed in four grand divisions.   There were in carriages one hundred and ten of the survivors of the revolutionary war, one of whom was at Lexington and Concord, on the nineteenth of April, 1775, and at Bunker Hill, on the seventeenth of June.†   The Mechanic Association, King Solomon's Lodge of Charlestown and the Masonic fraternity generally, and numerous other bodies and associations, joined in the procession.

The various bodies assembled at an early hour in the forenoon on and near the Common, and taking up the honored guests of the association at the State House, moved from that point at eleven o'clock to the hill.   Such crowds of people as lined the streets and filled the houses, on the route of the procession, have rarely been seen in Boston.   The arrangements were admirable,

---

* Hon. Hugh S. Legare, of South Carolina, Attorney General and Secretary of State, *ad interim*, was unable to attend the celebration, although in Boston for that purpose, by reason of sickness of which he died on the morning of the 20th.   He was buried at Mount Auburn.

† Phineas Johnson, aged 97 years, the oldest man present.   Captain Josiah Cleaveland, who came from Owego, N. Y., to attend the celebration, died at Charlestown, on the 30th of June, aged 83 years.   He was a native of Canterbury, Conn., and a volunteer under Colonel Putnam.   He continued in service through the war and was in several great battles and at the capture of Cornwallis.   He was buried at Mount Auburn, with military honors, and a monument was erected over his grave.

and so well conducted that, on reaching the hill, no difficulty
was experienced in establishing the whole body of the procession
on the easterly slope around the orator's stand ; and the great
audience, disposed in the form of an amphitheatre, was hemmed-
in on all sides by the vast multitude, who had come up, as it
were, to this Mecca of American Liberty, in patriotic worship.
The President of the United States and his Secretaries, the venerable survivors of the Revolution, the many distinguished persons present, and the government of the association, were seated
around the orator on the platform, and inspired while they
listened to the thrilling eloquence which fell in such Doric
beauty from the speaker's lips.

Mr. Webster commenced his oration in the most stately manner, cool and unimpassioned as a statue: "A duty has been
performed. A work of gratitude and patriotism is completed."
. . . Stating the peculiar circumstance that the projectors
of the work had relied upon voluntary contributions for its construction and had not been disappointed, he next referred to
the labors of the directors and committees of the association, and
spoke of the architect as follows : "The architect, equally entitled to our thanks and commendation, will find other reward
also, for his labor and skill, in the beauty and elegance of the
obelisk itself, and the distinction, which, as a work of art, it
confers on him." After mentioning the effort and services of the
Mechanic Association towards the completion of the work, he
spoke of the crowning labors of the ladies as follows : —

"The last effort and the last contribution were from a different source. Garlands of grace and elegance were destined to
crown a work which had its commencement in manly patriotism.
The winning power of the sex addressed itself to the public, and
all that was needed to carry the monument to its proposed
height, and give to it its finish, was promptly supplied. The
mothers and the daughters of the land contributed thus, most
successfully to whatever of beauty is in the obelisk itself, or

whatever of utility and public benefit and gratification in its completion."

We quote some further portions of this splendid oration, although it is accessible to the reader in other forms. These relate so distinctly to the monument itself and its high purposes, that they will not be deemed out of place in this connection, and the oftener they are presented to the people, read and pondered by them, the better will it be for the country and "all succeeding generations" : —

"The Bunker Hill Monument is finished. Here it stands. Fortunate in the natural eminence on which it is placed — higher, infinitely higher in its objects and purpose, it rises over the land, and over the sea, and visible, at their homes, to three hundred thousand citizens of Massachusetts — it stands a memorial of the last, and a monitor to the present and all succeeding generations. I have spoken of the loftiness of it purpose : If it had been without any other design than the creation of a work of art, the granite of which it is composed, would have slept in its native bed. It has a purpose; and that purpose gives it character. That purpose enrobes it with dignity and moral grandeur. That well-known purpose it is, which causes us to look up to it with a feeling of awe. It is itself the orator of this occasion ; it is not from my lips, it is not from any human lips, that that strain of eloquence is this day to flow, most competent to move and excite the vast multitudes around. The potent speaker stands motionless before them. It is a plain shaft. It bears no inscriptions, fronting to the rising sun, from which the future antiquarian shall wipe the dust. Nor does the rising sun cause tones of music to issue from its summit. But at the rising of the sun, and at the setting of the sun, in the blaze of noonday, and beneath the milder effulgence of lunar light, it looks, it speaks, it acts, to the full comprehension of every American mind, and the awakening of glowing enthusiasm in every American heart. Its silent, but awful utterance; its deep pathos, as it brings to our contemplation the seventeenth of June, 1775, and the consequences which have resulted to us, to our country, and to the world, from the events of that day, and which we know must continue to rain influence on the destinies of mankind, to the end of time; the elevation with which it raises us high above the ordinary feelings of life, surpasses all that the study of the closet, or even the inspiration of genius can produce. To-day it speaks to us. Its future auditories will be through successive generations of men, as they rise up before it, and gather round it. Its speech will be of patriotism and courage; of civil and religious liberty; of free govern-ment; of the moral improvement and elevation of mankind; and of the immortal memory of those who, with heroic devotion, have sacrificed their lives for their country."

There seems to be something more than mere foresight in the following burst of eloquence upon the theme of the "Union," in which is included that voluminous sentence, so often quoted, which we have put in italics : —

" Woe betide the man who brings to this day's worship feel-ing less than wholly American ! Woe betide the man who can stand here with the fires of local resentments burning, or the purpose of fomenting local jealousies, and the strifes of local interests festering and rankling in his heart. Union, founded in justice, in patriotism, and the most plain and obvious common interest; Union, founded on the same love of liberty, cemented by blood shed in the same cause; Union has been the source of all our glory and greatness thus far, and is the ground of all our highest hopes. *This Column stands on Union.* I know not that it might not keep its position, if the American Union, in the mad conflict of human passions, and in the strife of par-ties and factions, should be broken up and destroyed. I know not that it would totter and fall to the earth, and mingle its

26

fragments with the fragments of Liberty and the Constitution, when State should be separated from State, and faction and dismemberment obliterate forever all the hopes of the founders of our Republic, and the great inheritance of their children. — It might stand. But who, from beneath the weight of mortification and shame, that would oppress him, could look up to behold it ? For my part, should I live to such a time, I shall avert my eyes from it forever."

Happily the noble-hearted orator did not live to witness that attempted dismemberment which he so feelingly deprecated !

This profound and patriotic oration will live as long as the language in which it is written, and will form a prominent chapter in the history of the growth of races and nations. — It seems tame to turn from its study and the contemplation of thoughts which its perusal inspires to other incidents of the day, however pleasant these may be. The celebration was concluded by a grand festival in Faneuil Hall, at which were present all the distinguished guests of the association, except its modest and retiring architect, whose absence was regretted by all who knew him. His unwillingness to be noticed or made prominent in such an assemblage, we have no doubt, kept him from participating in the general joy of the occasion. He never submitted to the trial of hearing himself or his works commended before the public ; and probably did not hear the complimentary words of the orator upon his finished work.

The President and the members of his Cabinet were present at the festival, and responded to the calls of the chairman. The occasion, of course, was not political, and patriotic toasts only were proposed. The President gave " The Union : Union of purpose ; Union of feeling ; the Union established by our fathers." The States of Virginia and Massachusetts were coupled in a toast by the Secretary of the Navy, and the States of South Carolina and Massachusetts in another by a gentleman of Boston. The Monument, the Orator, and the Ladies, were the subjects of other sentiments. That referring to the Monument was as follows: "The Bunker Hill Monument — It bears no inscription, and it needs none, since the lessons of patriotism it is designed to commemorate, can only be inscribed upon the hearts of those who behold it."

Excepting the reference made to the architect by Mr. Webster, we are not aware that any allusion was made to him or his valuable and efficient services, during the day; but this was not a thing to disturb him. He felt sure that justice would be done to him in the future, and within three years from this time, one who knew him better than any of his associates and more of his devotion and labor in behalf of the monument, penned a brief record of his judgment in the following words: —

"But *the work is done,* and posterity *ought to know* that they are *more* indebted *to Sol₀. Willard than to any other person,* for the monument.* It was by his labors and taste that the plan was adopted and the stone quarry secured; the work done in a style that will be approved by generations to come. Let us render, then, to Mr. Willard, the honor that belongs to him. AMOS LAWRENCE."

"Boston, March 18, 1846."

If it was a happy day to anybody, that was a happy day to Mr. Willard which saw the monument completed.

---

* The italics are printed as marked by Mr. Lawrence in the manuscript.

CHAPTER XXVIII.

COST OF THE BUNKER HILL MONUMENT.

THE cost of the Bunker Hill Monument has always been a question of peculiar interest, not merely as a matter of curiosity, but as having some relation to the proper and judicious expenditure of the funds voluntarily contributed by the community at large and the specific donations of individuals. It was understood at the time of the commencement of the work, that its size and character were to be in some degree dependent upon the amount of the means at the disposition of the directors, and this matter was ostensibly considered in deciding upon the design. In the advertisement offering a premium of one hundred dollars for the design "which shall appear to merit the preference," no limitation in regard to cost is contained; but Mr. Willard says, "it will be perceived, therefore, that the size of the obelisk had necessarily to conform to the means available; and it was so decided by the committee on designs." Most of the sketches and plans made by Mr. Willard, at the request of the committee, were made under a limitation unknown to other artists and apparently disregarded in the end. At the time the design was decided upon, Mr. Willard was requested to prepare three separate sketches, in order "to test the question of cost," and Colonel Baldwin, in his final report, says the committee took "into consideration the funds already provided, or *probably attainable.*" Nevertheless, with an estimate of cost for the design proposed, amounting to one hundred thousand dollars, and funds on hand amounting to only about one-third of this sum, the directors determined to proceed with the work. This estimate, made by Colonel Baldwin, has been published by Mr. Willard and shown by him to-be an estimate for small blocks and the cheapest kind of work ; the inner walls to be left in a rough state, and a large part of the work to be done at the price, whatever the quality, of common cellar stone.   We quote a portion of Mr. Willard's remarks upon this estimate, in order that the subject may be properly understood and his services in the construction of the work properly appreciated :

" According to the estimate, there were to have been one hundred and forty-seven courses in the obelisk,* of eighteen inches rise and eighteen inches thick ; and, as no drawing accompanied the estimate, it is to be presumed that they were to have been from six to eight feet long, and consequently would have been about equal to posts and caps of the same dimensions.   This lot of stone is estimated at twenty cents per cubic foot, delivered at the site of the monument.   It will be seen at once, by those acquainted with the business, that twenty cents per cubic foot, for stone of that quality, is a low estimate ; that it would barely pay the prime cost, under the best management.   The transportation alone has generally cost about twelve cents per foot, leaving only eight cents per foot, for the quarrying, loading, bankage and tools.   The average price paid at the State Prison for such stone, for the last seventeen years, where competition has been allowed, and consequently, the stone has been obtained at the lowest market price, is about thirty-four cents per foot.

" The next item in the estimate, is for twenty-three hundred and forty-nine and two-thirds perches of stone for the interior.

----

* There are seventy-eight courses in the shaft of the monument, and six in the " pointed pyramid."

These are estimated at three dollars per perch, or at twelve cents per cubic foot; which was the price of common cellar stone at the time. It must be obvious, therefore, that the price was low, or that a very ordinary material was estimated for.

" The hammering, on the outside, appears to be estimated at about a fair rate. It should be noticed, however, that the inner walls were to have been left in a rough state; and in the design which has been executed, the fine dressing on the inner walls is about equal to the fine dressing on the outside; and consequently, there is nearly double the number of feet of fine dressing on the design which has been executed, that there was to have been on the one estimated for.

" The hammering of the beds and builds, amounting to one hundred and forty-seven thousand seven hundred and thirty-five feet, is estimated at six cents per foot. This again, it will be seen, is a very low estimate for decent work, including tools; and it will be obvious to every one acquainted with the business, that anything that could be done for six cents per foot, must necessarily be ordinary work; the lowest work of the kind in the Custom House bill of prices being twenty-five cents. The laying of three thousand five hundred and thirty-eight perches of stone, at five dollars per perch, including scaffolding and rigging, amounting for the whole mason work above ground, to seventeen thousand six hundred and ninety dollars, seems to be a moderate estimate; as it is understood that a sum of nearly the amount was carried in for the last contract alone, which was only about one-third part of the work.

" Of the remaining items no particular notice seems to be necessary. It must be obvious, however, that the foregoing estimate was intended for a cheap kind of work, in order to adapt it as far as possible, to the low state of the finances; and, notwithstanding the low rate, it amounts to the sum of one hundred thousand dollars."

Without any disparagement of the estimate made by Colonel

Baldwin for the work proposed, we have no hesitation in saying that no such work as that indicated by the prices fixed for it, would ever have been done under Mr. Willard's superintendence, or if done, would have been satisfactory to him. Colonel Baldwin's estimate was for the kind of work which the dealers and workers in granite wished Mr. Willard to adopt and which they were prepared to execute, namely, "small blocks," such as they were using for "posts and caps." Such blocks might make a "grand and striking object," when thrown together in "the form of an obelisk," but they would not constitute that character of "natural, inherent, durable greatness," of which Mr. Webster very early spoke and which the Directors' always desired.

Mr. Willard's views as to what the proposed work should be, and his efforts to secure a suitable quarry for the purpose. have already been stated in the preceding pages. The plan which he suggested and which was adopted for carrying on the work, and the details of some of the experiments instituted by him to ascertain the cost of quarrying, dressing and laying the stone, have also been given, — not so much for the purpose of establishing these definitively or applying the results obtained to the whole work, as to show the system employed and methods adopted under Mr. Willard's superintendence. That the system was successful was demonstrated at the time : the work was done in the best manner, by the best workmen, and at much less cost than any similar work.

We cannot but esteem it as fortunate that the monument was not built under Colonel Baldwin's estimate. As it now stands complete in its massive grandeur, it is a very different work, in material and finish, externally and internally, and in all respects of much higher character, than it would have been under that cheap estimate.

The actual cost of the monument, as stated by Mr. Willard, is based upon the results of the "three experiments" conducted by him during the progress of the work. In these are included the actual payments on account of the work, and they are as follows :—

1. Expenses from November 17, 1825, to February 28, 1859, - - - - - $56,525 19
2. Expenses from June 17, 1834, to January, 1836, - - - - - -   20,421 77
3. Expenses paid by the Contractor, - -   27,016 72

Aggregate, $103,963 68

Deduct for apparatus, - - 1,400
"   house burnt, - - 800
"   overcharge in transportation, 800

3,000 00

Total, - - - - - $101,963 68

Some other items of expense for iron work, lightning conductors and bankage, increase the above to the sum of one hundred and one thousand six hundred and eighty-eight dollars, ($101,-688.) In the above, the cost of the third experiment is not the amount paid by the association to the contractor, but the amount paid by the contractor for material, labor and superintendence, irrespective of profits.

Mr. Willard, in the publication by him already referred to, makes several comparisons between the cost of material and work in the monument and in other structures of the same material in Boston. The average size of the blocks in the monument is a little less than five tons, and at the cost paid for similar blocks at the Branch Bank, in State street, " eighty-seven thousand feet at five hundred cents per foot," for the granite alone, Mr. Willard very justly concluded, " would have amounted to an enormous sum." The market price, at this time, however, Mr. Willard admits, was about one dollar per cubic foot for blocks of fifty-four feet; or, taking the Railway price, at one hundred and one cents, and the Custom House price, seventy-nine cents, gives an average of ninety cents per cubic foot. At this price, the cost of the granite blocks would have amounted to over seventy-eight thousand dollars, and the whole cost of the monument over two hundred and fifty thousand dollars; and this sum, we presume, would have been a reasonable estimate for the work at the time, considering the condition of the granite business and state of the market.

There was at one time in the community an impression that in some way, or by somebody, the funds subscribed for the erection of the monument had been wasted or misused; and this matter assumed a somewhat tangible shape in a so-called report, printed in 1832, by the party which the year previous attempted to assume control of the corporation, but we believe no answer or explanation of the charge from that source was deemed expedient. Mr. Willard, however, referred to it, in 1835, in a letter from which we make the following extract :—

" The work commenced by the directors required one hundred and fifty thousand feet of granite to complete it, the market value of which was more than seventy cents, and consequently the stone alone, delivered at the site of the monument, would have cost the sum of $105,000, had we paid the market price of ordinary stone. The fitting, hoisting and setting, including the mortar, iron-work, &c., would probably have come to something more than $15,000, which with the cost of the stone, would have amounted to more than $120,000. The cash in the Treasury at the commencement of the work, with $7,000 obtained from the State, amounting to about $33,000, was all that could have been safely relied on by those who commenced it. It must be obvious, therefore, that a work was begun on a scale and magnitude out of all proportion to the means at the disposal of those who had the charge at the time, and could not have been prosecuted had it been necessary to pay the customary prices for the stone. It must also be obvious that the reports

27

of a waste of the funds, which have been current these ten years past, are wholly unfounded, for nothing can be more self-evident than that the managers could not have wasted what they never had. These reports have undoubtedly arisen either from gross ignorance of the state of the facts, or an intention to deceive; and have probably been circulated by those who had contributed little or nothing to their amount.

"It should be observed, however, that the sum of $4,720 85, spent according to the Treasurer's Report for 1830, in laying the corner-stone, and which appears to have given the only ground of complaint of a waste of funds, had it been appropriated to the work, would have increased the whole sum to only $38,000, which is less than one-third part of what was required to complete it, had we paid the market prices. It must be clear, therefore, that the whole sum available, with or without that spent in laying the corner-stone, was wholly inadequate to the purpose intended, had we pursued the usual course in carrying our work into execution.

"All the important bearings, however, were well understood at the time. It was well known that the granite business was then in the hands of men of mercenary views, without science, and was consequently conducted in an unskilful manner. It was proposed, therefore, to keep the work in our own hands, and after going through the usual course of advertising for proposals without receiving any that were satisfactory, the work was commenced under my superintendence about the fifteenth of November, 1825."

We copy the following statements and remarks, upon the subject of this chapter, from Mr. Willard's printed book, and commend the conclusion arrived at to the consideration of his friends, the members of the Monument Association and the contributors to the work : —

"It has been shown that the actual cost of the obelisk was about one hundred thousand dollars; this being the total cost, notwithstanding all the impediments that have attended the work. Had it been well sustained, and completed in the course of about three years — which would have been a reasonable time — it would have made a great difference in the final cost. It must be obvious, however, that whatever the difference might have been, it cannot be accurately ascertained; but is estimated at twenty thousand dollars, leaving eighty thousand dollars as the probable cost of the obelisk, had the work gone on without interruption or embarrassment.

" The suspensions at different times were disadvantageous to the economy of the work. . . . . But notwithstanding the unfavorable circumstances that have attended the work, it is presumed that, in regard to economy in the execution, it will not suffer in a comparison with any work whatever, that has been executed in modern times. And such a comparison would probably exhibit its merits more clearly than could be done in any other way.

" It is found by comparison, that the Washington Monument, in Baltimore, contains but about half the number of cubic feet of material that are in this obelisk. It consists of a column of about nineteen feet diameter at the base, set on a pedestal, and altogether about one hundred and sixty feet high. It is well executed, but of cheap construction. The foundation is of slaty granite, in small pieces, and the body of the work is of bricks, faced with limestone, and in ashlar courses of about one foot rise. And, notwithstanding, has cost, as stated on good authority, about two hundred and twenty thousand dollars. And, consequently, has cost twenty thousand dollars more than twice as much as the obelisk.

" It will be seen also that the obelisk will compare still more favorably with the work now going on at the Custom House, in Boston. It appears by the debate in Congress, that this Custom House, which it is presumed contains about an equal quantity of granite with the obelisk, has already cost the sum of seven hundred thousand dollars, and requires three hundred

thousand more to complete the work. The whole amounting to
a million of dollars, and consequently equal in cost to ten such
obelisks as that on Bunker Hill. And it is presumed, that
the columns and pilasters alone, which are attached to the body
of the work, have cost as much as two such obelisks.

"It must be obvious, therefore, that if these works have been
executed at fair rates, the obelisk has been built at a very low
rate; and could not have been executed at such a price had not
the work been skilfully planned, and had not the plan been well
sustained by close attention and hard labor.

"It has already been shown, that the work done on the obelisk, had the association paid its full value, would have cost
them the round sum of two hundred thousand dollars; whereas,
the actual sum paid out for the work is but about *half* that
amount; and, consequently, there has been a clear saving of
one hundred thousand dollars, by the course taken in carrying
it on. And as the saving of that amount is equivalent to contributing the same amount in cash, it follows, that those who
have planned and conducted the executive parts of the work,
have in effect, borne half of the expense. by contributing to that
amount in cash or its equivalent."

These statements and remarks, which have been before the
public under Mr. Willard's authority, since 1843, have never
been disputed, questioned or even criticised, and are believed to
be entirely accurate. By the lowest terms of the market value
of material and labor, had the association purchased in the usual
way the one, and paid the customary profit on the other, —
instead of owning the quarry and employing their own workmen, — it is not possible to make the cost of the monument
less than two hundred thousand dollars; and there is, therefore,
today, (to say nothing of Mr. Willard's unpaid work on the
design, his time and expenses in finding a suitable quarry, &c.)
not less than one hundred thousand dollars, chiefly represented
by his thought, skill and labor, in the grand structure that now

crowns the glorious battle-ground of Bunker Hill : and the truthfulness of Mr. Lawrence's record, "that posterity . . are more indebted to Solomon Willard than to any other man for the monument," must be considered as demonstrated.

In stating the actual cost of the monument at about one hundred and one thousand dollars, ($101,688,) or even its contingent cost, had a different course been pursued, at double that sum, it is to be considered, that no allowance is made for compensation of services rendered by the respective committees who had the work in charge, or for superintendence, beyond the necessary expenses, nor any *profit*, as such, other than the ordinary day-wages or piece-pay of the workmen allowed to them. It is not too much to say, that the work actually done in behalf of the monument, — by the long and patriotic services of its devoted Treasurer, by its diligent and talented Secretaries, its influential and eminent Presidents, its able and intelligent Committees and its distinguished Boards of Directors, — and not paid for in any way, was many times larger than the real work of building the monument, which, excepting the profits gained by the last contractor, is all that was ever compensated for at a money valuation.

The whole amount of money which was collected or received and expended by the association and its auxiliaries in the work, — for expenses of organization, meetings, ceremonies and celebrations, printing and publication, interest on loans and debt, and various other charges, — it would be almost impossible now to ascertain ; but probably all these, together with the actual cost of the work itself, will hardly amount to a greater sum than the cost as reported of the Washington Monument, at Baltimore, (nearly a quarter of a million dollars,) and less than one quarter part of the probable cost of the Custom House at Boston.

CHAPTER XXIX.

LOCATION AND DESCRIPTION OF BUNKER HILL MONUMENT.

THE town of Charlestown, and by inheritance the city of Charlestown, is made historical by the Battle of Bunker Hill, in the opening of the American Revolution. Like Boston, it was originally a "trimountaine" peninsula, having most prominent in its outline three distinct elevations: the Town Hill, upon which Governor Winthrop's company built their stockade houses and buried their dead; Breed's Hill, upon which the battle was mainly fought, and Bunker's Hill, the highest of the three and nearest the neck of the peninsula. It seems to be conceded that the order of General Ward, which brought on the battle, was intended to apply to Bunker's Hill, (now generally written Bunker Hill.) and that Breed's Hill, being much nearer to Boston, was taken possession of as the preferable position, or by a mistake, the consequences of which have proved so momentous in the history of the country. The anomaly in history that the Battle of Bunker Hill was fought upon Breed's Hill, is probably not very remarkable at this day, and the attempt made some years ago, on a local map, to change the names of the two hills, was simply ludicrous.

The summit of the hill is about fifty feet above the level of tide-water. The first address of the Monument Association to the public, speaks of it as "the most interesting spot in our country." The "Circular" of 1824, gives a more elaborate description of the spot and its suitableness for the purposes then in contemplation.* The views from the hill are briefly indicated by Mr. Everett, in his Faneuil Hall speech, of May, 1833, in which he called upon his listener "to place himself, in imagination, on the summit of the beautiful hill where the battle was fought; look out upon the prospect-of unsurpassed loveliness that spreads before him, by land and by sea; the united features of town and country; the long rows of buildings and stores in the city, rising one above another upon the sides of her triple hills; the surrounding sweep of country, checked with prosperous villages; on one side the towers of the city churches, on the other the long succession of rural spires; the rivers that flow on either side to the sea; the broad expanse of harbor and bay, spotted with verdant islands, — with a hundred ships dancing in every direction over the waves; the vessels of war, keeping guard with their sleeping thunders, at the foot of the hill; and on its top, within the shade of venerable trees, over the ashes of the great and good, the noble obelisk, rising to the heavens and crowning the magnificent scene."

From its prominence in the landscape and its position at the head of Massachusetts Bay, it was always regarded as an eminently suitable spot for the erection of the proposed monument. That the engagement which here took place, — the first in the war which may be properly called a battle, — and the consequences which flowed from it upon the future relations of the colonies, made it of all others, the place for the erection of such a memorial, was abundantly shown at the time of its commencement. That the time for its erection was fitly chosen, — after the war of independence had been confirmed by a war for national consideration, — recent unhappy events have only too plainly demonstrated.

The majestic structure which now rises from this renowned

---

* Ante, p. 64.

hill, and by its massive proportions gives grace and grandeur to the scene, is variously spoken of as simple, grand or sublime, according to the taste or sentiment of the beholder. But as a work of art, or as a mechanical creation, it is very rarely that its excellencies are appreciated, or the skill and labor which it embodies understood. It is called both by Mr. Webster and Mr. Willard, an " Obelisk," but in the words of the vote adopting the design, it is more accurately spoken of as " *in the form of an Obelisk*," being composed of sections, or courses, built up as masonry, instead of a single block or shaft. The numerous Egyptian obelisks which ornament modern Rome ; those of Heliopolis, Luxor and Carnac, all come within the authorized definition of the term, each being " a lofty *monolithic* quadrangular shaft, tapering gradually from the base to the summit, which terminates in a pointed pyramid." These almost without exception, are covered with inscriptions in hieroglyphic characters, and are variously regarded as religious, historical or merely ornamental structures, and by some have been even supposed to be for scientific purposes. It is highly probable that they were personal monuments, erected by kings or rulers to commemorate their reigns, and thus to some extent historical ; and as they were all erected many centuries B. C., may have been dedicated to some of the heathen gods and regarded as sacred. Some of those now standing in Rome have been surmounted with globes, crosses or statuary.

The object and purposes of the Bunker Hill Monument are fully set forth in history ; but should the material of this structure prove more durable than history, the time may come, centuries hence, when its purpose will be as obscure as that of the Egyptian obelisks and pyramids are today. But of this we may be quite sure : it will never be removed from the place it now occupies to adorn some future Rome, or bear down to times more remote the effigy of some temporary ecclesiastic.

The monument differs from an Obelisk *externally*, only in the fact that it is not a monolith ; but internally, as in the arrangement of space, there is no similarity, and no comparison between the two can be made. As a work of art, the merit of the monument does not consist in its form, or external appearance, but rather in its planning, scientific construction and impressiveness as a whole. The formation of an obelisk, from a single block of granite, the height, dimensions of base and apex being furnished, would seem to be, in the earliest times, a comparatively easy task, involving but few of the scientific principles which are to be found impressed on nearly every block of stone in the Bunker Hill Monument. To erect an Egyptian obelisk in sections, or courses of masonry, without interior apartments, would be a much more difficult work and require vastly more skill and labor, than would be required to hew it out of a single block of whatever size. Such a work would be equal, supposing the structure to be of the same magnitude, only to the external walls of the present monument.

There are instead of one, as in a monolith, *four* wrought surfaces in this great work, extending to the whole height of its parts, and each differing in its diminishing line from all the others ; and, in addition to these, there is a lofty flight of circular stairs, between the inner wall of the monument and the outer wall of the cone, extending to the domed chamber, nearly the whole height of the structure. Of the four wrought surfaces, the three inside of the work are circular — two of them fine hammered — the height of the courses and the degree of the angles being different in the cone and the main work. The monument, therefore, is far from being a simple obelisk, or even two obelisks, one within the other. In its exterior form it is a quadrangular structure, 221 feet 5, in height, terminating at the top in a pointed pyramid. The sides of the square at the base, are 30 feet, diminishing to 15 feet at the base of the pyramid. Were it not for the hollow cone in the interior and the elaborate stairway winding around it, there would be within a circular chamber, conical in form, about 215 feet high, diminishing in diameter from 17 feet at the base to 11 feet at the

28

spring of the arch of the dome. But the architect, to whom
the details of the construction were entrusted, determined to
provide for a commodious stairway by the erection of a hollow
cone in the centre of the work, the proportions of which would
be such as to afford between it and the monument proper, the
desired space. This has been accomplished in a most successful
manner, rendering the ascent of the monument perfectly easy,
safe and convenient.

A sectional view of the monument, drawn and published by
Mr. Willard,* more clearly than any words can do, shows the
manner of building and some of the peculiarities in the construction. The Foundation consists of six courses of heavy
blocks of granite, laid alternately as headers and stretchers,
the sides of the first course being fifty feet, covering the
whole square excepting the corners. The second course falls
back three feet ; the other courses fall back in the same manner to a square of thirty feet, and the seventh course is the
first of the monument. Inserted in the stone at the northeast
corner of this course, marked with an asterisk (*) in the
engraving, on its under side, is the deposit which was placed
in one of the temporary foundation stones in the presence of
General Lafayette, on the 17th of June, 1825.

The outer and inner courses of the monument are each 2 feet
8 inches rise, and 78 in number, to the base of the pyramid.—
The inclination in the outer wall, on each side of the structure,
is 7 feet 6 inches from the perpendicular, equal to 2¼ inches
diminution in each course—so that each side of the monument is
built on an angle of less than two degrees inclination. The interior surface has a lesser diminishing line, in order to maintain
the largest practicable width for the stairway.

The Pyramid which forms the top and apex of the monument
is composed of six courses of stone, including the cap-stone, and

---

* " Plans and Sections of the Obelisk," &c.

its vertical section forms an equilateral triangle of fifteen feet, its base being fifteen feet square. Its perpendicular height from the base line to the apex is thirteen feet. The two courses below the cap-stone are composed of two blocks each, laid transversely to each other.

The Cone, or hollow column, in the centre of the monument, at the base, is 10 feet in diameter from outside to outside, 6 feet 8 inches in the clear, and the wall 20 inches in thickness. At the top the diameter is 6 ft. 2 inches outside, 4 ft. 2 inches in the clear, and the wall 12 inches in thickness. The variation from the perpendicular in the line of the outer wall is about one foot eleven inches in the whole height—equal to one-eighth of an inch to a foot ; and owing to the diminution in the thickness of the wall, the angle of its inner side is still smaller, not exceeding one-twelfth of an inch to a foot in height.— There are one hundred and forty-seven courses of stone in the cone, of 1 foot 4 inches each. Thus this portion of the structure is a series of conic sections, each block being of different angles on the sides, bevelled at the ends and forming the section of a circle. There is not, therefore, in the cone, a single block of stone having any right angles ; and the only blocks in the structure that are of similar dimensions, or that could be used in duplicate, are those which occupy corresponding positions in the same course.

If this cone could be seen separated from the monument, which encloses it, it would present the form of a regular diminishing column of 10 feet diameter at its base and 6 ft. 2, at its top, hollow in its full height, flat at the top and smooth hammered on its exterior surface. Alone, it would constitute a monument of gigantic dimensions, towering far above all surrounding objects, filling the eye with its proportions, and excelling in height any similar monument in the world. But, as built, there winds around this cone a flight of stairs, conceived with judgment and executed with skill, extending from the base to its top, enclosed by the grand and massive structure, "in the form of an Obelisk," of dimensions excelled only in the pyramids of Egypt. As there was originally a long discussion whether the monument should be in the obelisk form or a column, it is singular that as built it should unite the two — one within the other.

The Steps in the circular stairway are 294 in number, and of course, owing to the gradual *batter* of the walls in which they rest, each step must vary in dimensions from every other step, excepting in their height. The rise of the steps is 8 inches, doubling in the walls of the cone, and the latter doubling in the walls of the monument. The narrow openings on the north side of the monument for light and ventilation, occur in each circle of the steps around the cone, at the broad stair, and are seven in number. Thirty-nine steps are required to complete the first circle, and forty for the second. The third circle has thirty-eight steps; the fourth, thirty-seven; the fifth, thirty-five; the sixth, thirty-three; the seventh, thirty-two; the eighth, forty. Now, if in our mind's eye we surround this lofty stairway with a quadrangular structure, of the dimensions already stated, as the monument proper, and comprehend at a glance its gigantic proportions, its large interior spaces and its exterior surface on each side of the quadrangle, with a height perfectly dizzying to the sight, we shall have a clear general conception of the Bunker Hill Monument, with an idea, however imperfect, of its extraordinary character, which it is not easy for a mere beholder of the work to realize.

The monument proper of course is its external form, irrespective of its internal arrangement or construction. The character as well as the purpose of the work is expressed in this, and by this its excellence is to be estimated. The interior may be ever so complex and successful, it would weigh but little against a failure externally. To this test the Bunker Hill Monument has been subjected, in its proportions and details, and it stands today, not only the loftiest, but the most sublime and impressive monument in the world. The blocks of which it is composed, so great in number and in variety of form, were all quarried and hewn to size and shape, in the wild crags of Mount Wollaston, so that comparatively speaking, scarcely was the sound of maul or chisel heard upon the hill in its erection. There are in the monument more than six thousand six hundred tons of stone, and not a single block, excepting those in the foundation below the surface of the ground, which is rectangular in its form.

" In the construction, the courses are alike, except diminishing as they recede from the base upward.   In order to preserve the bond, however, the headers are shifted to opposite sides in each succeeding course, namely : in the first course, the headers show on the east and west sides, and in the second on the south, and so on."*

The base of the monument is surrounded by a solid granite platform, just above the surface of the ground, and supporting on its outer edge a handsome iron fence, with appropriate granite posts at the corners.

We have been somewhat particular in describing the monument in order to show that it has claims as a work of art, not generally understood or conceded to the architect.   To those " architects and engineers" to whom Mr. Willard especially dedicated his printed volume, much that we have said may be deemed superfluous and unnecessary : to others it may prove to be more suggestive.   As compared with the Egyptian obelisks, in respect to the skill and labor required in the work, it must be equal, irrespective of inscriptions, to a large number of them ; and in the more scientific work of preparation, planning, drawing, modelling, &c., the difference is still more appreciable.

----

* " Plans and Sections of the Obelisk," &c

It is no part of our purpose, in this way, to institute a comparison between ancient and modern art, but simply to show the
large excess of work in the Bunker Hill Monument, the skill
and judgment manifested in its conception and exercised in its
erection, and its title to consideration in art.

As a whole the completed monument has fully equalled the
expectations of its builders and the public — and probably, of
a more exacting party, the Architect.   But from the latter, not
one word do the public or private records afford, expressive of
any opinion, or indicative of any claim to consideration in connection with this crowning work of his life.   That he was satisfied with the design for the work, as finally drawn by him and
adopted by the committee, and gratified beyond expression at its
completion, there is every reason to believe.   His extraordinary
interest in the work is sufficient evidence of this; and he felt,
or had a right to feel, that the monument was an enduring
memorial of his own merit as an artist, and of his skill, genius
and perseverance as a mechanic.   He never spoke or wrote of
this, and the feeling, though it may have dignified him as a
man, never otherwise escaped him.   His native modesty forbade
him to make any claim in his own behalf, and in his printed
volume, as in his letters and reports, he invariably spoke of
"those who have planned and conducted the executive parts of
the work."   He always had faith that justice would be done
to him.   For the credit of the Bunker Hill Monument Association, for the encouragement of a laudable ambition in men,
his merit should be rewarded, his faith and constancy duly
honored.   We must cherish the faith of man in men, for the
benefit of those it may inspire.

The completed monument realized to the directors their first
conception of the work, announced long before any design had
been decided upon, and before the question had been discussed.
Their first remark was that " it would be distinguished by simplicity and grandeur, rather than by elaborate or elegant ornaments," and this remark quite perfectly describes the finished

structure. Mr. Everett, in speaking of the monument before it was finished, said, "What is already done is as substantial as the great pyramid of Egypt. The foundations have been laid with such depth and solidity that nothing but an earthquake can shake them. The part already constructed will last to the end of time."

The Executive Committee, in 1834, spoke of the monument as follows : "It may hereafter be said of this monument, with more propriety and more feeling than the Greeks were accustomed to speak of the Statue of Olympian Jupiter, that 'to have lived, and to have died, without having seen it, was to have lived in vain.' "

The monument is without any inscription : the following eloquent exposition of its purpose, and the lesson it is intended to teach, is the language of the certificate of membership issued in the joint names of the Bunker Hill Monument and Mechanic Associations, in 1833 :—

"The Law of Nature ordains equality among men in political rights and duties. The American Revolution established the dominion of this law, but at the cost of Valiant Patriots, who devoted their lives that future generations might rise to the dignity of Free Citizens, qualified to make their own rules in social and political order. The People of this day, in the full enjoyment of the benefits for which these Patriots fought and died, and humbly acknowledging their dependence on Divine Providence, for all the good that has been gained and secured to them, unite in raising a monument on the field of battle, to commemorate the events of the

SEVENTEENTH OF JUNE, 1775,

as the most eminent of the early achievements in the cause of rational freedom. If in the delusions of prosperity, or the gloom of adversity, or in the tendency to change which is stamped on all human purpose, the spirit of that day should be perishing, let this MONUMENT renew it with all its glorious and dutiful associations."

MEASUREMENTS OF BUNKER HILL MONUMENT.

By Charles L. Stevenson, Civil Engineer.

Dimensions of the Obelisk.

Height of obelisk to base of pyramid, .	208 ft. 5
Height of the monument to the apex, .	221 ft. 5
Sides of the square, first course, . .	30 feet.
Sides of the square at base of pyramid, .	15 "
Thickness of wall at the base, one-fifth, .	6 "
Thickness of wall at the top, . . .	2 "
Circumference of chamber in the top, .	36 "
Height of chamber, ...	18 "
Diameter of chamber, ...	11 ft. 6
Height of each course in the monument,	2 ft. 8
Diminish in each course, . .	2¼ inches.
Number of courses to base of pyramid,	78
Number of steps in the circular stairs,	294
Height of riser, ...	8 inches.

Foundation 50 ft. square, 6 courses, 2 ft. each, 12 ft. deep.

Dimensions of the Cone.

Height of the cone, from the flooring, . .	196 ft. 9
Diameter of the first course, .	10 feet.
Diameter of the top course, . .	6 ft. 2
Thickness of wall, at base, one-sixth, .	1 ft. 8
Thickness of wall at the top, . .	1 foot.
Height of each course, ...	1 ft. 4
Number of courses, ...	147
Diminish in each course,	6-10ths of an inch.

Dimensions of the Pyramid.

Vertical height from base line to apex, .	13 feet.
Number of courses in the pyramid, .	6
Sides of the base, . . .	15 feet.
From the base line to apex,	15 "

CHAPTER XXX.

MR. WILLARD AS ARCHITECT AND BUILDER -- 1824 — 1835.

WHILE the work upon the monument was going forward, Mr. Willard's duties at the quarry and on the hill were such as to allow him little time for any other service, or the progressive self-culture which he always desired. In addition to his general superintendence and oversight of the various processes, new contrivances for facilitating the work, working-models and plans for the hammerers, were often required, while questions as to the quality of the stock, the difficulties of transportation, the employment, payment and discharge of the men, made frequent demands upon his time. He was almost daily at the site of the monument, or at the quarry, and had little time to perform the necessary office-work. He was, however, very frequently called upon for information and advice by architects, builders and individuals, and it was always given, generally without fee or subsequent employment. Designs and plans were furnished in the same way. During the suspensions of the work on the monument, Mr. Willard was variously engaged as architect, builder and quarryman.

The United States Branch Bank, on State street, which was designed and built by him, was completed before the work on the monument was commenced. The corner-stone of the Bank was formally laid on the fifth day of July, 1824. The heavy columns in the portico of this building, were cut from a huge

29

boulder of granite in the town of Westford, Massachusetts, known as the Chelmsford granite. They were twenty-four feet in height, including the cap, and four feet in diameter at the base, being six-diameter columns. The building was very much admired for its pure style of architecture, and a professor in Harvard College requested of Mr. Willard a statement of its proportions to be used "in an exercise in perspective." This building has since been remodelled, in order to enlarge its accommodations, and its claims at this day to architectural merit may well be questioned.

The plan of the monument at Concord, in commemoration of the fight at the "old North bridge," was furnished at the request of Mr. Everett, in 1825, but on account of the indecision as to its location, was not completed until 1836. It is a plain obelisk, elevated upon a pedestal, but unfortunately is in several pieces. The plan made by Mr. Willard, was at once adopted by the Building Committee, of which fact Mr. Everett informed him, and requested to know the fee for preparing it. To this note Mr. Willard replied — "I did not think of making any charge, and am sorry you should give yourself any trouble about it." This little circumstance is quite characteristic of both gentlemen — Mr. Everett would have freely paid the fee out of his own pocket; Mr. Willard did not desire it of anybody. In the same note he wrote to Mr. Everett, "many of my friends are in a habit of adding an *Esq.*, to my name in the superscriptions of their letters, supposing me possessed of the little vanity which it would gratify; but as I have no claim to such distinction, it would be more pleasing to have it omitted." In a subsequent note from Mr. Everett he scrupulously complied with Mr. Willard's request.

The inscription upon the Concord monument, is cut on a marble slab. It was written by Rev. Dr. Ripley, of that town, one of the energetic and authoritative clergymen of the old school, whose faith in God was not simply that He ruled the universe by all-wise laws, but, in temporal matters, by special acts of

Divine government, rewarded the just and upheld the right. — His thorough belief in an over-ruling Providence was as real as his own existence. The spirit of this old Christian Patriot is manifested in the terse and .emphatic inscription on the Concord monument, which stands upon land given by him and formerly a part of his farm.

The Norfolk County Court House, at Dedham, was designed by Mr. Willard, and erected in 1826. It was then and still is a really beautiful building, constructed of granite found in the immediate neighborhood, with light Doric porticos having four columns in each front. Its dimensions were 48 by 98 feet, with projections. It was universally regarded as one of the truest and best specimens of architecture in the country. In February, 1827, when it was formally opened for public use, Mr. Samuel P. Loud wrote to Mr. Willard, inviting and urging him to be present on the occasion, casually remarking, — "The Dedham people and people generally, I believe, are delighted with this building." It has since been enlarged and altered — often a fatal process upon any work of real merit — but is yet regarded, next to the monument, as Mr. Willard's most successful work in architecture.

The Franklin Monument, in the Granary Burying-ground, was erected by a few citizens of Boston, in 1827. It is of pyramidal form, composed of several blocks taken from the Bunker Hill quarry. The design was furnished by Mr. Willard. The inscription is upon a copper tablet let into the shaft. Its height is twenty-five feet.

The Harvard Monument, in the old Burying-ground, in Charlestown, designed by Mr. Willard, was erected by the alumni of Harvard, in 1828. It is an obelisk, strictly conforming to the legitimate definition of the term, fifteen feet high to the pyramid. The base of the shaft is four feet six inches, diminishing one half in the height, and its weight about fourteen tons, (or about 180 feet cubic measurement.) The inscription upon this monument is on a marble slab, set into the shaft. —

The block was taken from the Bunker Hill quarry, and at the price paid for the monument stone, cost about forty-five cents in the ledge — one quarter of a cent per cubic foot.

Upon the suspension of the work on the monument, in 1829, Mr. Willard gave his time and attention, not merely to the furnishing of designs, but to the business of quarrying stone; introducing it, in fact, as a building material, and taking contracts himself. In a letter to Mr. Joseph Grennell, of New Bedford, with whom he had just completed a contract, in November, 1831, he wrote as follows : —

" The high price demanded for granite for fifteen years past, and particularly for blocks of large dimensions, has had a tendency to discourage the use of it ; and my object in engaging in the stone business was not to make money, but to make experiments in order to remove the obstructions to the extensive use of granite as a building material, and to ascertain the lowest price at which it could be afforded with the common facilities for doing business. I left the profession of architect, which I had followed ten years in Boston, and took charge of a corps of quarrymen, at the Bunker Hill quarry, in Quincy, six years ago the fifteenth of the present November. The committee of that work had previously advertised for proposals for furnishing the stone required, and received but one, and that was sixty-two cents per cubic foot, for the raw material delivered in Charlestown. A combination had taken place among the dealers in stone to keep up the prices, as is usually the case. The quarrying of four thousand tons was finally done by the day, by men under my charge, and cost the association but thirteen cents and three mills per cubic foot, delivered on a wharf in Charlestown. Since the work has been discontinued, I have been making experiments at my own expense. While I conducted the public work, my services were gratuitous, and since doing business on my own account, I have merely charged my employers for their work what I supposed would be the prime cost, well managed, taking all risks on myself, without any compensation for the excessive labor and anxiety that I have had on their account."

Mr. Willard furnished at different times, many designs for churches, hospitals, dwelling houses, stores, &c., and plans for remodelling churches and other edifices. In July, 1829, he was consulted concerning the monument to the memory of Thomas Addis Emmet, the Irish patriot and distinguished barrister, which was afterwards erected in Saint Paul's Church yard, in New York; and in the fall of the same year was employed by Mr. Andrew J. Allen, in reconnoitering the route of the Fitchburg railroad — a road which was built fifteen or sixteen years later by other parties. In December, of the same year, he drew outlines of several different routes, extending them as far as Brattleborough, in Vermont. In 1830, he made several designs for churches, including one at Bangor, Maine, and the Bowdoin street church, in Boston, which last he contracted for and built of rough granite at very low rates. The style and architecture of the edifice, although heavy and sombre, the more so from being of rough stone, was much commended for its good proportions. The next year, Mr. Willard examined the route for a railroad from Boston to Taunton and Somerset.

In 1831, application was made to him to furnish stone for two houses in New Bedford, and he proposed to deliver it on a wharf in Quincy, in 8-inch ashlars, at fifteen cents a foot, and he made up the account of cost as follows : For bankage onequarter of a cent; quarrying, four cents; dressing edges, seven cents; transportation, two and three-quarter cents; profit, one cent; total, fifteen cents. The cost of stone-cornices, with three cubic feet of stone and seven feet of dressing, he stated at one dollar and seventy-four cents per running foot. These prices were scarcely up to the prime cost of the article at that time ; were manifestly too low to be a safe guide to other dealers, and however intended, were in some degree unjust towards them. — Large contracts were made with Mr. Joseph Grennell, and Mr.

Joseph R. Anthony, of New Bedford, and the stone supplied, as well as the prices charged, gave great satisfaction to those gentlemen. At the same time, Mr. Willard fulfilled a contract with Mr. Martin Brimmer, of Boston, and supplied the stone for the fence and gate-way of the Granary Burying-ground, one block of which, — that nearest the Tremont House, — is about thirty-five feet long. The work on the gate-way, (the winged globe and inverted torches,) and on the corner-posts, (winged hour-glass,) was executed at Quincy, under the general superintendence of Mr. Willard, and is still among the best granite sculpture in the city.

The new Court House for Suffolk County, in Boston, which has been since enlarged, was designed and built by Mr. Willard, and completed in 1835. There were eight granite columns in the two finely-proportioned Doric porticos, — only one of which now remains, — four in each; they were twenty-five feet six inches in height, four feet six inches in diameter, and measured about fifty tons each. They were among the first of these heavy columns, after those of the Branch Bank and Quincy market, brought into the city. A team of sixty-five yoke of oxen and twelve horses was required to draw them from the railway in Quincy to Boston.

CHAPTER XXXI.

NEW YORK MERCHANTS' EXCHANGE — 1836 — 1841.

In June, 1836, a contract was made by Mr. Willard with the New York Merchants' Exchange Company, to furnish the stone for their new building, and the contract continued for over five years. Mr. Isaiah Rogers was the architect, and the company, by Mr. Willard's suggestion, purchased the right to take the stone required from the Wigwam Quarry. During the progress of this work a voluminous correspondence became necessary in relation to the plans, transmission of the stone, payment of the workmen, &c., and lastly pertaining to the final settlement of the accounts, amounting to nearly four hundred thousand dollars. Of course in a large portion of this correspondence there is nothing of general interest concerning Mr. Willard, or illustrative of his character; but in the lesser portion, there are a few passages of interest which may properly be referred to or quoted.

The contract was dated the 22d of June, and the consideration to be paid to Mr. Willard for all his services was five dollars a day. He assumed the agency of working the quarry, employing the men, shipping the stone, &c., and the company paid the expenses of his necessary visits to New York. In a letter of January, 1837, Mr. Willard refers to some difficulty experienced in the progress of the work by the masons waiting for material. "It must be quite obvious," he says, "that if the

masons wait, there are too many of them employed; or too few
employed in preparing the material at the quarry. We found
in building the monument that about four-fifths of the money
was expended in preparing and getting the materials to the site
of the building, and one-fifth in fitting, hoisting and setting the
stone: the fitters were employed in working off the quoin-heads,
facing the headers, matching-in the steps, &c., and the blacksmith's work, coal, &c., was also included. Those who did the
hoisting were a distinct gang, and were employed in adjusting
the machinery, getting the blocks of stone to a convenient place
for hoisting and in raising them. Under the head of mason's
work was included the cost of the mortar, setting of the stone,
adjusting the scaffolding, &c. The three gangs were about
equal, and the expense of the three amounted to about one-fifth
of the whole sum paid out, and consequently each of the gangs
to one-fifteenth. The relative proportions may vary in different buildings. In a building partly of bricks and rough stone,
the cost of the mason's work to the whole cost may be greater
than in the experiment noticed. This experiment, however,
goes to show that the mason's work is comparatively a small
part of the whole. . . . No waiting ever occurred at the
monument in consequence of a want of proportion in the different
gangs, and as the expense of the mason's part was found to be
about one-fifteenth of the whole, a useful rule may be drawn
for proportioning the gangs in other places: if for every effec-
tive mason that is employed, there be fourteen other men engaged in preparing the material, there will be no waiting. . .
I do not think it good policy to crowd on more men than can
work to advantage, as it defeats the purpose it is intended to
advance. Idle men are a dead weight, and worse than useless,
—whether they be idle from want of material or room to work—
as they increase the expense without forwarding the work. It
may be easily shown that the wages of thirty idle men at three
dollars per day would amount to more than the interest on half
a million of dollars at six per cent. per annum."

Mr. Rogers, in a letter of March 30, 1837, says, he understands the arrangements at the quarry are superior to any other in Quincy, and this from "a Quincy man is saying much." "I feel very much gratified," he added, "to see the narrow feeling giving way to liberal and just views of your services; and I hope before the stone for the Exchange is finished, if your health is spared to you, those contracted beings who have been so prone to throw false impressions upon your exertions and valuable experiments, will be willing to appreciate some of your past services."

Mr. Willard's efforts to extend the use of granite as a building material, by putting it at prime cost, — tending to reduce the profits of others engaged in the same business, had the effect to prejudice them against him, especially as they were too immediately interested to be able to appreciate his purpose.

Mr. John A. Stevens. president of the Exchange Company, visited the quarry in August, 1838, and expressed himself as follows respecting the work in progress: "I was pleased exceedingly with things there. I do not believe granite has been worked so extensively and beautifully in such masses since the times of the Egyptians. The bases, consoles, flutings and caps are equally admirable." We do not know where the Egyptians have left any work at all comparable to that to be found in the New York Merchants' Exchange.

Up to January, 1840, Mr. Willard had employed at the quarry from forty to ninety men, engaged exclusively on the work for the Merchants' Exchange. and had received from the company and paid to them, and for contingent expenses, the sum of $255,794 91, — more than double the amount expended on the monument. During this period of three and a half years, Mr. Willard had devoted himself to his work and workmen, with such assiduity and kindness as to command the entire confidence and respect of employer and employed.

A very large amount of stone was required for this building, including eighteen fluted columns, of over thirty tons each,

30

(similar to those in the Court House and Tremont House, in Boston,) and more than fifty other blocks of twelve to sixteen tons measurement. The finished columns were thirty-two feet eight inches in height, and are superb specimens of work. — After the first column had been successfully obtained, Mr. Willard wrote, "I do not apprehend much difficulty in getting the whole out, although our neighbors in the stone business appear to be much concerned about it. I presume we can get them if anybody can and at less than half the cost to them."

In July, 1840, Mr. Willard wrote as follows : " We are now drilling a line of holes eighty-four feet long, and have a fair chance of getting two columns at the next split." On the fifth of August, he wrote, " our long split is wedged off about an inch, and I think will make what was intended. Our quarrymen have had to proceed with great caution on account of the great length." This block must have measured from one hundred to one hundred and fifty tons. Another block was partly got out which it was expected would make four columns, but it was not successful. One year from this time, during which much of the stone for the Exchange and Custom House, in Boston, had been got out and forwarded, Mr. Willard wrote, July 8th, 1841, as follows : " We expect to get through shortly and to have the greatest hoorah and throwing up of caps that ever was in Quincy ! We have saved three cartridges for the Yankee, to be fired off when the last column is loaded." Four months later he wrote : "We are about getting the seventeenth column to the wharf. The eighteenth we expect to get finished on Tuesday next, and the whole, column and architrave, afloat in the course of next week."

Two years time, after most of the other work was done, was required to get out and finish up these columns. The cost of them is stated in an estimate of work remaining to be done in June, 1839, at $1,500 each ; but in a later statement made in October, 1841, two of them, upon which extra work was ordered by Mr Stevens, are put down at $4,000, and Mr. Willard in one of his letters said, "The prime cost of getting out one of these shafts is as much as the prime cost of a Doric column with its capital, for which $5,200 is paid at the Custom House." The estimated work upon each was equal to four men for forty-five days. There were great risks in getting them out, and no less than five blocks which were split off failed to answer for column, and one was rejected after it was rounded.

Mr. Willard wrote on the fifth of November, "Our unsettled accounts are of long standing and I should like to have them settled in the shortest possible time. How would it do for you to spend a few days in Quincy, in helping to count up? We have to work hard and live poor, and sleep on a board, and have no accommodations to brag of near the quarry; but there are two houses about a mile off where they keep all the good things necessary to make life comfortable, where I presume you can be accommodated."

The work at this time was nearly completed and the splendid edifice, wrought out of the rocky ledges of Quincy and shipped to New York, stone by stone, stood in symmetrical beauty as the Merchants' Exchange, in the great commercial metropolis of the nation. "So far as regards the architectural taste of the building and its execution," Mr. Willard most submissively wrote to Mr. Stevens, "I never doubted that they would be considered respectable." Mr. Rogers, if he ever saw this letter, would hardly consider the remark very flattering to himself. — The building, however, still attests the taste and genius of the architect as well as the skill of the superintendent of the quarry and the industry of the men.

During the whole time of the work on the Merchants' Exchange, Mr. Willard was particularly careful of the interests and welfare of the men employed and many of them became very much attached to him. Much of his correspondence was in their behalf, seeking prompt and seasonable payment of their wages, and urging in particular cases, their claims to consideration. At different times, owing to the somewhat stringent

circumstances of the company, although he himself remained
unpaid to the last, he advanced out of his own pocket hundreds
of dollars to the workmen, to relieve them from pressing neces-
sities or embarrassment. Some of the men were disposed to be
troublesome, notwithstanding Mr. Willard thought the "advantage was entirely on their side, as they had been employed at
high prices through the dullest of times." Two of them went
to New York to obtain the balances due to them and there made
false reports about the work, which reached Mr. Willard. He
thought the men were "too ignorant and simple to be very dangerous to anybody. For young men they have both appeared
to be uncommonly craven and avaricious." After alluding to
the jealousies existing in Quincy, in regard to the work, he
suggested to Mr. McCormick that it was "descending too much
for you to ask them anything about the work, as it only flatters
their vanity to be taken notice of, and you must perceive that
you would not get a favorable opinion at any rate. Our affairs
are always open to examination and if there is anything wrong,
it might be easily found out by the personal inspection of the
president, yourself or Mr. Rogers." In allusion to this matter,
Mr. Stevens immediately wrote him, "You need give yourself
no uneasiness as to the effect of any impression made by what
discharged men say about your work. We leave the management of the quarry with great confidence to you — at all times."

The work was completed in December, 1841, having been in
progress five years and four months. It was a great and very
costly enterprise, and owing to the depression in mercantile
affairs which occurred during the progress of the work, the
company became greatly embarrassed. When the affairs were
finally settled, a considerable amount was found to be due to
Mr. Willard and his workmen, but all were finally paid, Mr.
Willard and others, receiving for their claims the new five per
cent. bonds issued by the company.

Mr. Willard made seven or eight visits to New York while
the work was going on, and no doubt gave Mr. Rogers much

valuable assistance in his plans. IIis memorandum of personal expenses at this time affords an insight to his methods and an idea of the cost of travel and the expense of commodities, as compared with the present time. , The cost of a journey to and from New York, in 1837, in his prudent way, was twenty-five dollars. In 1842, the items of expense for the same journey are recorded as follows : Fare from Quincy to Boston, 37 ; dinner, 33 ; fare to New York, 2.50 ; supper, 50 ; breakfast, 50 ; blacking boots, 12 ; board at Holt's, 1.50 ; fare back, 3.00 ; supper, 50 ; lunch and fare to Quincy, 90 — total, $10.22. — Personal expenses of most kinds were about half what they have been for same years past, while the expenses of travelling have been in most cases largely reduced and the facilities proportionably increased.

The following is a specimen of charges among his entries : — Paid for ——, court fees 25 ; justice fees 90 ; lent him $5. — Among the other items are subscriptions for several new roads, for the public library, contributions to various individuals and to various laudable purposes — all showing his interest in public and charitable objects and his readiness to contribute something to each.

CHAPTER XXXIII.

THE objects and purposes for which Mr. Willard avowedly engaged in the stone business, naturally excited the opposition and ill-will of all who were previously in it, and it is not strange that they should endeavor to keep up the prices of their work to a profit standard; not by any direct "combination," as he supposed, but by a common personal interest.   They looked upon his course with jealousy and suspicion, and his proceedings as inimical to them, and no doubt said harsh things about him.   Yet he did nothing but what he believed he had a clear right to do and would be justified in doing.   He was honest almost " to a fault," and did not consider that a wrong done to himself might be an injury to another.   Moralists may say no man has a right to do work for another without reasonable compensation, for thereby he enriches the party for whom he labors at the expense of those who obtain their living in the particular branch of business to which the work performed pertains.   It probably never occurred to Mr. Willard that in furnishing granite to builders at the prime cost, derived from an average, he was doing a wrong to those engaged in the same business who were dependent upon a reasonable profit on their labor ; yet it might have been so.

Not seeing the matter in this light, Mr. Willard continued his efforts to increase the demand for granite, expecting that all parties would find their interest ultimately in small profits upon large sales, and in this view doubtless his proceedings were justifiable. The success of his efforts, — his almost alone, — in introducing the free use of granite as a building material, as seen in the public buildings of Boston, New York, Philadelphia, and other cities; in the dry docks of Charlestown and Norfolk; in churches, cemeteries and other large public structures — all subsequent to the commencement of the monument — is the incontestible evidence of his sagacity and foresight. The opening of the Bunker Hill quarry led to the discovery and opening of other quarries, caused the building of the first railroad in the country, and gave an impulse to business which has adorned our cities with a class of splendid and substantial buildings, both public and private, which for durability and beauty, are wholly unsurpassed. In no part of the world, we believe, is a more excellent material to be found; and hard and heavy as the blocks are, they are new worked and handled with a facility which Mr. Willard foresaw, and by his inventions did so much to attain.

In 1841, commencing before the New York Exchange was completed, he furnished the stone for the Merchants' Exchange in Boston, which was also the work of Mr. Rogers. The tall plain and fluted pilasters in the front of this building are much the largest in Boston, and were raised into position by means of screws. The corner pilasters are forty-one feet eight inches in height, six feet wide and weigh about fifty-five tons. The emblem of commerce and navigation, forming the centre-piece in the front elevation, — an engaged globe, showing parallels, meridians and ecliptic, surmounted by the American eagle, with cornucopias of productions and coin resting upon bales below, and projecting from behind the globe, at the sides, a ship's mast, trident, anchor, and caduceus — although wrought by a stone-cutter nearly a quarter of a century ago, is still the most elaborate piece of granite sculpture in the city, and though it has been harshly criticised, was considered to be well done for the time

and the material.   The art was in its infancy, and it is but recently that higher achievements have been accomplished.

In 1841–2, and more or less subsequently, Mr. Willard
was occupied in the superintendence of the work on the
monument, as already related in these pages.   During this time
the work on the " two Exchanges" was completed.

But Mr. Willard began to feel that he had completed his
experiments and was satisfied with the results, and he did not
care to continue any longer in the business, — not even now to
make money, which, in his mode of life, without a family, he
did not need.   Applications to him were therefore declined, or
turned over to other parties.   In February, 1842, he wrote, —
" I have never intended to remain permanently in Quincy.   The
principal work, — the monument, — that led me to this place
sixteen years ago, is nearly finished, besides the two Exchanges,
which have incidentally come in.   I have made no further arrangements ; but, as the times are unfavorable for disposing
of what I have in Quincy, I may be detained for some time
to come."   Notwithstanding these remarks, it appears that Mr.
Willard and Mr. Rogers, only a month previous took a lease of
the Wigwam Quarry of Mr. Belknap, for five years.   We presume that this was mainly Mr. Rogers's transaction, as Mr.
Willard enters the payment of the tax upon the quarry in this
wise: " Paid Mr. Rogers's tax for ledge, $16, made out to
A. E. Belknap."

He interested himself, however, in the affairs of the town,
of which he had been a citizen since 1825, and superintended the erection of a School House, in 1842, giving the
land to the town, and of a Town House, in 1844, both neat and
substantial buildings of native granite.

Mr. Willard also laid out and publicly opened the Hall Cemetery, in the neighborhood of the quarry, doing much of the
work with " his own hands, without money and without price."
In this cemetery, a few years later, he raised the Rejected
Column, above-mentioned, intended for the New York Exchange.

It was removed by himself and four men, with the aid of his machinery, a distance of more than forty rods, and erected in the centre of the cemetery, as a monument, and it forms a most conspicuous and impressive object in the grounds. A suitable foundation was prepared for this remarkable shaft, which was erected as left by the workmen, and Mr. Willard deposited in its top a complete set of stone cutter's tools. It is about the same height and somewhat heavier than the finished columns. It is still a matter of surprise that he was able to move and raise a column of over thirty tons weight with the small force he had. The land for the cemetery was given by Mr. James Hall, at Mr. Willard's solicitation. Mr. Hall was a very wealthy man, — a bachelor, — and had unbounded faith in Mr. Willard. After the cemetery was laid out, Mr. Willard suggested to him that an iron fence for the front was needed. He inquired what it would cost. Mr. Willard replied, "about a thousand dollars," and Mr. Hall, jocosely remarking, "you have got the land and now you want money," gave him the desired amount.

Harboring, it would seem, some vague ideas of change of place, or possibly of resuming his profession, Mr. Willard still continued a citizen of Quincy, although simply a boarder in a private family. Without the slightest ambition for position, and no desire for wealth, or taste for display, he did not engage in any business or professional pursuit for either purpose. What property he had, besides some notes and bonds, was located in Quincy, capable of use and improvement and requiring his attention. Naturally enough, — for he could not be an idler anywhere, — he gradually fell into the pursuit of an amateur farmer and occupied himself in the cultivation and improvement of his land. He bought agricultural books, subscribed for agricultural newspapers, became, somewhat later, a member of the Norfolk County Agricultural Society, and went very systematically into the study and practice of the art. The occupation was not entirely new to him : he had worked in his early years

upon his father's farm in Petersham, and had "dabbled" a little
in agriculture while engaged in working the quarry.   In 1839,
as if the matter had been already talked about, Mr. McCormick
sent him the famous new potatoe of that time, the " Rohan," —
one of which, he said, " will produce a barrel," — a feat in
agriculture which coopers or grammarians must regard as mar-
vellous.   The " Red Dutch" and " Pine Apple," though new,
were thought to be inferior, as they cost only half the price, —
fifteen dollars per bushel, — of the " Rohans."   Mr. Willard
wrote to his correspondent that " owing to previous engagements
in other directions, his experiments in the farming line would be
necessarily few this season.   I intend, however, to take particular care of the ' murphys' sent, in order to give a good account
of them at the end of the year."   It is just possible that this
" good account of them" may be found in the proceedings of the
Norfolk County Society, but we doubt if he ever sent any such
account to his correspondent.

It is not probable that either Mr. Willard's speculations or
experiments in agriculture, at this time, were of any particular
value ; and we have not found among his papers any statement
of their results, or any account of sales of produce.   We presume his operations were not very extensive, though they
served to occupy his mind and engage his interest.   He may
have entered more zealously into the business in later years,
when he sought to interest others, and especially the young, in
the art, by appropriating small portions of his land to their
use and encouraging them to cultivate it for their own benefit,
while he in fact was desirous of cultivating in them habits of
labor and industry — buying off the rude and indolent boys that
they should not molest the workers.

CHAPTER XXXIV.

INTRODUCTION OF GRANITE AND MACHINERY.

WE have only incidentally mentioned, or briefly spoken of, Mr. Willard's efforts to introduce granite as a building material and at the same time to improve the prevailing style of architecture. Mr. Willard felt persuaded that an improvement in the material for building purposes, so decided as that which he, in fact, had introduced, would gradually effect a change in the style of building and in the general architecture of the times. Granite, as a building material, excepting in a few instances and those mostly under Mr. Willard's superintendence, had been used in small pieces, or blocks of moderate size, for cellar walls, underpinning, posts, lintels, &c.; and his first measure was to introduce the material in large blocks, such as were in themselves massive and durable — which, as he saw at once, would absolutely necessitate changes in the style of architecture and in the character of public buildings, stores and other substantial structures.* A good deal of feeling was manifested when he determined that such blocks should be provided for the Bunker Hill Monument, because no one of the dealers in stone was prepared to furnish them — neither to quarry them, to

---

* A sample of the small blocks may be seen in the front of Saint Paul's Church, Boston, and of larger ones in the United States' Court House, (formerly the Masonic Temple,) on the adjoining premises ; and both together, the large above the small, make an awkward appearance in the Navy Yard wall, on Chelsea street, in Charlestown.

manipulate or to transport them. The means to do these things had to be created, and in consequence of his unchangeable determination, his enterprise and inventive genius, they were created and his purpose fully accomplished. It was found to be practicable to get such blocks out of the new quarry, as well as out of boulders, and they were got out, wrought and transported to Charlestown, by means prepared for the purpose. The effect was just what Mr. Willard supposed it would be upon the style of buildings required in the city, and finally in other cities, and in distant parts of the country, where our superb granite at this day finds a market. Evidence is not wanting — and is, in fact, so abundant in what we every day witness as not to need suggestion — of Mr. Willard's foresight and skill in this matter. As the civil engineer under whose superintendence the government dry docks of Norfolk and Charlestown were built, proposed to construct Bunker Hill Monument of small blocks, it is probable that similar material would have been used for those works except for the success which attended Mr. Willard's efforts in introducing large blocks for the monument.

The following are the remarks of Mr. Willard on this subject, published by him after the completion of the monument : —

" There are other important considerations, connected with these experiments, however, and advantages growing out of them — only secondary to the main purpose ; namely, the effect they have had in improving the style of building, and the taste in architecture, by the introduction of a building material not before in use; and showing that it can be worked into any moulded or ornamental form required, for the exterior of the best structures, and at a reasonable rate. And thereby having supplied a desideratum which had always existed, until the commencement of these experiments.

" A strongly marked improvement in taste, and in construction, immediately followed the commencement of this work ; as will be obvious on viewing the public structures which have

been erected since that time. Improvement in construction may
be noticed in the Dry Docks in Charlestown and Norfolk, executed soon after the commencement of our work. And many of
the buildings recently erected in, Boston and New York, will
show improvement in architectural taste, and mechanical execution. And particularly the Astor House and Exchange, in
New York, and the Tremont House,* Exchange, and Custom
House, in Boston. A change for the better may also be seen
in the recent blocks of stores of which the same material forms
an essential part.

"In a pecuniary point of view these experiments have also
been advantageous. In establishing the credit of a new building material it created a new demand; and consequently, a
business has grown out of them since the work was commenced;
and, in a space of a few square miles, amounting, as estimated,
to three millions of dollars. which would not otherwise have
been done at these quarries, and of which the work on the
obelisk is but about one-thirtieth part."

Mr. Dearborn, in his "Boston Notions," mentions thirty or
forty new blocks of stores and single buildings, all of granite or
of granite fronts, one of which (the store of the late Benjamin
Loring, on State street,) was erected in 1823 ; another, (of the
late Andrew J. Allen, on State street,) erected in 1827 ; the
Masonic Temple, (U. S. Court House,) and a granite block on

* The Tremont House was built in 1828 — the corner-stone having been
laid on the 4th of July, by Samuel T. Armstrong, President of the Massachusetts Charitable Mechanic Association. The stone was hammered at the State
Prison, under the direction of Mr. Samuel Lawrence. The ornamental parts of
the entablature, the facade and the portico, were executed by Mr. Samuel R.
Johnson, of Charlestown. The Tremont House was one of the earliest of the
first class hotels in the country. The inscription under the corner-stone says—
"A desire to promote the welfare and to contribute to the embellishment of
their native city led the Proprietors, Thomas Handasyde Perkins, James Perkins, Andrew Eliot Belknap, William Harvard Eliot, and Samuel Atkins Eliot
to undertake this work."

Washington street, erected in 1831; a block on Washington
street, in 1832; Amory Hall Block, 1835; Lawrence Block,
Milk street, 1844; the Cruft, Oregon, Quincy, and Brooks
Blocks, in Pearl street, in 1845-6 and 1847; Bowdoin and
Morton Blocks, Milk street, 1845; Old South Block, 1845;
Horticultural Hall, on the site of the present Parker House, in
School street, 1844; Sewall Block, Milk street, and Sanford
Block, Franklin street, 1846; and many more during the last
twenty years, — all, excepting the first mentioned, were erected
subsequently to the commencement of the work on the monu-
ment, and most of them after its completion.

After the blocks were split off from the ledge, means were
required to raise them and to transport them, and these, as we
have said, had to be invented and constructed, as no machinery
equal to the purpose and otherwise reliable, was then in use. —
The hoisting apparatus, which was first required, was provided
by Mr. Almoran Holmes, and respecting it and him we may
safely adopt the honest, generous and feeling language of Mr.
Willard, who knew and appreciated him:

"Holmes's Hoisting Apparatus. This was used for setting
the first fifty-five thousand feet of the granite in the obelisk.*
This apparatus, with various modifications to adapt it to different purposes, appears to have been the original invention of Mr.
Almoran Holmes, of Boston. He was a practical seaman, and
a bold and skilful hand in this department of engineering. He
had recently given his attention to the different kinds of machinery required for the hoisting of heavy weights, and, from
his early training, was well prepared to direct in all difficult
cases, and particularly where rope purchases were required. —
He finally lost his life by a casualty which occurred at Long

---

* All the remaining stone were hoisted by steam power; and the same
power was used, for more than a year after the completion of the monument, to
carry visitors to the top, passing up through the cone.

Wharf, in Boston, in lowering a diving-bell. He had the entire charge of contriving the apparatus and hoisting the first thirty-six thousand feet of granite in the obelisk; but, previous to the recommencement of the work in 1834, the fatal accident occurred, which deprived the association and the public of his invaluable services.

"This hoisting apparatus is remarkable for its compass, and the ease and grace with which it performs its work. With a gaff or arm, of fifty feet, it will command a circle of one hundred feet in diameter. It will take a weight at the point of the gaff and land the same at any part of the outer circle; or on any point of a concentric circle, until it arrives at the foot of the derrick, and vice versa. It is consequently well adapted to buildings of magnitude, in setting the stone work; and for wharves, and other places of deposit, in stowing the materials in the most compact manner; and reloading them when wanted. — This apparatus, with some variations, has come into general use, and is so well contrived for the purpose intended, as to leave little to be wished for, in regard to apparatus for hoisting.

"Something of the kind is said to have been used at the Bell-Rock light-house, for setting the stone work; and it is quite possible that this apparatus, and indeed every other modern invention for the purpose of hoisting, may have been in use before. The great works of the ancients that have come down to us, prove that they must have had an apparatus of great power of some kind; and it seems quite probable that this, as well as other inventions of modern times, may have been repeatedly invented and lost, within the last four thousand years."*

Other machinery was required for the handling, lifting and hauling of the large blocks of granite from the Bunker Hill ledge, for the monument, and the still heavier blocks which were

---

* A part of this apparatus is seen in the engraving representing the first course and corner-stone of the monument.

subsequently required, from ten tons to a hundred tons, or even to one hundred and fifty tons measurement. This machinery was furnished by Mr. Willard, and we copy his brief and unpretending account of it, with the illustrations and explanations given by him : —

"The Lifting Jack has been found to be a useful machine for turning heavy blocks of stone. It is a compact and powerful machine, calculated for hard service, and, for some purposes, seems to be better ada ;ted than any other power. It consists of a rack, and one or more wheels and pinions, according to the power required.

"Something of the kind has been in use from the earliest times ; but was not used in the granite business until the work on the monument was commenced. Those in use were constructed for other purposes, and not adapted to hard service. — They were generally made of thin plates of iron, bolted to a large stock of wood, having a feeble rack, and without proper boxes for gudgeons. They were also weak and of rude workmanship, and, when put to hard service, either broke or wore down and out of gear in a short time.

"In order to adapt it to hard service, thicker plates were used, and these plates were screwed to a hoop of iron. This iron hoop extended to the foot of the jack, and the foot was bolted on, giving the whole a firm bearing on the ground ; a piece of wood was bolted between the sides, leaving a groove for the sliding of the rack.

"It was considered important that the best of materials should be used, in order to obtain the greatest strength, with the least weight. And, consequently, the whole was made of the best of wrought iron and cast steel, except the boxes, which were of bronze, or composition. The rack and the wheels were of wrought iron, and the pinions of cast steel.

"The Pulling Jack. This jack is constructed much like that for lifting : but is always in a horizontal position. The crank pinion is extended two or three feet, and turned by four arms about three feet long. The rack has a claw at the end to receive a chain, which may be led to places which are inaccessible, and dangerous for using the common jack. It is a powerful and convenient purchase for canting and hauling out heavy blocks of stone.

" The power of the one used is about ten tons ; but, by the addition of a shieve, the power is nearly doubled — amounting to twenty tons. If more is necessary, it is obtained by adding another jack. This machine was contrived and first used at the Bunker Hill quarry.

" The Hoisting Apparatus was contrived at the Bunker Hill quarry and first used in loading a large mass of the granite for the obelisk. It is calculated for raising weights too heavy for shears, or derricks, and has been found convenient for loading any stone from five to fifty, or even sixty tons in weight. A horse, or timber frame, is set over the stone to be raised, supporting a screw and nut. A chain from the weight, leads to a shackle, which is connected with the screw. The nut is then turned round by long arms, and the weight raised to a proper height for the carriage to pass under it, and when properly adjusted, the weight is lowered to its bearings.

" For blocks of granite of great length, such as columns and pilasters, &c., two horses and screws were used. In unloading the same, the apparatus was placed over them, and the weight raised sufficiently to clear the carriage. The carriage was then drawn out, and the weight lowered to the ground. Many hundreds of loads have been raised in this way without accident, and with facility and economy."

These several machines are still in use at the quarries, gigantic specimens of Holmes's derrick, towering over the ledges, being the most conspicuous objects in West Quincy.

32

CHAPTER XXXV.

MR. WILLARD continued to reside in Quincy, and gradually gave up all idea of leaving the neighborhood. It can hardly be said that he continued to do business as heretofore, or if so, it was only for a short time. His book concerning the monument, was published in 1843, and that had occupied some of his time, and gave much satisfaction to his friends.

He had furnished the first granite paving stones ever used in Boston, laid in front of the Tremont House: they have been since a good deal used and are still made in quantities at the ledges in Quincy. He had also furnished the working plans and stone, for the astronomical observatory at Cambridge, designed by Mr. Rogers. Mr. Willard's method of planning the foundation and support for the great refractor, of heavy granite blocks, in the form of an inverted cone, was thought to be a very ingenious and successful piece of work. In 1843-4, he attended Mr. Glidden's lectures, at the Lowell Institute, and studied Egyptian antiquities. In '44, he furnished the stone for a Savings' Bank building, in New York, and superintended the erection of the Town House, in Quincy — and these were among the last of his engagements. He sold his tools and purchased farming implements; sold his lot at Mount Auburn and took one in the Hall Cemetery; sold some of his real estate,

and, (after the interest on his Exchange Bonds failed,) supported himself on the proceeds.

For a year or two after the building of the Town House, he
was interested and engaged in the erection of a School House,
in the village which he had done so much to create. It is in
the centre of the population, on a broad plain almost hemmed-in
by the ledges; is a neat and handsome building, and the
remarkable circumstance about it is, that it is not constructed
of the substantial material so abundant in the vicinity. A good
deal of the work inside of the building was not only planned
but performed by Mr. Willard with great care and nicety, at his
own expense. The Selectmen did him the justice to confer his
name upon the School. The Hall Cemetery and the Willard
School are in proximity to each other, while the men whose
memories they are intended to perpetuate, long united in
friendly bands here, now rest side by side, and after a brief
separation, are again united in heaven. Mr. Willard died a
year or two before his friend, although the youngest, and
was deposited in his tomb.

Before commencing the School House, Mr. Willard seems
to have been indisposed to undertake any work for money.
Unfortunately, perhaps, for a proper understanding of his life
at this time and subsequently, the papers which he left at his
death, were scattered, and a portion of them destroyed by fire,
so that none of them have been available in writing this memoir.
He was now about sixty years of age, without a family to look
after, without any ambition to gratify, with no desire for office
or position, with no "entangling alliances," and only himself
to support. He sometimes remarked that he could be rich
if he wished to be, but he did not want money. He might
have left a "large fortune, but he had no aspirations for wealth."
With regard to resuming his profession, he undoubtedly felt
that he was now too far advanced in life to put himself into
competition with younger men. He was not inclined to be idle,
but rather disposed to do something which nobody else would

think of or venture upon. He had already laid out and opened upon his own land two or three new roads or streets, without any cost to the town, and his attention was again turned in that direction. The enterprise which he began, and worked upon almost up to the hour of his death, was the building of a road from the village, near the ledges, to the " new state," towards Milton. This road would open to easy access several hundred acres of valuable woodland, belonging to the Adams and the Quincy estates, and, as Mr. Willard thought, would at once double the value of the wood. It may well be supposed that the proprietors of those extensive lands were willing that Mr. Willard should build a road into them.

This was the last labor in which he engaged. He undertook it alone, and worked alone, without the expectation or hope of reward, without the stimulant of fame, present or to come, but simply from the habit of industry and the desire to accomplish something useful, no matter how much labor was required to do it. The road was to be two or three miles in length, when completed, ranging through the woods, over hills and vallies, crags and ledges, across swamps and meadows, and amongst entanglements almost insurmountable by human effort. One of the head quarrymen, accustomed to rugged work in a rough country, went over the route with the bold explorer, on one occasion, and declares the undertaking the severest experience of the kind in his life. Nothing would induce him to attempt the same route back, and he still considers it wonderful that they escaped without breaking any of their limbs.

Mr. Willard labored upon this work unflinchingly, as if he meant to accomplish it, and he would have accomplished it, had his life been spared. He felt so confident of this, though it would have occupied him for several years, that he had actually projected and partially surveyed another similar road of greater length in a different direction. He was devoted to his work, manifesting the same indomitable spirit he had displayed in the building of the monument; and for the first time, in the hearing of his friends, at the end of his last day's labor, admitted that he was tired. When the scene of his work was visited, after his death, great surprise was expressed at the extent and severe character of the labor he had performed during the day. It was considered almost incredible that some of the rocks moved by him could have been moved by one man. No further progress has been made on the road.

Mr. Willard's habits were very regular, and it had been for years his custom to rise early in the morning and retire at the unfashionable hour of nine o'clock in the evening. Although considerably fatigued with his day's work, on the twenty-sixth of February, 1861, he retired apparently in his usual state of health, and not the slightest apprehension was felt in the family concerning him. The only remark made during the evening relating to himself was, that "he did not feel very well and had probably worked too hard." He arose and came from his room at about the usual hour, the next morning, Wednesday the twenty-seventh, and while waiting for breakfast, talked of the state of the country and the then impending war. Six of the States had at this time passed the ordinance of secession ; forts, arsenals, mints and navy yards had been seized, and the confederate convention was engaged in preparing a constitution in the interest of rebellion and slavery. Mr. Willard, at this early time, seems to have feared the success of the rebels. and was apprehensive that the Bunker Hill Monument, to complete which he had sacrificed so much, would be destroyed by them. Those who were with him declare that he was so much affected by this thought that he shed tears as he spoke. Mr. Samuel Ela, with whom Mr. Willard boarded, and who was one of his reliable men in the Monument and Exchange work, told him he thought it would all come out right in the end, and that he need not trouble himself about it at present.

Soon after this conversation, breakfast was announced to be ready and Mr. Willard, Mr. Ela and another who was present, proceeded to the breakfast-room ; but as Mr. Willard was moving his chair and about to sit down at the table, he fell sideways upon the floor, in apoplexy, and never spoke again. A physician was sent for, but before he reached the house, Mr. Willard had breathed his last, living only about twenty minutes after he was placed upon his bed.

Mr. Willard's sudden death, without any previous sickness in his life, produced a deep sensation in the town, and the whole community felt that they had lost a friend and one of their most estimable citizens. He was known by everybody as an earnest, public spirited, unselfish man, and in various ways a benefactor to the town. The death of no other man in Quincy would have more generally or more deeply stirred the hearts of the people. Their love and respect for him was manifested on the occasion of his funeral : all the work at the various ledges was suspended ; the bells of the town were tolled ; the schools dismissed and the children formed in procession ; a band of music was present on the occasion and every mark of consideration and respect which was practicable with the town authorities and the people, was bestowed upon him. His name was given to one of the ledges, and his memory will ever be green among the people who have been benefitted by his labors. One of his townsmen* says of him, " he combined as many virtues in his character as often falls to the lot of one man. If 'an honest man' is 'the noblest work of God,' he was that man. His conscientiousness was remarkable, but his benevolence knew no bounds. His desire to do good to all around him was the theme of his whole life. He had not an enemy in Quincy — all who knew him honored and loved him. The name of Solomon Willard will never be forgotten here. Like all men of good deeds, he was diligent in every good work to the last.

" It may be said of him that he daily went about doing good. I never knew a more disinterested man than he was ; selfishness

---

* Dr. W. B. Duggan.

formed no part of his character. He had a fine mind and was a devoted lover of science. His conversational powers were pleasing and instructive. He was well read in Geology, and latterly, in agricultural science.' But the prominent business trait in his character was mechanical genius.

"He was a donor to the town in many instances. The granite engine-house lot, a part of the school-house lot, and many new avenues through his land, were public gifts from Mr. Willard. At the first mention of any public improvement, he was the first to offer his counsel and services.

"In all the relations of life, he was just. pleasing in manners and divested of all ostentation, having a good word for every person he met. His society was always attractive and he left a good impression on the hearts of all who knew him. . . The brightest gem in his character was charity and good will to men.

"I never knew his theological views. His life was one so virtuous and good, he was certainly a practical Christian. Many years before his death, he selected a piece of land, covered by a beautiful grove, through which coursed a silver stream of brook-water, designing to erect on this lovely retreat a chapel for the worship of God. He gave it the name of Chapel Lot.

"The little children of his neighborhood loved him as a father. In their pastimes, he whose head was covered with the snows of nearly four score years, advised and counselled with them. On the return of each vernal period, he would select small sites of his land as garden lots, for any little boys to cultivate as they might choose, often assisting them in their labors."

CHAPTER XXXVI.

PERSONAL APPEARANCE AND CHARACTER OF MR. WILLARD.

FROM what has been already said in these pages of Mr. Willard's life and labors, a tolerably accurate idea of his character as a man is readily to be inferred. He was ever thoughtful, studious and industrious; thinking about matters which other people overlooked or neglected, and seeking to fill his mind with knowledge that could at some time be made available. From his habit of thinking, and his making a practical use of the knowledge he obtained, he exemplified the truth of Cowper's well-known lines : —

> "Knowledge and Wisdom, far from bein gone
> Have ofttimes no connection. Knowledge dwells
> In heads replete with thoughts of other men ;
> Wisdom in minds attentive to their own.
> Knowledge — a rude unprofitable mass,
> The mere materials with which Wisdom builds,
> 'Till smoothed and squared and fitted to its place,
> Does but cucumber whom it seems to enrich.
> Knowledge is proud that he has learned so much ;
> Wisdom is humble that he knows no more."

Mr. Willard had learned much and was humble.

As boy and man, workman and pupil, he was always seeking improvement and endeavoring to qualify himself for some higher service. While with his father he served him dutifully and

faithfully up to the day of his freedom, using his leisure time
in his own improvement. The superfluities and luxuries of life,
and what others esteem as the luxury of idleness, had no at-
tractions for him. He was little disposed to "recreate" for the
sake of recreation, or "indulge" merely for the pleasure of the
indulgence. He "patronized" nothing that did not bring with
it some other advantage than mere gratification of passion or
desire. "Dulce et utile," was a rule with him, but utility was
his more general practice. Perhaps he carried his reserve and
self-restraint too far, but not to indulge in what others appeared
to enjoy was no deprivation to him. Abstinence was natural or
the result of preference : contemporary young men might prefer
to spend their evenings in amusement or gaming, while he made
use of his to gain admission to the Athenæum, where he could
hold communion with the wise and learned of past and present
times, and make himself acquainted with the history of man
and his achievements. It might be supposed that his retired
and studious habits would lead to moroseness or perhaps to
misanthropy, but it did not do either in his case. He was
genial, cordial, and cheerful, in his way.

As a carpenter, carver, designer, architect, builder, and as a
teacher, Mr. Willard was among the first and best, and in some
of these pursuits was rather in advance of his time. The opinions of those who knew him most intimately, and among these
some of the professional master mechanics and builders of the
present day, are all to the effect of that expressed by Mr. Carey,
in 1861, already quoted, who says, "I have been acquainted
with nearly all of the principal artists and mechanics who have
resided in Boston, for the last fifty years, and I think I have
never known a man of greater original powers of mind, combined with uncommon practical skill in executing, than Solomon
Willard."

Mr. Willard's habits were exemplary ; his indulgences, even
in innocent enjoyments, were very few. He did not find his
pleasure in what are considered the "smaller vices," and was no

33

"faster" in his daily habits than in his daily walk. He seldom
visited places of amusement or recreation, and his invitations,
unless to lectures or where instruction was combined with enter-
tainment, were unaccepted. He appears to have been rigid in
these things, — not in the hope of reward, not in the austerity
of the bigot, not from any vain show or pretence of goodness,
but from principle, because he could find better employment,
more profitable to his thoughts, more congenial with his tastes,
more consonant with his reason and judgment. He preferred to
cultivate his higher nature, as a sentient being, without any
stringent theological notions, whatever he might have thought of
these. He followed the emphatic injunctions of Solomon, builder
and king, and sought wisdom as the highest good, — as more
precious than gold, for he readily parted with his first earnings
for books and instruction. He sought at all times the development and cultivation of his intellectual nature; and his life
shows that his moral and physical capacities were not neglected.
He desired to know and understand whatever pertained to his
profession or pursuits, and spared no effort, labor or cost, in the
accomplishment of that purpose.

Intellectually, therefore, though not an educated man, Mr.
Willard was a well developed man. He was a deep thinker and
careful reasoner upon subjects which he understood; although,
of course, his writings lacked the finish of scholarly composi-
tions. It is a matter of regret, perhaps, that he allowed himself to become interested in so many pursuits instead of limiting
his efforts to some one of them. He did, in fact, for some years
previously to engaging in the erection of the monument and becoming interested in the stone business, confine himself to architecture and considered that his profession. Had he persevered in
this pursuit, he would undoubtedly have excelled in some of its
branches, and especially in construction. He had good taste in
design, but both genius and skill in execution. Nevertheless, if
he made a mistake in leaving a profitable profession for a pursuit more onerous and undistinguished, the advantage has been

gained to the public in the introduction and use of a valuable building material at reasonable cost.

From an examination of the papers and letters of Mr. Willard, the conclusion is inevitable that he was not only an original, scientific and skilful mechanic and artist, but that he was eminently practical in the various departments of labor, improvement and progress. His mind was ever active in suggestion and invention — never yielding to obstacles or at a loss for means and contrivances to overcome them. He was not only fertile in originating ideas of improvement, but quick to adopt and follow out the suggestions of others, and free to give praise or credit where either was due. He was tenacious of his own claims and modest in the presentation of them.

Mr. Willard was a man that could not be frivolous ; nonsense, however essential it may be to some lives, or however necessary to the equilibrium of things, was never a current coin with him. There is a difference of natures in this respect — in what may be called the unbending of the mind. Frivolity and nonsense, where not constitutional, is one method, (sometimes it becomes chronic) ; a meditative, perhaps we may say, a ruminating habit, is another method; others are found in any rational recreation in which the mind is not kept at tension. Mr. Willard's mind, we should say, was rather meditative than speculative ; thoughts and ideas could never be said to strike him — they planted themselves in his mind by a process, as it were, and grew there. On passing him in the street, instead of saying he is thinking of something, you would be almost sure to say he is going somewhere — so slow and inconspicuous were his thoughts. When he did think, his ideas were practical, carefully considered and mature, and were not to be killed like some other things which grow, by the first frost.

In personal appearance, Mr. Willard was sedate, — almost grave. This was his constant bearing, the garb in which he was habited, the air in which he moved. The mantle of thoughtfulness seemed always to cover him, and this was manifest in his

gait as in his countenance.   Physically he was a large man, tall
and stout and slow of movement.   He never spoke quickly or
hastily but moderately, and knew well the advantage that despatch has over hurry.   There is no record that on any occasion,
or for any purpose, he ever moved faster than his accustomed
walk ; but he moved steadily forward, and would probably walk
farther in the course of a day than most other men.   One
thing was pretty certain, he would accomplish whatever he
intended to do, be it much or little.   He was a moderatist in
all things, never doing extreme things or holding extreme opinions ; yet strong in his feelings, firm in his convictions, probably
a little prejudiced, and very likely often dogmatical.   Human
nature, however bestowed, is entitled to its weaknesses, and no
doubt Mr. Willard had his full share of these.   He did much
in the way of intellectual discipline, — more or less required of
every man, — and kept his thoughts and passions subordinate
to his sense and judgment.   He was one whose better nature
was always most apparent.

Mr. Willard can hardly be said to have been widely known.
He was known, when in the profession, by architects and artists,
and subsequently by quarrymen, stone-cutters and builders ; but
was little known personally to the public.   In fact, in the latter
years of his life, he was in Boston only on occasions of especial
interest to himself.   The last time he was seen by the writer was
in September, 1860, at the Ninth Exhibition of the Mechanic
Association held that year.   He spent his time in the quiet
hamlet of West Quincy, and latterly in a spot almost unvisited
by other men, and sought neither publicity or popularity.   He
had qualified himself for a work and had accomplished it.

Some persons thought Mr. Willard was eccentric ; but Mr.
Everett said the only thing he knew of him that was eccentric
was his readiness to do anything for anybody for nothing.   This
was his trait through life, and his later years, in a quiet and
unostentatious way, were almost entirely dedicated to the public.   The little village, in a retired part of which he lived, was

his field of labor, and its improvement and prosperity, his personal care. It is said that Washington was made childless that he might be the "Father of his Country:" Mr. Willard, in the same sense, having no family of his own, was father of the village which had grown up from the impulse which he had given to the stone business. It was now his home, his pride and his care.

It is a living and throbbing memorial of him, and his memory, within sound of the hammer and drill in its inexhaustible quarries, can hardly be forgotten. The children of the town, and their children's children, will become familiar with his name in the school house; the workmen will be reminded of him by the machines which they use and the ledge which bears his name, and all will recognize his work and his benevolence in the Cemetery, where the "Rejected Column" rises with so much massive grandeur, and is, in so many ways, significant of him who placed it there.

Such was Solomon Willard, and such the service he rendered to the public in his day and generation. He has left prominent evidences of his ability and skill in invention and execution; of his industry, perseverance and public spirit; of his generosity, magnanimity and benevolence, and his name and memory remain registered and enshrined in the hearts of the people among whom he lived. One record more, in justice to him, remains to be made: the duty of making that belongs to the Bunker Hill Monument Association; and it is to inscribe upon one the blocks of granite in their monument, the name of " Solomon Willard, Architect."

APPENDIX.

BEACON HILL MONUMENT.

A brief notice and description of Beacon Hill Monument will be found on pages 31 and 32 of the present volume. The suggestion there made respecting the rebuilding of this early historical memorial of the Revolution, has attained to practical importance by the ready action of the Bunker Hill Monument Association. At its annual meeting on the seventeenth of June, 1864, at which the suggestion was presented, a committee was appointed to consider the subject.* It is due to a member of that committee, Mr. Robert C. Winthrop, to say that, had the suggestion so distinctly made by him in his classical and patriotic oration in aid of the Washington Equestrian Statue,† been known to the writer, he would have taken great pleasure in the previous pages in awarding to him the honor, so justly his due, of first suggesting the rebuilding of this beautiful column. As it is, simply claiming to have made the same suggestion from a conviction of its propriety, we yield to him the precedence, with the high satisfaction of knowing that we were seconding the thought of a gentleman of so much intelligence in history, so much fervor in patriotic feeling and so much taste and appreciation in art.

The Beacon Hill Monument was erected " by the voluntary con-

---

* William W. Wheildon, Robert C. Winthrop, Frederic W. Lincoln, Winslow Lewis and J. Huntington Wolcott, Committee.

† " An Address delivered in aid of the fund for Ball's Equestrian Statue of Washington, 13 May, 1859."

tributions of the citizens of Boston," in 1790; and was undoubtedly the earliest public memorial intended "to commemorate that
train of events which led to the American Revolution, and finally
secured Liberty and Independence to the United States," if not, in
fact, the first public monument erected in the country. The monument on Bunker Hill in memory of Gen. Warren, was erected in
1794; the monument in memory of the slain at Lexington, was
erected in 1799, at the expense of the Commonwealth.

Upon the application of the committee above mentioned, the
legislature has passed an act, April, 1865, authorizing the Bunker
Hill Monument Association to rebuild the Beacon Hill Monument,
on some suitable site to be selected and provided by them; and
also to receive from the Commonwealth the original tablets or inscriptions, now in the doric hall of the State House, to be used in
the reconstruction of said monument. Under the auspices of this
patriotic association, it is to be hoped the Beacon Hill column will
be restored to the public in its original proportions.

WILLARD MEMOIR — LETTER TO THE PRESIDENT OF

THE MONUMENT ASSOCIATION.

CHARLESTOWN, July 10, 1861.

DEAR SIR: The Committee appointed at the meeting of the Bunker Hill Monument Association, on the 17th ult., to "prepare a
suitable notice of the late Solomon Willard," find it impracticable
to prepare any sketch of his life and connection with the Bunker
Hill Monument which would be worthy of him, or creditable to the
Association, in season to be included in the pamphlet report of the
proceedings of the day, as contemplated by the vote of the Association. Mr. Willard was one of those men so common in the history of this country, and generally included in the term " self-made

men," having by his own industry and genius risen from the mechanical profession in which he was bred, to prominence as an artizan and architect ; and his life is an example of industry, perseverance, self-instruction and skill. .. He was eminently careful, cautious and reliable ; intelligent, ingenious, and devoted to whatever he undertook to accomplish. His zeal and ardor and energy, in connection with the commencement and progress of the Bunker Hill Monument, were such as to constitute a marked feature of his life, and lead the Committee to believe that it is due to his memory and to the honor of the Association, that a more complete sketch of his services, so liberally and earnestly rendered, than they are now able to present, should be preserved among its memorials. To him not less than to the noble, patriotic and generous men of his time, who first and last engaged themselves in this great national enterprise, many of whom have passed to that future state of hopefulness and reward promised to the faithful, is the country indebted today for the monument which marks forever the first great battle-field of Liberty and Independence. Long may it stand, a proud memorial, as it is, of patriotism and gratitude, indicating the spot, and perpetuating the remembrance of deeds, upon which and through which a nation was born and the rights of the people justified.

Very respectfully,

In behalf of the Committee,

WM. W. WHEILDON.

Hon. G. Washington Warren,

President Bunker Hill Monument Association.

FIRST REPORT OF THE COMMITTEE ON THE MEMOIR OF SOLOMON WILLARD.

COMMITTEE :

WILLIAM W. WHFILDON,   NATHANIEL COTTON,
FRED. H. STIMPSON,   URIEL CROCKER,
        AMOS A. LAWRENCE.

THE Committee, appointed on the seventeenth of June last, to prepare a Memoir of the late SOLOMON WILLARD, Architect and Superintendent of the Bunker Hill Monument, respectfully RE-PORT, in part, —

That they were wholly unable to prepare such Memoir in season for publication in the pamphlet report of the ceremonies and pro-ceedings of that day, as intended by the association, and accord-ingly so informed the President, in a note of the 10th of July, which is contained in the pamphlet referred to.

The Committee have had several meetings, and the members have given such portions of time to the collection and prepa-ration of material as they have been able to spare from other en-gagements. In this service they have succeeded beyond their ex-pectations, and find reasons, from the documents and facts which have come to their knowledge, which not only justify the associa-tion in the measure proposed, but seem to demand the service at their hands.

The Committee believe that the purpose of biography, toward eminent or prominent men, is not merely to do honor to the dead — a cheap reward to them — but to afford examples of encouragement, hopefulness, and character, to the youth of our country, who are so frequently and so early in life compelled to rely upon their own exertions for advancement and success ; and, at the same time, to give assurance that those efforts and that success, when attained and resulting in benefits to the community, shall be properly appreciated and duly honored.

The Committee are led to believe that in nothing which has yet been given to the public, has reasonable justice been done to Mr. Willard, and especially in relation to the great national structure of which he was architect and patron, and to which he devoted, with a zeal and interest which knew no fatigue or flagging, some of the best years of his life, the only adequate compensation for which, in lieu of any other reward, is to be found in the work itself. Nor have his character and services, — the latter variously rendered in this city and elsewhere, — nor the means, self-inspired and self-created, by which he was enabled to secure the one and perform the other, ever been presented as they ought to be to the youth of the country and to the consideration of the public judgment. Such an example as his life affords, cordially attested by those who knew him best, of untiring industry, unyielding faith and unimpeachable integrity, in word and deed, — raising himself from the laborer to the artist,—ought not to be lost ; and the Committee will feel it to be their duty, if further time be allowed to them, with such authentic materials as they may possess, to do some degree of justice and honor to his memory, and make some suitable record of the valuable services so freely rendered by him to this association.

In behalf of the Committee,

WM. W. WHEILDON.

Boston, 17th June, 1862.

The Report was read and accepted, and the following vote passed by the Association : —

VOTED, That the Committee, appointed June 17, 1861, to prepare a Memoir of the late SOLOMON WILLARD, be authorized to publish said Memoir, when completed, in such form as they may deem suitable ; and that it be printed with the approbation of the Standing Committee.

HISTORICAL MONUMENTS IN MASSACHUSETTS.

Acton Monument, at Acton, in memory of Davis, Hosmer, and Hayward, who were killed at Concord, 19th April, 1775. Built by the State Legislature, 1852. Granite, in obelisk form.

Beacon Hill Monument, erected in 1790; taken down in 1811. — Its tablets are preserved and it will probably be rebuilt on Boston Common, on a spur of the original hill.

Bunker Hill Monument, at Charlestown, 1825–'43. Built of granite, 221 feet 5 inches in height.[*]

Concord Monument, at Concord, to commemorate the fight at the North Bridge, April 19, 1775. Granite obelisk. 1826—1836.

Cushman Monument, in the cemetery at Plymouth, in memory of the Pilgrim Fathers, erected in 1858, of Quincy granite, in the obelisk form.

Danvers Monument, at Danvers, in memory of seven citizens of that town, killed at West Cambridge, April 19th, 1775. Granite in the obelisk form.

Duston Monument, at Haverhill, in memory of Hannah Duston, on the site of the house from which she was taken by the Indians. Authorized by act of legislature, 1856.

Forefather's Monument, proposed to be erected at Plymouth — on an elaborate and costly design. Corner-stone laid in 1859.

Harvard Monument, in the old burying-ground at Charlestown, in memory of Rev. John Harvard, founder of Harvard College, erected in 1838, by the alumni. Granite obelisk. ·

---

[*] Height of the column of Alexander, at St. Petersburg, (including pedestal, capital, bronze dome, angel and cross,) 150 feet ; of the Monument of London, stated to be "the loftiest *column* in the world," 202 feet ; of the Arch of Triumphe, at Paris, 152 feet ; of the Column of Napoleon, Place Vendome, 135 feet and the statue 11 feet ; Colonne de Juillet, 154 feet ; of the Trajan Column, at Rome, 125 ; of Antoninus, 123 ; of Pompey's Pillar, at Alexandria, 100 ; of Cleopatra's Needle, about 70 feet.

Lexington Monument, at Lexington, in memory of seven citizens of that town and one of Woburn, killed on the 19th of April, 1775. Erected by the State Legislature in 1799. In 1850, a corporation was established for the erection of a new and larger monument at Lexington.

Ladd and Whitney Monument, in Merrimack Square, Lowell, in memory of two soldiers killed in the streets of Baltimore, on April 19, 1861. Concord granite. Dedicated, June 17, 1865.

Monument at Bloody Brook, Deerfield, erected in 1838, in memory of Capt. Thomas Lothrop and seventy-six men, out of eighty under his command, who were killed by 700 Indians, at Bloody Brook, September 18, 1675, old style.

Monument at Somerville, in memory of citizens of that town killed in the war of the Rebellion. Built by the Somerville Light Infantry, of marble, 1863.

Monument at Mount Auburn, in memory of Lieut. Underwood and Midshipmen Henry, Reid and Bacon, of the U. S. Exploring Expedition, erected by their associate officers and scientific corps.

Wadsworth Monument, at Sudbury, in memory of Capt. Wadsworth, killed by the Indians, in King Philip's war. in 1676. Completed and dedicated in November, 1852.

Warren Monument, on Bunker Hill, erected in 1794 ; taken down in 1825, to give place to the present structure. A miniature model, in white marble, is deposited in the present monument.

West Cambridge Monument, in memory of twelve persons who fell in that town, on the 19th of April, 1775, on the return of the British troops from Concord. Erected 1847. Granite obelisk.

NOTE.

There are many monuments, of a more or less public character, erected by private munificence, in our cemeteries and in every city and almost every town in the Commonwealth, in memory of prominent and eminent citizens.   One of the most conspicuous and beautiful of these is that erected a few years ago, by Mr. T. Bigelow Lawrence, at Worcester, in memory of his great-grandfather, Colonel Timothy Bigelow, of revolutionary renown.   This monument was publicly dedicated on the 19th of April, 1861, the 86th anniversary of the day on which he rallied his company of minutemen and started for Concord.*

The Monumental Urn, generally regarded as a memorial of Dr. Benjamin Franklin, which for more than half a century stood in the centre of the enclosure in Franklin Place, in Boston, was erected about 1793, and was removed when that beautiful place was surrendered for the erection of warehouses in 1858-9. It was purchased at Bath, England, whence the plan of Franklin Place, in its elliptical form, was derived, and in which city such ornaments were common.   It is made of oolite, or white free stone of which the ancient fashionable city which rejoices in the possession of a statue of "Beau Nash," is mostly built.   It is now over the grave of Mr. Charles Bulfinch, Mr. Willard's earnest friend, at Mount Auburn.

* An account of the "Ceremonies at the Dedication of the Bigelow Monument," was published by Mr. Lawrence, in 1861.

STATUARY IN MASSACHUSETTS.

THE SAVIOR, a copy from Thorwaldsen, on the apex of the pediment of the church of the Immaculate Conception, Boston, marble.

VIRGIN MARY, in a niche in front of the same church.

Washington, by Sir Francis Chantrey, in the Doric Hall of the State House, in marble.

Washington, by Houdon, in the Boston Athenæum, a copy in plaster of that belonging to the State of Virginia, at Richmond.

Franklin, by Horatio Greenough, in front of the City Hall, Boston, cast in bronze at Chicopee.

John Winthrop, by Horatio Greenough, in the Chapel at Mount Auburn, in marble.

John Adams, by Randolph Rogers, at Mount Auburn, in marble.

James Otis, by Thomas G. Crawford, at Mount Auburn, in marble.

Joseph Warren, by Henry Dexter, at Bunker Hill, in marble.

Alexander Hamilton, by Dr. Rimmer, of Chelsea, Commonwealth Avenue, Boston. Presented to the city by Mr. Thomas Lee.— Cut in white granite, probably the first in that material in the country.

Joseph Story, by W. W. Story, at Mount Auburn, in marble.

Nathaniel Bowditch, by Ball Hughes, at Mount Auburn, cast in bronze at Boston. The model is in the Boston Athenæum.

Daniel Webster, by Hiram Powers, in front of the State House, cast in bronze at Munich.

Horace Mann, by Miss Stebbins, in front of the State House, cast in bronze at Munich.

Hosea Ballou, by Edw. A. Brackett, at Mount Auburn, in marble.

Josiah Quincy, by Story, yet at Rome, ordered by the alumni of Harvard College, and is to come to Boston.

Aristides, in Louisburg Square, Boston, imported by Mr. Joseph Iasigi, and owned by the residents on the Square ; in marble.

Columbus (lifting the veil from the Earth,) in Louisburg Square, imported by Mr. Iasigi, and owned by the residents : in marble.

Beethoven, by Thomas G. Crawford, in Music Hall, cast in bronze
at Munich, the gift of Mr. Charles C. Perkins, of Boston.

Wounded Indian, by P. Stephenson, in the hall of the Mercantile
Library Association, Boston, in marble.

Venus de Milo, (armless,) heroic size, in the Reading Room of the
same association. A copy of the original found in the island of
Milo, in 1820, and now in the Louvre.

The Arcadian Shepherd Boy, by W. W. Story, in the Public Library, Boston, presented by several citizens.

Madonna and Infant, St. Mary's Institute, Boston, in plaster.

Guardian Angel, a group, at the House of the Guardian Angel, in
Roxbury, carved in wood.

Charity, two groups, on Octagon Hall, in Roxbury, formerly on
the old Boston alms house.

NOTE. There are many others in the Commonwealth, but we have
not thought it expedient to extend the list. Those named are of
life or heroic size, and are open to public inspection. Of ancient
and classical statuary there is a large collection in the Boston
Athenæum, and more or less in private possession. There are also
at Mount Auburn, besides numerous monuments which are superb
and costly works of art, many elaborate specimens of sculpture
and statuary in addition to those already mentioned. The same
may be said of Forest Hill and other cemeteries.

The Equestrian Statue of Washington, by Thomas Ball, has
been moulded by that artist and exhibited to the public in Boston.
It is to be cast in bronze, but has not yet been placed in the hands
of the founders.

Statues of Ceres, Flora and Pomona, which have been modelled
by Martin Milmore, of Boston, are to be erected in the front of
the new Horticultural Hall, Tremont street, Boston. Ceres will be
eleven feet high ; Flora and Pomona, eight feet. In fine granite.

A statue of the late Edward Everett, whose services have been
so frequently mentioned in the preceding pages, is soon to be provided for the city of Boston, the necessary funds having already
been raised by voluntary subscriptions for the purpose.

First Course and Corner Stone (*) of Bunker Hill Monument.

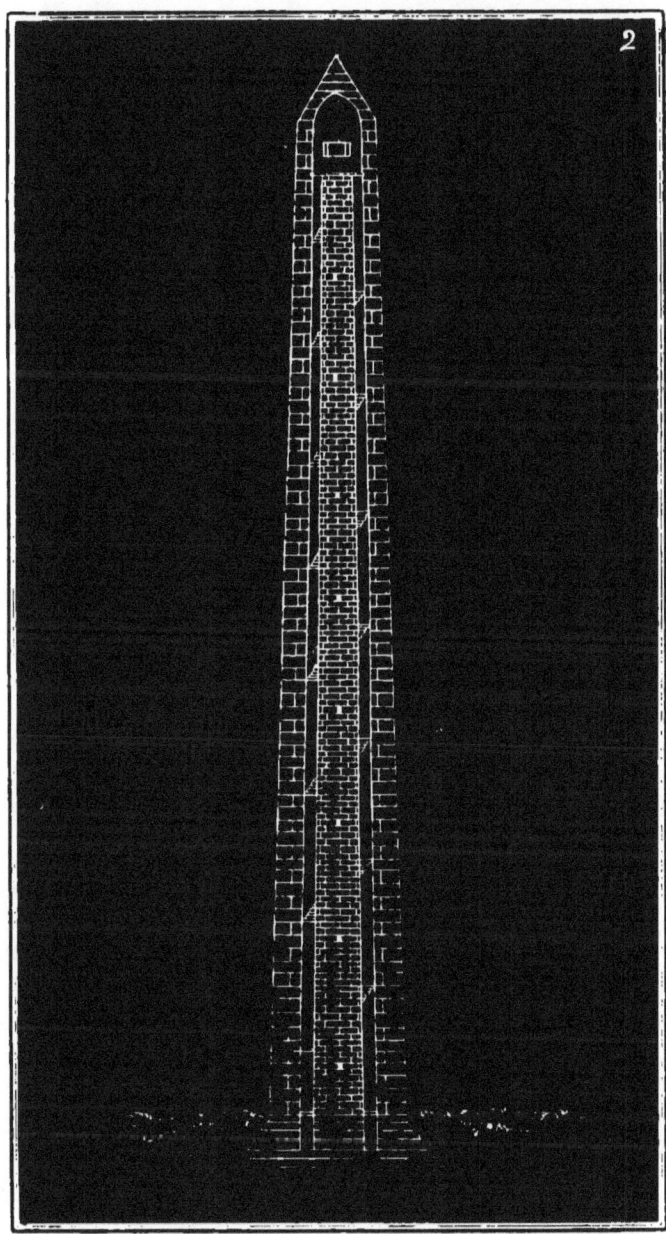

Sectional View of the Monument.

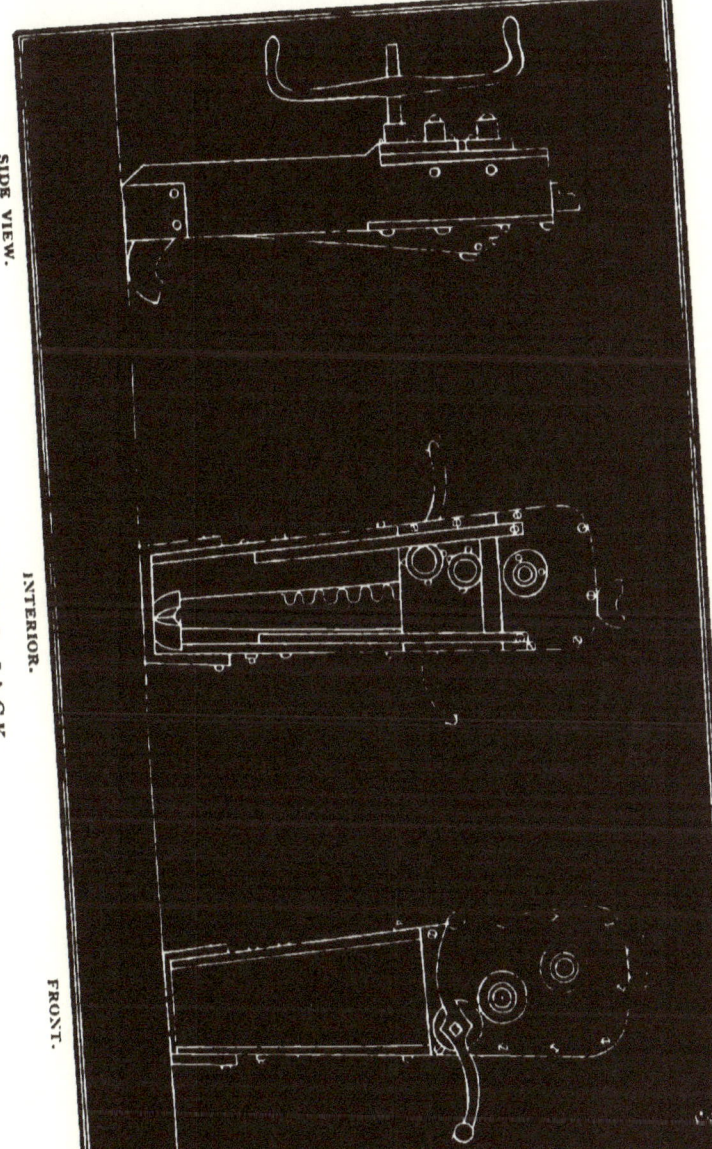

SIDE VIEW.

INTERIOR.

FRONT.

LIFTING JACK.

PULLING JACK.

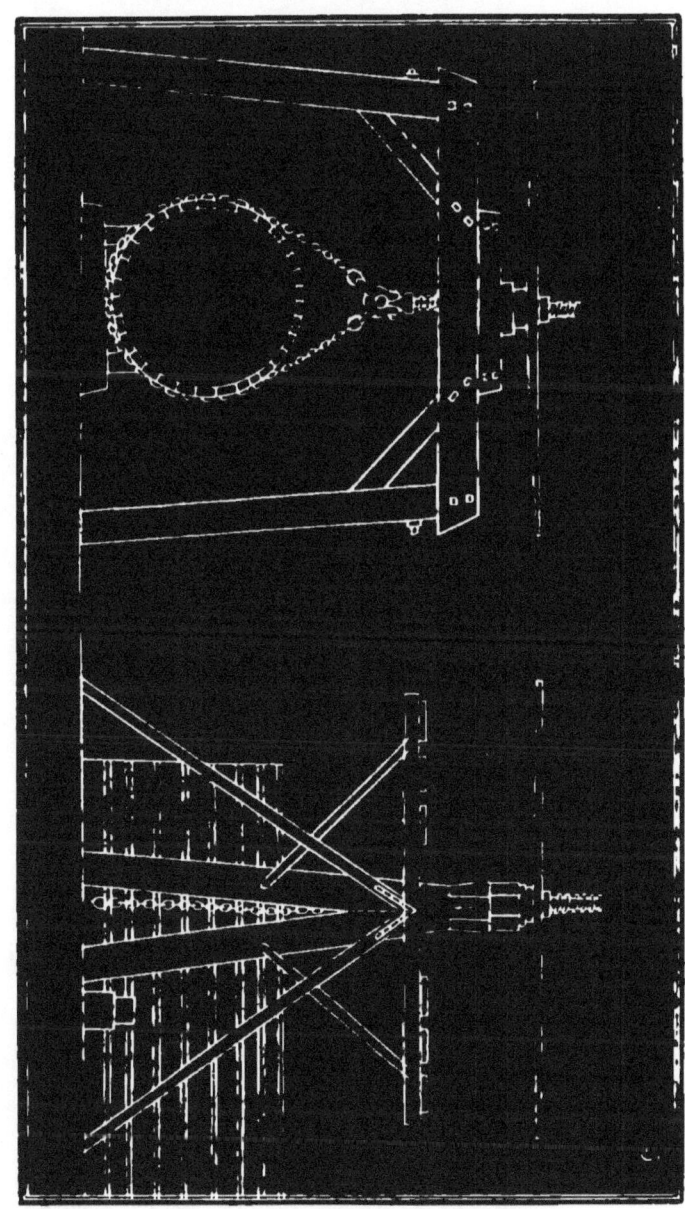

HOISTING APPARATUS.